THE WINTER OF MY LOVE

AN UNFORESEEN PREGNANCY IS JUST THE
BEGINNING OF THEIR STORY

J. L. LORA

Larimar

THE WINTER OF MY LOVE

Copyright © 2019 by Janny L. Lora

This book is a work of fiction. Names, characters, businesses, organizations, places, events and incidents either are the product of the author's imagination or are used fictitiously. Any resemblance to actual persons, living or dead, events, or locales is entirely coincidental.

For information contact J.L. Lora at:

P. O. Box 47022

Windsor Mill, MD 21244

http://www.JLLora.com

Book and Cover design by Deranged Doctor Designs

Copyediting by Nina S. Gooden

ISBN: 978-1-950453-00-9 (eBook)

ISBN: 978-1-950453-01-6 (Trade Paperback)

First Edition: March 2019

❀ Created with Vellum

the Winter Of My Love

J.L. LORA

For Vera, Angil, Nina, and Lynn

Ruth,
I hope you enjoy
Winter + Grayson's
story. May they
steal your heart

Nora

Grayson

"Something's happened to your sperm."

My pencil scrapes over the paper, leaving a coal scratch over the area where the parking lot is supposed to go.

And *I couldn't disagree more. Absolutely nothing's happened to my sperm. Literally.* It's been pooling inside my testicles because I'm too damned busy to arrange a date and too tired to masturbate when I get home.

My primary lawyer doesn't know that, and I'm sure as hell not going to tell him. I go back to the blueprint proposal for the new factory campus. I don't have time for whatever gossip the rumor mill has cooked up about me this time.

"Grayson, did you hear me?" Elias' voice is sharp, with twinges of being fed up.

"I don't have time for gossip, Elias. This proposal is taking—"

"I wouldn't bother you if it wasn't an emergency."

For fuck's sake. No, Grayson. Remember the HR training. Stay in the dialogue, make it safe for him, and focus on the desired outcome: getting him the fuck out of here. "Make it quick."

"Alice disappeared. She hasn't been seen for the past two days and she never got impregnated."

My blood trips inside my veins. His words are meshing together and try as I might, I can't make sense of them. Then they all hit me at once and in a breath I'm up on my feet and around the desk. "Elias, you know I don't have a fucking sense of humor. If this is some bullshit prank, you're going to need a surgeon to remove my fist from your throat and a sandwich cart. I will fire your ass so fast no one in the world would hire you again."

His jaw tightens, the icy glint in his eyes tells me he would punch me. If he could. But his voice is soft and measured. "Grayson, threatening me won't change the facts. I wouldn't jest about this. I'm repeating what was told to me. If you answered your phone and didn't have all your calls routed to me like I'm your secretary, the clinic could have told you personally—"

I hold up a hand. He's not wrong, but I pay him more than well enough to deal with shit for me when I'm swamped. "You told me it was under control. A couple of days ago, Alice came in here and assured me she felt good and all was going according to plan. You backed her up. Now you come to me with this bullshit?"

Elias presses a hand to his mouth. "All was supposed to be well. We had a pregnancy confirmation and it was evolving according to plan."

"But you went to the appointment with her."

"I couldn't go, Grayson." His voice rises. "You sent me to the closing for the buildings near Havre de Grace. I wouldn't have made it on time. She went into the appointment that day by herself and I met her for lunch after. She showed me the procedure confirmation. I had no reason to doubt her. The positive test two weeks later confirmed it was all done. I can't be in all places at once."

I go back around my desk to check my calendar but I hadn't added any reminders. *Fuck me. This is not happening.* "Tell me what they told you."

"The clinic director called this morning. The doctor who performed the procedure has gone missing. When they looked through his files, they realized what happened. According to their records, Alice showed up to the clinic the day of the procedure but the video surveillance footage shows her leaving fifteen minutes later."

I press my palms flat on top of my desk. *A clear head must prevail when dealing with a crisis.* "Have her found. I want to make sure she never opens her mouth about this to anyone. I need her silence."

Elias clears his throat. "There's more. Alice didn't get to do the procedure but..." He adjusts the knot in his tie. "...the doctor recorded that your specimen was used. Implanted in another patient, who was settled in the adjacent room. They suspect the missing doctor messed up or was helping Alice..."

A wave of cold knifes through my stomach, chilling my whole body. I stop him with a shake of my head. I've gone senile because everything out of Elias' mouth today is something out of a B-rate movie. My embryo is growing inside a stranger's body. "If you're joking—"

"I'm not," he says in his litigation tone.

"Could this other woman be working with Alice? Because if she's part of this, I will make her pay." I run my fingers through my hair. This is ridiculous.

"There's no evidence the woman was in on this. The clinic director wouldn't tell me much at first, trying to adhere to the HIPAA Privacy Rule. I threatened to bury them in litigation, a malpractice lawsuit, and all the publicity your money could buy. She forked over all of what they know thus far. She suspects Alice and this doctor worked together on this. They're currently questioning all the employees on duty that day. The impregnated woman is a school teacher who went in for a routine procedure, a device called an IUD. She has not been notified."

I can't fucking believe this. This kind of shit doesn't happen. Least of all to me. I've had those embryos frozen for years. Since Astrid... No, I can't let myself think of that. "The teacher. Who is she?"

Elias never would've come to me without as much information as was available. That's a mistake no one working for me would ever make.

Elias clear his throat. "She teaches art to elementary school children, at a private school, and tutors. She's also an artist whose work has been featured at *Artscape* a few times. She's of Hispanic descent, has a decent credit score but no real money. She rents a place near Patterson Park, drives a beat-up Camry, and does not have a criminal record."

This is a fucking nightmare.

"Go see her. I need her to come and meet me. I didn't plan it this way but that's still my embryo in there. Tell her I want to negotiate. Have contracts drawn up. I'll pay her for any inconvenience. I don't care how many zeroes it takes."

Elias' eyebrows lift but he nods. I turn away. The sky is bright out and I can see almost all the way to Fort McHenry. If I were the type of man that enjoyed these things, I would leave work and go home. I would go to my rooftop terrace to think about this mess.

His footsteps tap toward the door but there's one more thing.

"What's her name, Elias?"

"Winter Alexander," he says and closes the door behind him.

It's the right call. I don't want to be bothered by anyone. I can almost picture Astrid looking down on me with her sad eyes, flattened lips, and with that understated disappointment she used to wear so seamlessly. The same sad irritation that had lingered in her features when I tried to console her after every failed IVF treatment.

Promise you'll have our baby, Grayson.

I'd been a fool to say yes. I was bound to disappoint her again but I couldn't deny my wife her last wish. I'll do whatever it takes to fulfill it. I will make this happen.

Because I can't fail her this time. No matter what.

I sit back behind my desk, pushing to the side the blueprints and notes that have robbed me of countless hours of sleep. I open a new browser window and enter a search: Winter Alexander in Baltimore.

It takes a few clicks but soon a face fills my screen. It's from an artist showcase. An all-black outfit covers most of her body. Tons of

4

hair, golden amber skin, and a smile like she's trying to hold the happiness inside but can't. Her almond eyes make me pause. They're deep amber, like McCallan 18 swirling on a Baccarat tumbler.

I hope she's just as open when I meet her as she looks in the picture. Because I didn't choose this Winter woman, but she's going to carry that pregnancy to term. *No matter what it costs me.*

Winter

I'm not going to fight death anymore. I'm going to lie here and let her take me. Another cramp slithers up my torso but there's no bracing for it. My stomach has been trying to shove its way out of my body for days. Thankfully, the end is near. I just wish it didn't have to be so painful.

Slow breaths. Don't inhale too deep.

I keep my energy centered on breathing and rubbing a hand over my belly until the pain subsides.

I stretch my legs out on the bed and stare at the ceiling. If I concentrate on counting the blue stripes, the nausea is not as bad. I don't focus so much on how shitty my body, my head, my whole life feels right at this moment. I concentrate on the damned stripes on my ceiling. I knew someday they would come handy for something other than falling asleep at night, which is good because I haven't been needing to count lately to knock myself out. I seem to fall asleep just by blinking.

The banging on the door jackhammers through my skull and I sit up fast. My heart pounds along with the rest of me. *I fell asleep thinking about how easily I fall asleep these days.*

"Winter." Lauren's voice comes through loud and clear through my cracked window.

Shit, I was supposed to go out with the girls tonight. I groan.

The knocking continues. I roll myself out of bed and shuffle down the stairs. They won't go away until they've seen me. The downfall of

5

having friends is they care. One look at me and they exchange identical looks of what can only be described as horror.

I bet I look like the human version of a Jackson Pollock painting.

"Oh no. You still don't feel well," Adri says in that mommy tone that is so natural to her. Her fingers brush over my cheek like I'm a five-year-old with a tummy ache.

I'm not. I'm just your average thirty-year-old, dying because a volcano is erupting inside my body. Meanwhile, she and Lauren stand flawless in killer outfits, bang-up makeup, and perfectly-lined lips.

Nothing makes you feel worse about being sick and looking like shit than seeing other people at the peak of their health. I stare at them with their glorious, shiny hair and glowing skin, looking like they are illustrated with Titian's magic brush, and repress the urge to slam the door on their faces.

I'm a hater.

I shove away the green monster and myself out of the way so they can come in. Lo ruffles my tangled hair, like I'm Bronwyn, Adri's daughter.

Adri heads straight for my kitchen and I don't even bother to stop her. She won't listen to me anyway.

Lauren grabs a bottle of water from my coffee table and hands it to me. "I can't believe you're still sick. Did you go to the doctor again?"

I move to the chair and sit because standing is near impossible. "I left messages for her to call me. I'm still waiting—"

I've been abandoned by my doctor. *What else is new?*

Adri rushes back into the living room. "You don't have anything in there. How am I supposed to make you soup?"

The thought of food makes me want to beg for a swift—*Final Destination* fast and fulminating—kind of death. "You don't have to Adri, I can't even hold—"

She holds up a hand, pulls out her phone and goes back to the kitchen.

Lauren grabs the throw from the couch and drapes it over me. "Why didn't you call me? We would have brought you food or medicine or whatever you needed. You would've been better by now."

6

THE WINTER OF MY LOVE

"I didn't have the energy. Between the nausea, the throwing up, the cramping and the headaches, I haven't had the energy to do anything but lay around."

"Throwing up? Headaches? Do you also wake up feeling like a semi-trailer rolled over you all night?" Adri asks from the kitchen entrance.

"Yeah."

She comes closer and feels my forehead. "No fever but you do look pale. Do your nipples feel like they're going to fall off because your boobs are so heavy?"

I nod. *How does she know?*

She smiles. "One more question, have you peed on a stick yet?"

A fresh wave of nausea rises up my chest and tickles my throat. I press my hand to my chest, massage it and force a laugh. "What? Pee on a stick? As in a pregnancy test? No. It would be immaculate conception and we all know I am far from the good *Virgen María*."

Lauren snickers. "Damn, girl. Has it been that long since you got the pipes cleaned?"

I can't help but join her. "You're one to talk. Unless there's something you want to tell us."

It's our running joke because it's been so long since either of us enjoyed a little man attention. Although, her drought is a choice. She has that hot Chase Blake after her. I don't know how she resists that hard body or that mouth.

Lauren sighs. "Sadly, my pipes are still clogged, too."

"My pipes are clean and shiny, "Adri blurts out. She's happier than anyone I've ever seen, since reuniting with her high school sweetheart. She, her boyfriend Cam and their daughter, Bron, are the perfect, most beautiful family.

I'm so jealous I could gag or maybe I'm just queasy again. *Hard to tell.*

"Shut up, Adri. Winter and I don't want to hear that shit during our backed-up period." Lauren turns a frown on me. "If you're not prego, and you had the IUD installed, then something else is going on. We

7

need to get you to a doctor. Let's go to the ER or one of those urgent patient care places."

I shake my head so hard it hurts. No force on heaven or earth can get me inside a hospital. Not while I'm conscious, anyway. I hate sterile environments and I would be all alone with the doctors while they examined me. *Nope nope nope. Not happening.*

"You're acting like one of your students, Miss Alexander. Let us take you to the doctor. You're probably dehydrated and need an IV."

My legs go weak. IV? As in a needle shoved into my arm and breaking through my skin? *Fuck no, with a capital F. No needles. No one is going to poke at my skin and not find my veins only to keep poking me until I have black marks. Just no.*

"You know what, the two of you should go out and do girls' night like we planned. I just need to shake this off. If I'm not better I promise I'll go to the doctor."

"One, you're a liar and a bad one at that. Two, we are not doing girls' night without you," Lauren says.

Adri's eyes narrow on me too. "Cam is sending my mom's *Sopa de Pollo* over. She makes it for when Bron is sick, so we keep a lot of it frozen. We won't stay long, so you can get some rest, but we're not leaving here until you've eaten and are comfortably settled."

Lauren nods and they do that gang up thing that comes natural to lifetime friends. I'm still learning the ins-and-outs of friendships.

"I'm not hungry." My protest makes me sound like my students when I ask them to read about art and not just try to paint it.

Lo sits next to me. "I need you to get better soon. I can't keep going out without a drinking partner. It gets me in trouble."

It's futile to fight it so I relent. "Okay."

Adri smiles at me. "Good. Now why don't you take a shower? You'll feel brand new after you smell fresh and eat some hot soup."

She's in full-on mom mode and I want to tell her she's thirty years too late. But being nasty to my only friends won't get me closer to lying in bed and going back to wallow in my misery. What *will* get me closer to there is doing as they say. I choose the path of less resistance.

She also just insinuated I stink. I feel too shitty to be indignant, so I head to the bathroom.

An hour and a half later, I can't help but appreciate the friends that took care of me.

The chicken soup was delicious and I do feel human again after the shower and the bottles of Gatorade Lauren made me drink. My eyes well. *What's wrong with me?* I never cry.

The knock on the door makes me laugh and I shake it off. They forced me to give them a key just in case but they're still knocking. I make my way to the door, careful to keep my eyes off the White Tara, my half-finished canvas. I haven't touched it in days and it's staring at me with accusatory eyes, like the novices at the group home had, back when something went missing.

I open the door but don't find my girls there. Instead, there is a tall man who seems vaguely familiar. Perfectly-pressed clothes, coiffed hair parted in a perfect line at the temple, and a world apart from the hipsters in my community classes. Eyes dark and frigid, like a January morning. He must be an IRS agent or an auditor of some sort.

Either way, I don't care. I just want to go back to my bed and enjoy how human I'm feeling right at this moment. "Can I help you?"

"Hello Miss Alexander. My name is Elias Saunders and I'm a lawyer. May I come in?"

And probably a serial killer, too.

"No. You may not."

His face remains unperturbed and he insists. "This is a serious matter."

"Whatever it is, you can tell me right here."

He leans forward and my hand balls into a fist. If he comes any closer, I'm going to knee him in the balls and break my fist on his jaw.

"It's about your procedure at the Better Maryland Obstetric and Research Clinic."

The blood whooshes from my head into my ears. I clutch my chest. Something went deadly wrong and he's come to tell me I'm dying. They found cancer in my ovaries or my blood cells or I have some incurable cognitive disease.

"Please don't be scared. I just need to talk to you."

I nod and step back. Not going much further past the entrance. "Don't close the door."

He nods and steps in. "Miss Alexander, I'm here representing Spencer Grayson. I'm sure you've heard his name. Mr. Grayson owns Grayson Global Corporation and several businesses in the Charm City area. He's sent me here because of a matter that involves both of you. I came here to inform you that you've been impregnated with Spencer Grayson's child."

2

Winter

I blink a few times. I don't think I heard him right. He just stands there like he's waiting for me to do something. And then I get it. He has the wrong person.

Laughter bubbles from my aching insides and I clamp a hand over my mouth. I'm exhausted and when I'm this tired, I get punchy and I laugh uncontrollably. Unfortunately for Elias Saunders, representative of Grayson Global Corporation, he gets my giggles for a long time. At the end of my fit, I'm tired, a little nauseous again, and hungry enough to eat a Porterhouse steak.

To his credit, he remains patient and his face doesn't even betray if he is breathing.

"Thank you for that. I've been so sick I'd thought I'd forgotten how to laugh. You can leave now, Mr. Saunders. I don't know Spencer Grayson. Yes, I've heard his name, who hasn't? But as you can tell, we don't exactly run in the same circles. He must have slept with some other woman named Winter."

Probably a fake name from a hooker.

11

"Yes, I'm well aware, Miss Alexander, that you don't run in Mr. Grayson's circles." I could have done without the sardonic smile playing about his lips. I'm about to tell him where he can go but he keeps talking. "However, it all has to do with the procedure you had done six weeks ago."

Say what?

"During your procedure—"

"Stop." I don't need this shit. Today, least of all days. I've been throwing up the lining of my stomach all afternoon, and he stands there in his designer suit and a face that betrays the stick firmly stuck up his ass. He looks as out of place in my modest little apartment as the *Mona Lisa* would look in an abandoned Rowhouse in Baltimore.

I'm a teacher, though. I preach politeness to my students. I'm going to channel my own lessons. "I don't want be rude, Mr. Saunders, but I don't feel well. Please leave."

"I'm serious Miss Alexander."

He looks it, too. But he can't be. Can he? *Have you peed on a stick yet?* Adri's words whisper in my ear again. Everything begins to rush up and my hand shoots to cover my stomach. "I'm sorry. I'm going to be sick. Stay right there."

I dash toward my bathroom with the food knocking at my throat's door and the little voice in my head screaming that I probably left a murderer in my living room.

Five minutes later, I no longer feel well and Adri's mom's delicious *sopa* has joined the Baltimore City waste. But I don't have time to dwell. I need to face Mr. Saunders and send him away. I rinse my mouth and make my way back to the living room. He's standing exactly where I left him. With a slight curl on his upper lip.

Now the man thinks I'm disgusting. *I want to die.* "I'm sorry about that. I need to be alone."

But he doesn't move. "I understand and I'm sorry to inconvenience you..."

Yet there's no apology or anything else in his face, except for the blankness and the lingering disgust twisting his mouth.

"...but Mr. Grayson would like to meet with you. What's happened to you is a great violation to you both. He wants to discuss dealing with the clinic and moving on from this in a favorable way for both parties."

Ugh, this guy. Just fucking go. "What? You're still on that? You can't be serious. I am not pregnant."

He sighs, long and dragged out, like my caseworker every time she had to tell me that my mother got out of jail or rehab. Except, there's no apology in his gaze. No regards for how I feel. No hope for ice cream after. No reassurances that this time things may be different and that the system will be there for me.

"Miss Alexander, six weeks ago, you went to the Better Maryland Clinic to have an IUD placed to relieve the ailments associated with your uterine fibroids. You had an appointment with Doctor Lawrence. During this procedure, instead of placing the IUD, you were impregnated with Mr. Grayson's embryo. It is a regrettable error, which is being thoroughly investigated."

I open my mouth but he waves a dismissive hand.

"You dropped off a specimen five days later and never heard back."

My stomach turns again and I'm grateful there is no longer anything there. *Oh my God. No. This is not happening.* I massage it, praying away the nausea and Mr. Saunders, who doesn't seem to have an off button.

"That specimen was put through a test, which detected the presence of a hormone called Human Chorionic Gonadotropin. It confirms that you are, indeed, pregnant. Mr. Grayson would like to make plans for the embryo. You can come to his office tomorrow. Is ten in the morning good for you?"

I nod like an idiot. Because I don't know what else to do or what else to say. I've gone numb. It can't be a prank or a joke. He knows so many things. But it has to be. "How…how could this happen?"

He shakes his head. "We still don't know but like I said there's an ongoing investigation. Tomorrow, when you come to Grayson Global, feel free to bring a lawyer. Mr. Grayson will pay for the fee." He pulls out a card from his pocket and hands it to me. "We can have a car pick you up if you would like."

I shake my head. I don't know these people. I can't get in a car with them.

"As you wish. We'll see you tomorrow."

He turns on his heel and walks out. I rush to the door and close it. I click on the two deadbolts and shuffle back to the living room.

I sit in my couch for I don't know how long. Elias Saunders came, bombed my world, and left me sitting in the wreckage.

Pregnant? No, that can't be? *I can't be.*

I shrug a jacket over my robe and head out into the street. I don't know how I made it to the Rite Aid pharmacy. I don't know how I made it back. I don't know when I called Lauren.

I don't even know how much time has passed. It's all a red blur as my friend stands at my bathroom door, pale and open-mouthed. I'm sitting on the floor surrounded by three different brands of pregnancy tests, different names and different looks. One with two pink lines, the other with a blue plus sign. But it's the third test that says in digital letters, clear blue as the sky, what the others can only hint at: *pregnant.*

Meaning me. *I'm fucking pregnant.*

Lauren's face is no longer glowing. A gray shade creeps over her creamy brown skin.

"I got impregnated." I laugh and laugh and laugh until I have to turn around and hug the toilet again.

3

_____

Grayson

My office phone buzzes, snatching me out of my thoughts. The digital clock is blinking with the time. It's ten o'clock.

Shit.

"Mr. Grayson?" Sandra calls out. "Miss Alexander is here to see you."

Fuck.

My chest tightens a little and I wish I had five more minutes. There's a quick knock and Elias steps inside.

His expression is as bland as the tan color of his suit. "Are you ready?"

Goddamn it, no.

I'm caught off guard like an amateur but I shove it into the mental vault along with Astrid, my anger at Alice, and my fear that this woman won't agree to carry my embryo to term.

I get up from my chair and take a breath. I tell myself this is nothing but a transaction right now and no one is as good at closing a business deal as I am.

Footsteps tap against the marble floor and Elias opens the door fully.

"Miss Alexander, nice to see you again," he says, as affable as I've heard him. His words ring as genuine as a Dollar Tree diamond.

"Thank you. I'm sorry about yesterday." The rasp in her voice is the first thing I get to know about her. There's a smoky quality to it, like it's been stored in a barrel and aged. It's at odds with the photos I've been studying since yesterday. No one with a pronounced dimple in her cheek should have a voice that deep.

And then the teacher comes to view, hair pulled back, eyes wide and the politest smile I've ever seen. It spreads across her lips and stops firm on her cheekbones. She stands at my office door and her amber gaze missiles to mine. Like I'm exactly where she thought I would be and I am exactly who she expected me to be.

I'm a pretty good judge of people. I'm willing to bet money she's already made up her mind about me. *Too bad.* I still don't know what to make of her.

I take her all in, glossing past the shapely legs in worn leather boots, the curves hugged snuggly in her dark-gray dress, and the swelling breasts pushing against the top. *Are they the result of the pregnancy or have they always been that full?* I dump away the thoughts that won't do any of us any good and zero in on her sharp, like eagle on prey, eyes.

She scans me too, never moving past my face but somehow making me feel like she sees me. All of me. All at once.

She Googled me. It's in the narrowing of her eyes and the tight line spreading flat across her plump lips. As if she's not surprised by what she sees and knows all she needs to.

So, I smile at her like I would with a reluctant seller. Because for the first time in a very long time, I'm at a disadvantage.

I need someone. I need this woman. I need her womb and her body. Not in the way I normally would. I don't want to twist her luscious body into a pretzel and pound her with my cock for one night until she's biting those lips and arching her back.

Not this time. I need more from this teacher than moans and her fingers squeezing at my back or tangling on the sheets as she begs me to go harder or faster.

I need her to grow my child inside her, to nurture and nourish him with her body. I'm prepared to give her what she wants. Money is no object but the still, small voice screams that it's going to take a lot more than that. And though I believe in my initial hunches, I don't care because either way it is going to happen.

I need this child. For Astrid and for myself.

"Come in, please." I signal to the chair and extend my hand.

She walks in the room and takes my hand in her smaller one. I expected softer skin and her nails are uneven, like she's been chewing on them.

"Winter," she says and when she takes the chair across from mine, I catch a whiff of soothing fruit, maybe grapefruit and peppermint. It's not overwhelming but understandable in her condition.

"It's nice to meet you. I wish it were under different circumstances."

Now why the hell did I say that? And why did my voice deepen like I meant it?

She stiffens. I don't know if it's because I reminded her of the reason why she's here or because she thinks I'm a sleaze ball. I did kind of ogle the shit out of her.

"Would you like something to drink?"

She shakes her head.

"Let's get on with it, then," Elias says.

I peel my gaze from Winter to stare at him. "Do you have somewhere more important to be?"

His face reddens. "No, but I believe Miss Alexander is missing school to be here."

My gaze returns to her and she gives me a slight nod.

"Elias told me he explained to you what we know happened and since you didn't bring a lawyer, I will have mine litigate for the both of us. The clinic needs to answer and pay for this error."

She holds up a finger. "How come the clinic never called me? And how come you know about my procedure? That's confidential information."

Elias clears his throat. "Better Maryland has bigger problems right now than a HIPAA violation. I made sure the director understood that."

He is not going to elaborate. He's made his point. The evidence is in her rounded eyes and semi-opened mouth. Elias can do a lot with a few words. It's what makes him a good lawyer and I bet good money, a shit ass human being.

"How could this happen?" Her skin is pale and her hand massages over her throat in a way that shouldn't still be so familiar to me.

She's fighting nausea.

I grab my iPhone and send a message to my secretary for some tea. I look back at her and I'm taken aback by the cold glint in her eyes. "I hired a surrogate to carry my frozen embryos. She chose that clinic. That should have been my first clue that something wasn't right. The day of the procedure she went in and left soon after. Doctor Lawrence, for reasons unknown to us, went through with the procedure anyway, implanting the embryos inside you."

Her hand shoots to her stomach. *She's going to be sick.* Where the hell is Sandra?

The quick knock comes through and my secretary walks in. Her smile, unflappable as a seasoned nurse. "Here you go, hon." She hands over the tea and excuses herself from the room.

Winter blinks a couple of times but takes the tea, wrapping both hands tightly around the mug. Her chest is heaving a little, which tells me she's close to retching. Though by the green tint on his face, I think Elias may beat her to it.

She takes a small sip of the tea and then another.

I continue telling her everything we know, my gaze still on her as she sips. "The day we found out, I sent Elias to you. The clinic will compensate you for this. If they don't offer, we will sue them. This is not just an error, one or more of their employees was in cahoots with my hired surrogate. I am certain this is not just a botched attempt. This is a plot. Against me, of course."

Color gradually returns to her face. "Why would someone want to do that to you?"

I shrug. "I'm a wealthy man. I paid Alice a lot of money to do this. She may think they could get more money. I briefly wondered if you were part of the whole thing…"

I don't know why I added that, maybe because I need to see her reaction for myself.

Her eyes go round and after a second, she laughs. Not, not just laughs. That throaty, dark sound is more than a laugh. It's a "fuck off into a dark corner of hell," if I've ever heard one. The glacial tone in her eyes lets me know she just about despises me right now.

"Let me assure you, Mr. Grayson, I never would have put myself in this situation. Not for any amount of money in the world."

Yeah, I went too far. "I apologize for implying you did. I hate that you got caught up in this. This is why I insist on compensating you as well."

Her eyebrows knit together. "Compensate me for what, exactly?"

"Grayson, perhaps—"

I wave away whatever Elias is trying to say.

"I would like to hire you to have my baby, Miss Alexander. I understand there will be a lot of inconveniences to you and your life-style. I would like to do whatever I can to alleviate those uncomfortable glitches."

The fire that ignites in her gaze is enough to tells me that I'm definitely about to be on the receiving end of a go-fuck-yourself.

She leans forward and stares straight into my eyes. "Mr. Grayson, I'm sure in your daily life you meet a lot of people that would do anything for money. *I* am not one of those people. You sit here, talking about a human life like it's a small business loan or maybe some asset you are trying to acquire. You make it sound like it's a UPS package with 'fragile' stamped on it that must be delivered after purchase. There's no talk about love or family."

My skin goes hot, too. She's assuming a lot of shit after sitting here just a few minutes. "You don't know anything about me, Miss Alexander."

19

She places her mug on my desk, her smile sharp like an ax swinging my way.

"What else is there to know? You're not even fully here. You're on your cell phone or chastising your employees. You're all about earning your cash, no matter what it costs but we're not talking about cash here. I have no desire to have any of my own, but children are not stocks and bonds. They cannot be bought. That's what you're trying to do, buy my womb. Maybe you feel like it's a rite of passage or whatever but you can count me out. I won't ever condemn a child to a life of coldness. I'm going to terminate this pregnancy as soon as I can."

She stands and heads for the door.

4

Winter

My skin is on fire as I leave Spencer Grayson's office and head toward the elevator. The nerve of that man. The secretary from earlier calls out to me, probably because I look deranged as I stalk across the carpet. I want to ignore her but I can't. This woman's kindness made me feel better. I would have had to excuse myself and go vomit without her.

I stop and turn to her, mustering a smile. "Thank you so much for the tea. I badly needed it and it settled my stomach."

Her expression shifts from concern to a don't-mention-it smile. "Oh, honey, don't thank me. I only brought you the tea. Mr. Grayson's the one who requested it."

As if he could be conjured by only mentioning his name, Grayson appears at the door. I pivot on my feet and continue on my way. He catches up to me at the elevators.

"Please listen to me."

"No." I punch the down button on the elevator. "I need to go back to work." I turn away from him but his hand closes over my wrist and brings me to face him.

"Winter, please." He moves in closer, his breath fanning over my face, and he's whispering now. "You can't terminate. I'm willing to do whatever it takes, no matter the cost."

I grind my teeth so hard it hurts. "Don't you get it? It's not about the money. It's about a child, a human life."

He frowns, those gray eyes overcast with confusion. "My child would have the best life."

I step closer, whispering as he is. "Yeah, all your money can buy, but what about love, affection, attention, a real home? I can't let someone knowingly go neglected like that. I'm sorry this happened but I can't do it. It's easy for you to ask—"

"Easy?" He scoffs. "Only someone who doesn't know me would think this is easy for me. Then again, you never intended to hear me out. You came in with your mind made up."

"No…" I trail off and I hate myself for it because he's right about that.

I spent most of the hours between last night and this morning looking on the internet for information on him, for articles as to what type of person he is. There are tons. From the *Forbes* and *Newsweek* types with experts like Warren Buffett hailing him as a King Midas, to the opinion articles on his style of business and his swallowing of small companies. And then there were the gossip rags. The salacious articles were plenty, with interviews of jilted ex-lovers. All of them alluded to the coldness that had hit me when I was in his office, when instead of treating this with warmth, he acted like he was hiring an accountant. He'd been on his phone while I asked him questions about how this came to happen.

My gaze snaps to his secretary's desk. She said he asked her to bring me the tea. *Had it been then? Have I been so wrong?*

He grasps both my hands in his and God, when did we get so close?

"Look, don't make any decisions now. Just give me a chance. Let's talk about this in a different place. Just please promise me you won't terminate. Please. Take some time to think about it. I'll call you this evening and we can arrange a time to meet and talk about this."

His fingers are tight on my wrist. He's not hurting me but the desperation in his eyes pierces right through me. I want to tell him no, that my decision is final and there is no way I'll become his rented womb. But there's something in that gaze, a slight edge, an anguish. Something that tugs deep at the tight knot on my chest.

"Not tonight. Come by tomorrow after my private lessons. I won't do anything until then but I'm not promising you anything. I'm just going to hear you out."

There's such relief in his eyes I can barely look at him when he says, "Thank you."

The ping of the elevator jolts us away from each other. The door opens. I walk in and he's still staring. "I'll see you tomorrow, Winter."

I don't take a breath again until the doors close and the weight of his gaze is off me. I sag back against the elevator wall, a hand pressed to my chest.

Lauren is waiting for me outside. She never went home and insisted on driving me. Just knowing she was waiting outside for me made me feel less alone. And for the first time in my life, I don't want to be alone.

I jump in the car, fasten my seat belt and lean my head back against the seat.

"Are you okay?"

I nod but can't say anything else, not with the way my heart is pounding. She puts the car in drive and gets going. I close my eyes and when I open them again, I have to blink a few times. We are at a diner half a mile from La Salle Academy where I work. I come here sometimes for lunch.

"What are we doing here?" I ask.

"We need to eat something before you go to work. You didn't eat anything this morning. Neither did I. I was too nervous. This is a crazy flashback to Adri being pregnant with Bron. I always get nauseous or hungry around pregnant women. I take sympathy pains to a new level."

No, she takes the word friendship *to a new level.* "Let's get us fed then."

23

She waits until the food is in front of us to pounce. "So, what happened?"

I pop a fry in my mouth and then go through the whole meeting. "…and he asked me to think about it. I'm supposed to talk to him tomorrow."

"Is this what you want to do? Think about it? Let him convince you? You know I'm here for you but I want to make sure this is what *you* want because you are the most innocent victim here and this is the weirdest conception known to man. No offense."

I nod. "None taken. I should want to terminate with no talks …"

I can still see his pleading gray eyes and feel the warmth of his hands around my wrist as he begged me to hear him out. What if I'm wrong? I still think he's cold. Why would he want a baby if he was an unfeeling man?

"What's making you doubt?" Lauren puts her burger down. "And before you answer, you know I'll be here for you no matter what. No one's a better auntie than me. Ask Bron. But I want to make sure you are not coerced into this."

"He's not forcing me to think about it. This is something I need to think about. I went in there with my mind made up about him but I don't think that's fair. You know?"

On the drive back to the school, I'm trying to find a way to put it all on hold so I can get through my day.

"So, what's he like? Is he as hot in person as he is in photos?" Lauren asks.

There's a fluttering in my belly but I manage a half-hearted nod. "He's good looking."

She chuckles and I have to look out of the window. It's not necessarily a lie but he's more than good looking. Spencer Grayson's the kind of hot that makes your legs drift apart before you can remember to glue them together.

I'm not going to get caught up in that, though. We have a messy situation on our hands and I promised to listen. That's all I'm going to do. Just listen.

5

Winter

Students like Ayla and Bron are the reason why I teach.

I love these girls. Love their talent and maturing strokes. Love the way they check each other's canvasses to make sure they're keeping up. Love the knowing smiles when they catch each other mid-peek. Bron's stroke is nature's touch at its best. She inherited it from her father and no doubt from observation and wrist emulation. Her strength is often in the overall picture.

Ayla's stroke is the result of her dedication and the hours of practice she puts into it. Her dad, Oliver, always gushes about what a hard worker she is. She is strongest in the details. Often, I'm taken aback by her ability to make certain objects the focal point in a scenery.

The giggles break from their throats and fill my living room, making me smile. They're as different as a Matisse and a Cézanne—one as light as the tint in her eyes and the other deep-shaded as the center of an onion. Bron's beautiful curls are exuberant as she is, while Ayla's braid, which she has mastered, keeps her hair neat and tidy.

They're fun and stand up for each other fiercely. Wouldn't the world be a better place if all girls were like Ayla and Bron?

"Your dads should be here soon. If you continue giggling, you won't get much further than this." My voice carries none of the stern emphasis I wish I could put on it. I always get caught up in them. It's beautiful to experience childhood like this, in a new way, through the eyes of two amazing little girls.

"Miss Winter?"

"Yes, Bron?"

She turns around to look at me. "My *abuela* is coming this weekend and she's staying for a while. Can she come to our lesson next week?"

"Of course. I'm looking forward to telling her how wonderful her *Sopa de Pollo* is. Thank *you* for sharing it with me."

She smiles. "You're welcome. Mom says she's going to have Abuela fill a whole fridge with it so she can have enough for all of us."

"Hey, we should sell your grandma's *sopa* for the school bazaar instead of cookies," Ayla says and then her eyes widen. "Ooooor maybe we can ask her to teach us to make it and we can have a soup stand at the games."

Bron's mouths opens into a perfect O. "You're a genius. We'll make so much money when it's cold."

I can picture Adrianna's face and Ayla's dad, Ollie, shaking their heads at this idea but I don't laugh. I bet they can convince them to let them try. Their parents are gaga for their babies.

Babies.

My stomach roils. How can I love other people's children so much and be literally sickened by the idea of having a child of my own? Would I love a child that was like these two? *Heck yeah.* The thing is, my child will never be like them. It couldn't be nurtured the same way. Flowers don't thrive in arid soil.

The knock on the door makes the three of us jump.

"That's probably my daddy," Bron says.

I usher them to go wash their hands and head to the door. My stomach has mostly behaved today. Maybe it's all the ginger tea and crackers I picked up on my way home from work yesterday. I open the door and standing in my threshold is Cameron Blake, like it's normal for a gifted, famous artist and former athlete to stand at my door.

"Good afternoon, Winter."

"Hi, Cam. Come in. They're washing their hands. Their strokes get better every day. Their messes, not so much."

He laughs. "At home, either. Thank God we have designated areas or I think Adri would kick us out."

His eyes do that smolder thing when he says Adrianna's name. I've made a point to watch for it. He infuses it with something. I can't quite put a name to it. But it always bleeds into his smile.

"Daddy."

Bronwyn rushes back to the living room with her hands still soapy and a smile from ear to ear. She stops in front of him and climbs on her tiptoes. Cam, wearing an identical smile, pulls her into his arms and presses a kiss to her cheek. His face goes completely unguarded with adoration whenever he looks at her. He doesn't even seem to notice her wet hands on his shirt.

"I just came to say hi and I'll be right back."

"Okay." He doesn't let her go.

"Daddy, don't be a baby." She giggles and wriggles away but turns around. "I'll be right back."

When Cam turns to me again, there's no bashfulness or shame in there. A girl barely half his size has him firmly wrapped around her soapy pinky.

"You two are so cute together," I say.

His face reddens a little. "Thanks. Adri says Bron's got me wearing my feelings all over my face."

I chuckle. "Yes, she does and it goes both ways. She's always talking about you, and not just your paintings or your games anymore."

"I don't know how I ever made it through life without her." His voice rings with wonder.

"What was it like? You know, finding out about her? If it's not too personal."

His smile widens. "I don't mind sharing this, her, or what she is to

27

me. I was shocked. When she showed up at my exhibit so sure of herself and so much like her mother, I couldn't believe it. I was already half in love with her but when I realized she was mine, it was like the world shifted. She became my everything in a matter of hours. You know?"

I shake my head. I don't know what it's like to be or have someone like that in my life.

"It's crazy, Winter. Since I had thought I'd lost Adri, all I wanted was to paint and be alone, doing the occasional art show. The first time she smiled at me, I learned that art covers a void but it doesn't fill it. I was full of voids. Bron and her mother fill them with smiles and noise and infinite chaos."

He says chaos like it's the most wonderful thing in the world. Like it's something we should all shoot for. Like we're not really living if there's no chaos in our lives.

I don't understand. "You wouldn't have it any other way?"

He laughs heartily and shakes his head. It's the same reaction he had when someone asked him if he would ever consider going back to Major League Baseball during La Salle's last baseball game.

"Bron brought new colors into my life and changed my whole outlook. I was one hundred percent sure I was never going to have children. I didn't even want them near me. Now, I would have twenty if they were just like her. She's got me involved with her teammates and all her class stuff. And I don't mind at all."

"Wow." My hand flies to my chest. "You want more kids?"

He shrugs. "I want five or as many as Adri agrees to. I don't think it will be five but at least one or two more."

Normally when people say they want five kids, I roll my eyes thinking, *Yeah you say that because we all know it's not going to happen*. But I have no doubts Cam would welcome however many come. It's in his eyes.

My friend is a lucky woman.

And Bron is an amazing kid. Only someone without a heart wouldn't want a little girl so perfect. I'm glad she'll never have to know the loneliness of having no one because everyone around her, including me, would bend over backwards to make her feel secure. All children should live with that kind of security and love.

The walls of my chest tighten and I have to massage circles into it.

Cam frowns. "Are you okay?"

I nod, not trusting my voice. My mind races, trying to come up with something but the girls come back in the room.

He smiles at them and places a hand on Ayla's shoulder. "Are you ready for Saturday's game, Ace? I know St. Theresa's team is shaking in their cleats right now, worrying about your fastball."

The tiny smile doubles and grows on Ayla's lips. Her eyes are alight with a flame she reserves for baseball or painting. She nods hard and flexes her hand open and closed.

"We're so going to win," Bronwyn says.

Cam nods. "Yes, you are. But what's more important than a win?"

Ayla raises her hand. "A clean game where you do your best, don't hold anything back, and leave everything on the field."

Cam high-fives her and then Bron. "That's right. Are we taking you home, Ayla?"

She shakes her head. "My dad's coming."

"We'll see you tomorrow, then. Tell your dad I'll call him about practice. Let's go, Bron. Your mom is waiting for us."

The girls hug tight, clinging to each other.

"I'll FaceTime you," Bron promises and Cam and I have to look away to keep from laughing. They act like they won't see each other in months, when they have school tomorrow.

I walk them out and wave them away. I'm about to close the door when a towering form, broad shoulders and eyes that cut through the distance, steps out of the driver side of a parked navy-blue car.

My breath skids, my hand tightening around the doorknob. *Spencer Grayson.* Is it time already? I'm not ready for him. Not yet. I lost myself in the girls and the lessons but time's up and he's here to convince me of something I really don't want to do.

With every long step he takes toward me, I'm more pressed, more helpless to do anything but watch him. I'm more entranced by his gaze and ease. This man fears nothing and his gait is daring, as if the world should fear him.

No wonder he's so successful. He probably intimidates the shit out of all the people he does business with. Except, I'm not just intimidated by him. I'm dreading this whole conversation and whatever decision may come out of it.

His scent reaches me ahead of him, something citrusy wrapped in smoke and decadent enough to cause a stir inside my skin. Smells have sort of become my enemy but I would gladly spray my blankets in whatever he's wearing.

"Winter." My name slow-rolls from his tongue, like he's savoring it.

"Hi, come in." I'm proud of how steady my tone is.

Let's get this over with.

6

Grayson

I follow Winter inside her rowhouse. Her shoulders are rigid, her spine so straight it could crack if she trips. She walks in fast steps, as if she's trying to get away from me. I didn't miss the stiffening of her body when I got out of my car, or the wariness in her eyes the closer I got.

I'm noticing way too many things about this woman.

I hate that she needs to be so guarded around me. I'm not trying to hurt her. All I want is the child growing inside her. I need to make sure she understands that I'm not a threat or she'll never agree to carry the pregnancy to term.

In her living room, a young girl sits on her couch, intent on what seems like a baseball game on her iPad. She glances up at me, her eyes sparkling with open curiosity. She looks me up and down like she's missing nothing and memorizing everything. She must be one of Winter's art students.

"Ayla, this is Spencer Grayson," Winter says and her voice, though as raspy as last time, is now infused with something warm.

"Hello," Ayla says.

I close the distance between us and shake her hand. "It's nice to meet you."

Ayla nods, her gaze bouncing briefly to Winter and then back to me.

"Ayla's dad is coming to pick her up soon." Winter keeps her voice light but there's a message there. We will wait until the girl leaves to talk. "Can I get you something to drink? I only have water, ginger tea, and Gatorade."

"Water is fine, please."

She heads through a door and I take a look around the room. There are paintings symmetrically hanged, crowding every part of the wall. One of the biggest is of a woman in a red dress with amazingly pronounced curves, her arms raised over her head and her face to the sun. Her hair hangs down her back. It's so vivid you can almost hear the music and I wouldn't be surprised if the woman began to sway.

Did Winter paint this?

I move from that one and my gaze lands on the two canvases near the window. Each portrays a silhouette of a woman, one with muscles in a military stance with bright stars on her shoulders and drilling eyes. The other with a book in one hand and a finger in the air, pointed toward a building. Neither seems the work of the person that painted the ones on the wall.

"Are you Miss Winter's boyfriend?"

I whip about to find Ayla has gotten up from the couch and is now a few feet away. It's an odd first question when you don't know someone but I go with it. It's not like I can tell the kid I'm trying to make her teacher carry my baby. "No, we're friends."

She pins me with an I-don't-buy-it look. "I've never seen you before and I know all her other friends."

"Are any of these yours?" I counter, trying to distract her.

She nods and comes to stand next to me. "This one's Bron's. Her *abuela* is a vice-principal. The one to the left is mine. That's my grandma. She was in the army."

I get caught on the brightness of the gold features, the muscles, and

THE WINTER OF MY LOVE

sharpened eyes. "She's a tough lady. Look at all those medals and stars."

Ayla smiles. It's a shy, little curve of the lips. "She was a decorated soldier who fought in Desert Storm. It was a war a looooong time ago, in the nineteen-nineties."

A long time ago, huh? "You must be really proud of her."

"I am. She's really strict and people are really afraid of her but she's super sweet. She bakes me Snickerdoodles."

"You're lucky," I say

"Here's your water," Winter says, handing me a glass. "Ayla, your dad just pulled up outside." She heads to the door.

The little girl goes to the couch and grabs her iPad and a bookbag from the floor. "We'll have to finish this talk some other time. Daddy's late." Her eyes sparkle mischievously. Like she's happy her father is late to pick her up. Why is that? Doesn't she like spending time with her dad?

Winter returns with a man about my height, dark skin, and built like a Yankees' shortstop. They're smiling like they just shared a private joke.

"*Papi*, you are soooo late." Ayla singsongs but she's smiling hard as she crosses the room to hug him. His arms go around her, tight. Her head lingers on his chest for a while and then he kisses her cheek in sequence. One kiss after the next.

"I'm only twenty minutes late," he says in a strong *Latino* accent.

"Still late."

"Fine. Do you have all your stuff? We need to get out of Winter's hair."

Winter. He calls her Winter.

"*No te apures.*" She laughs. "I'm almost jealous of the Chick-fil-A that you and Ayla get to have for dinner."

"*Te traigo algo?*"

She rubs her belly and looks at me briefly. My stomach tightens for some reason I can't explain. He wants to come back and bring her food.

She looks back at him and shakes her head. "*No. Gracias.*"

The man turns to me and extends his hand. "I'm Oliver, Ayla's dad."

I'm still taken aback by Winter. She speaks Spanish, as does he. And not high school Spanish. This is the real thing. Elias didn't tell me.

I shake his hand. "Spencer Grayson. Your daughter is very talented. She was telling me about her decorated army grandma. You must be proud of your mother."

Ollie smiles. "She's my former mother-in-law, but yes, she's a very accomplished lady, just like my little Frida Kahlo here." He squeezes his daughter's shoulder. "We should get going. Someone needs her fast food so she can do her homework."

Ayla giggles. "It's not that bad. The newspaper yesterday said it's the healthiest of all the chains."

Oliver taps his index finger to his lips. "Hmm. I guess you'll have a salad instead of fries? Since you're so concerned about health nowadays."

The horror in her face is comical and Winter's laughter rings out. It's full-bodied and real and just a little bit too loud.

The little girl's cheeks bloom red as she grabs her dad's hand and heads to the door.

Oliver doesn't move. "Did you forget to say something?"

She turns around and goes to hug Winter. "Thank you."

Winter touches her forehead. "I'll see you tomorrow. You did excellent work today and you'll be awesome in Saturday's game."

Ayla nods, waves to me and turns to her dad. "Come on, *Papi*."

"Nice to meet you. I'll close the door behind me," Oliver barely gets out before Ayla pulls him toward the door.

"Did you miss me a lot today, *Papi*?"

Oliver sighs heavy and loud. "Every second of the day."

"Me, too. Can we watch an episode of *Vampire Chronicles* after my homework?"

He closes the door and Winter and I are finally alone. I'm looking at her. Her gaze is on her flip-flops.

"Please sit." She points to the spot that Ayla vacated a few minutes ago.

I wait until she takes the chair across from it before I sit. "How many kids do you teach at home?"

"Just Ayla and Bronwyn. You missed Bron."

"I saw a little girl leave with a man that looked familiar. "

She nods. "Cameron Blake, her dad, came to pick her up. Ollie called earlier to tell me he would be a little late to pick up Ayla."

"Why was she happy he was late?"

She chuckles. "Whenever he's late, she gets Chick-fil-A for dinner. Today he was late just to make her happy."

"Yeah, they seem really close."

"It's just the two of them." Her smile reaches all the way to her eyes and yet there's a hint of sadness there. Or maybe I'm imagining it.

And then she sighs and catches herself, her arms cross. One hand secured tight over the other like she's trying to prevent anything else from coming out. "You wanted to talk?"

"I'm not trying to hurt you, Winter." I surprise myself by saying it.

Her mouth falls open and her face goes blank. "I don't think you are."

"Are you sure? Because you seem a little scared."

"I'm not scared of anyone." There's conviction in her voice and fire roaring in her eyes. "I'm not comfortable with what you want from me. I never planned to get pregnant or be a mom."

"But you're a teacher," I say without thinking. *What the hell am I doing?* Questioning her choices is no way to ingratiate myself to her.

"I love children, in general. They're wonderful and honest. I just don't want any of my own."

A screw tightens inside my chest. She doesn't want a child and she's carrying one that was forced on her. It's lousy to try to convince her to carry a child she doesn't want. But I have no choice but to persuade her.

Because that's my child inside her and I *do* want him.

7

Winter

I don't like him in my house. I don't like how much space he occupies. And I definitely don't like the way he looks at me like I'm a porcupinefish fish at the Aquarium.

He's not the first or the last person to wonder why I don't have kids or don't want them. I get the same question and assumptions from others. The questions don't bother me much anymore. I guess once you get past the none-of-your-damned-business part, it's pretty common.

But Grayson's reaction bugs me. There's something subdued and restrained in his gaze, like he has a lot more to say. I don't know why though. And I shouldn't care anyway. This man sees me as a human incubator, so I see him as a threat.

"Why did someone like you have a woman inseminated? I'm sure there are women everywhere who would jump at the chance of marrying you."

His head rears back a little as if my question surprises him. I wish I can chew the words right back into my mouth. I was just inner-bitching about nosy people and look at me, as close to a mind-your-fucking-life as I've ever been.

Then he smiles, it's slow but the lines stretch all the way to the corners of his eyes, displaying the type of teeth my dentist would swoon over. It's the kind of smile I would have given extra fries for at McDonalds. The reason I watch *Luther, The Wire*, or Idris Elba clean his kitchen on a loop.

"Not as many women as you're thinking, and thank you for the compliment, but I have no desire to marry again. My relationships with women are strictly on the casual side."

A slow tremor rattles my clit and spreads to my body but I shake it away and don't let my mind drift further than him shrugging his shirt off for a quick and thorough fuck on my couch.

What the fuck is wrong with me?

"Um. But you're having a child." Even as the words pop out of my mouth, I wince at how archaic they are. In this day and age, many people choose to parent alone, via insemination or adoption. This man just doesn't seem like the type. I don't see him changing diapers or running a kid to playdates like Cam with Bron. Or letting his child climb all over him or bending over backwards to make her smile like Oliver does Ayla.

"I plan to be a single parent, Winter."

His voice shakes me and I wish he wouldn't say my name like a dark whisper that vibrates through my skin.

"Why?" I find myself asking and then reprimanding myself. *The real why here is: why do you need to know this?*

His eyes go cold and my arms tighten around myself. I deserve whatever is coming out of his mouth. Just because I'm involuntarily pregnant with his kid—*Jesus, what a nightmare*—doesn't mean I'm entitled to ask this stuff.

I need to explain. "I'm just trying to understand. You told me you don't do relationships but you want to have a child and that's the most involved, invasive, and deep-rooted relationship anyone can have with another human. I don't want to condemn an innocent child to a life of being ignored and emotionally neglected. There is nothing worse in life."

A new light flashes in his eyes, turning them another shade of intense, almost-blue gray. "I don't do romantic relationships with women. Astrid, my wife, died three years ago..." He looks down at the floor for a moment.

Way to go, Winter. "I'm sorry. I didn't mean to bring up painful memories."

His head snaps up.

"I don't ever talk about this...but it's important you understand, since you have me in your hands." His eyes stay on mine. "We found out Astrid had an aggressive form of ovarian cancer as we were going through fertility treatments. We had frozen embryos, but her body wasn't responding to the IVF. After some tests, the doctors found she was very sick. One of her last wishes was for me to have the child we both wanted so much."

The air shrivels in my chest. *The embryo is from his beloved wife.*

I remember reading about his wife passing away but I never thought twice as to that being the reason he may want this baby. I'd come to all sorts of conclusions, but never that this might be his last chance to have a child with the woman he loved.

"Our marriage wasn't perfect but we wanted children, at least one. The disease took her too fast...I do know it's harder to raise a child on your own, but that's what my father did. He was a dedicated man who got up every morning, fed me, ironed my clothes, took me to school and went to work. At nights, we did homework, talked about life, and we watched TV shows together. We had each other. That was enough."

Good God, did he lose his mom as a child and then his wife? "Did your mom pass away?"

All the warmth fades from his eyes. "No, she lives in Italy with her husband."

Oh.

His icy gaze is centered on me and suggests that I don't ask any more questions on the subject. "You see, Winter, one can survive without a mother."

The memory is instant. I'm standing by a window, my palms against the cold glass. Outside, the cops are taking my mom away. And I'm scared, so scared…that she'll turn around and come back.

The oppressive memory chokes the breath out of my lungs. The wave of nausea rises furious until I'm close to gagging. My fingers curl around my throat. My other hand over my mouth.

Grayson moves so fast I don't even register it. He's next to me in less than a second.

"Deep breaths." He pries my hand from my mouth and places my three fingers on the inside of the opposite wrist. He massages slow circles into it.

"Continue doing this and I'll be right back." He disappears into my kitchen and I mimic what he was doing without question.

He's wounded me, deeper than he would ever know.

Because the words he just uttered are the harshest, but truest in the world.

Because I know, oh, so well, what is like to lack a mother and to survive without one.

Because the only thing that ties me to the woman that birthed me is a DNA code.

Tears fill my eyes and I continue massaging rough circles into my wrist. My microwave beeps three times and moments later, Grayson comes back with a mug in his hand. He places it in my hand.

His fingers brush mine and he shoots me an apologetic smile. "I made a mess of your cabinets looking for the tea."

A whiff of ginger sends a calming wave through me like an announcement that things will get better. I concentrate on taking one slow sip after the other until my stomach begins to settle. He's still next to me, rubbing circles on my wrist as if he's not afraid that I may barf on him.

"How do you know so much about nausea?" I ask, mostly to distract myself from his nearness. There's a gray hair on his pant leg.

"Astrid always had a strong reaction to chemo."

An ache breaks out in my chest and I'm helpless to do anything but stare into his eyes until he looks away.

"I'm sorry, Grayson."

His gaze shoots to mine and he's on his feet the next second. "I should probably go if you're feeling better. You've probably had a long day and you need rest. Can we talk about this tomorrow again? Please don't do anything until I've gotten the chance to really explain. I know money can't sway you but if you decide to do this, I promise you, I will make this as comfortable as I can. And if you ever find a way, I can compensate you..." He shakes his head. "...just please give me a chance to convince you."

I catch another glimpse of that desperation in his eyes, of that desire I saw by the elevator. I can't handle that right now. I bob my head and stare into my tea.

I walk him to the door. He takes something out of his pocket and places it in my palm. It's his business card. "If you need anything, please call me. No matter the time. My cell phone is at the bottom. Lock your deadbolts."

I nod.

"Winter, thank you for hearing me out. I know this is not easy for you." He motions for me to close my door and I do.

I can't form words. I'm paralyzed with fear. And the reason is one I can't explain, even to myself.

I've already decided. I'm going to carry his child.

Grayson

The ride back home is quick. Winter's place in Patterson Park is not too far away from my Silo Point condo, but the weight of our conversation haunts me. The pressure on my chest doesn't lighten with the miles between us. I'm in for another sleepless night.

Part of me screams that I should have stayed and tried to convince her tonight but she didn't look like she could take much more pressure.

And then there is the rest of me. I didn't want to have to share more than I already did.

Her questions were normal, given our situation, but...I don't ever talk about Astrid. With anyone. I don't like to keep reliving how I failed my wife in more than one way. I couldn't love her like she wanted. I couldn't make her dream to be a mom come true. I couldn't even find a doctor to cure her.

She'd been looking out for me even as her body faded. She left fatherhood for me all set. I messed that up, too. I didn't see Alice as the opportunist she is. It was too easy.

Nothing involving people is ever that simple.

Now Winter's decision stands in a corner, looming like the proverbial elephant.

Tonight gave me no clue what she's going to do. I don't know what to make of her or the world she lives in. She teaches children but wants none. She is so sweet with Ayla and watches her and her father with fondness. It is a contrast to our conversation.

I just see those stormy eyes, the way she paled and became almost sickened by the prospect of having a child. That's what haunts me. I see her at the door, holding tight to the knob as if she couldn't wait to shut it on my face.

I pull out my phone and check through my messages to divert myself. Elias' name is on at least five unread emails. Sandra sent four more for my approval and I skim through those, making mental notes on what I need to do.

Nin, my gray-and-white Siamese kitten, is waiting for me on the other side of the door but doesn't move from her spot as I come in. Aloofness is something we usually have in common.

"Hey, Tyrant." I move past her and she follows me. I shrug off my jacket and head to the kitchen. I didn't pick up dinner and Aunt Millie went out with her Pink Ladies Society. I told her I wouldn't be home until late. I was too preoccupied trying to convince Winter.

A sandwich will do. And chips, of course. Who would eat a sandwich without chips? I take the turkey pastrami, Muenster cheese, and butter from the fridge. I slather the butter over the bread slices and smile. I can hear my dad saying, "You need butter, Grayson. A ham and cheese sandwich is nothing without the butter."

I put it on a plate and pull out Nin's treat bag.

"If Winter says yes, you will have to share me."

She meows and rubs herself along my leg, full-on needy now.

We move to the living room. I put the treats on her plate next to the couch. I sit and eat my sandwich with the TV on mute while the highlights of the Orioles game play on the screen. They lost again. My employees will be raging about this game all day tomorrow and claiming some small victory in the fact that they played their hearts out. And at least the Yankees lost too, overlooking the fact that theirs was the worst team in baseball.

I'm finishing a beer when my phone rings. It's an unknown four-four-three number but everyone who calls my cell is, because they've been given the number specifically.

"Grayson, it's Winter," she says before I can even say anything.

I was not expecting a call from her tonight. "Hello."

"I'm feeling better. Thank you for the tea and teaching me to do that thing with my fingers. It worked." Her voice is subdued and grave.

No way she's calling me just to thank me. A knot breaks out and expands in my throat. *Jesus, please.*

I clear my throat. "You're welcome. I'm glad you're feeling better."

"I probably should tell you this in person…" she starts.

My heart tumbles. "I can come back over there."

And beg you with everything I have to please change your mind, to not say what I know will come out of your mouth next.

"No, it's okay. I'm going to bed soon but I need to say it out loud and specially to say it to you."

Jesus. I want to tell her it's fine, that I already know, but the walls of my chest are shoving together, squeezing so tightly I can barely breathe. I close my eyes and wait for it.

"I'm going to do it, Grayson. I'm going to carry the pregnancy to term."

Heat flushes through my body and rushes straight to my head. I lean forward, my shoulders sagging, and the air whooshes out of my lungs.

God.

"Grayson?"

My hands have gone numb and I have to flex them open and closed. It takes a couple of breaths to regain my voice. "I'm here."

She's going to have the baby.

"It wasn't an easy decision because of what I explained earlier to you. But the same way I wouldn't condemn someone to a life of neglect, I couldn't deny a child the chance at a good life with someone who loves them. And you and Astrid have wanted this baby for a long time."

My heart is now pummeling my sternum and I can't form the words I want to because how do you really thank someone for something this big?

"Thank you," I manage to squeeze out.

"I know we need to talk about this some more and make arrangements. I want to make it clear up front that I am not doing this for money and that I will not be paid for it. I also know it's not as simple as just saying yes and you'll want to talk to me about it. I can come to your office tomorrow after work."

"Yes, that will work," I rush out.

"Okay, well. I'm going to try to get some sleep. I'll see you tomorrow."

"Winter…"

"Yes?"

My throat is on fire but I need to say the words again because they're the only thing I can say to this woman. She won't accept my money and what she is doing is worth even more than what I can pay.

"Thank you." My voice cracks.

There's a sharp intake of breath on the other end, followed by silence and more quick breaths. Then she says, "See you tomorrow."

I hang up the phone but continue to grip it tight in my palm like it's the only thing holding me and my body up. My breath comes out ragged, as scrambled as my thoughts. She's going to do it. She's going to have my baby. I look up to the ceiling, like I do after every victory in my life, hoping Dad is seeing this, praying I don't disappoint him.

"She's going to do it." I still can't believe I'm saying those words. I was so sure she wasn't going through with this. *What made her change her mind?*

I'll have to find ways to make this up to her, to show her how grateful I am. I don't like to be indebted to anyone, but no matter what I do or give her, I'll always be in her debt.

Nin jumps into my lap, her dilated eyes staring up at me, her body vibrating in purrs. I indulge her by massaging her fur with my fingers. She shifts her head around to get me where she needs me to scratch. "It's actually going to happen."

And I have to shove away the fear that hits me with full force. I'm going to be someone's father. As Winter warned me earlier, I don't do relationships but now the biggest relationship of all is in my future. I look forward to it, but I can't stop the dread from creeping in. Because loving and losing are sometimes synonymous.

My head drifts back against the back of my couch and I doze off with one thought. I'll protect that child from anything and I swear I will make it up to Winter for the rest of her life.

8

Winter

The door to the diner opens and Adri strolls in, followed by Lauren. I push my fries away and take a deep breath. *Showtime.*

I wave to them and they head my way. I want to talk to them about my decision before I meet with Grayson. This is another first for me. I am not used to consulting or informing anyone about my decisions. I make them and that's it. But things have changed and these women have become so much more in my life. They're my first real friends.

"I should be a little mad that you asked me to meet you here. *Mi Tesoro*, the finest bistro in all of Maryland, is open for business at one and you ask us to meet you here," Adri teases.

"I have a meeting with Spencer Grayson after this but I wanted to talk to you first."

"Oh, shit. You're jumping right into it." Lauren takes a seat across from me and Adri takes the chair to her left and my right.

I blurt it out. "I decided to carry the pregnancy to term so he can have his baby."

"Okay. We are here for you. Whatever you need." Adri says and Lauren just nods.

What the hell. "You don't seem surprised."

Lo shakes her head. "We're not. The minute you said you would think about it, and after your call last night telling me about his wife, I knew you would do it."

"And it's you," Adri says. "You are one the kindest people I know. Granted, this is a huge favor to do for someone. But no, it doesn't surprise me that you're willing to do it."

"Once I found about his late wife and how they'd always dreamed of having a baby, I couldn't say no. I mean, I'm already pregnant. I also think he will give this baby a good life. You should've seen the way he talked about it."

My friends exchange worried looks.

"My only worry is you, Winter," Adri says and her face goes somber.

"Why? I'm fine."

"There's a lot more to this than just carrying an embryo." Adri places one hand over mine and points at my stomach with the other. "A baby is growing inside you and you'll share things with that baby that no one will ever know. It's more than your body, you'll know when he or she moves, or is restless, and you won't be able to help yourself, you'll bond with the baby. It will be hard to give it up. I would have killed anyone who tried to take Bron."

The tingling in my chest is almost painful. I don't want to hear this kind of thing but I know that won't happen. At least not in the way she thinks. I'll care about the child in the human sense but I'll be able to let him go. Like I do when my students graduate. I'll be happy I was able to help him get to the world and that he'll have a family in Grayson. I won't get more attached than is necessary.

"It won't be like that for me. One, this is not my baby and two, I don't have your maternal instincts. I'm going through this because I think he deserves to live and he has a parent waiting for him. I know I'll feel things but you know about my history."

Never will I put myself in the position of becoming the cold

46

woman who shares my DNA. The one whose only interest in me was for a welfare check to finance her addictions. The one who keeps landing in jail and expecting me to support her. That's why I don't want Grayson's money. Children and money are not things that should go together. My life would have been different if the check I got from the state of New York hadn't made me a viable way of supporting her habits.

"You are not your mother, Win." Lauren says and something twists on my chest. She only calls me Win when we're drunk or when I don't get things that are clear to others. Usually, about family relationships and emotions.

"I'm not her but I don't have those emotions in me. I promise."

"We'll keep an eye on you and you need to come to us if you start feeling different. You should also keep your options open. Maybe you can ask Grayson to see the child from time to time," Adri says.

"I don't think that would work, unless that's something Grayson initiates. It's his baby. I'll need the two of you throughout this thing. I'm a little worried about today, though. I hope he doesn't have his lawyer there. Elias Saunders kind of gives me the creeps. Most likely, he *will* be there since I am sure papers will be signed."

Their expressions shift from warmth to stunned. Lauren looks away first.

Adri leans closer. "Don't trust him. You can use one of Cam's lawyers if you need one."

"You know him?"

"He's a friend of Cam's." She pulls out her phone and types something in.

But not her friend? And Cam doesn't trust him enough to use him as a lawyer. Everything is in all the words she doesn't say.

Lauren is staring out the window and I remember why he seems familiar.

"Elias is the guy who was after you when you came by that night at the rooftop bar," I say to Lo. "He's the one you were torn between with Chase."

There was no competition there, in my opinion.

Her eye roll says everything. "I'm not torn. I won't ever take Elias seriously. So, he's the one dealing with this for Grayson?"

"He's the one who came to me the first day. I couldn't place him. I also don't think he remembers me from that night."

"He only remembers people when they can do something for him," Adri adds. "Just watch your back around him. Though, I doubt he would dare risk his job at Grayson Global. Status is big for him. But don't trust him."

She hates the guy.

"But he's Grayson's lawyer."

"It doesn't matter. I didn't tell Cam anything, just that you may need his lawyer. He says don't sign anything until his lawyer looks through it."

My mouth drops open. "Are you crazy? I can't afford a lawyer that represents Cam. He's uber rich."

Adri rolls her eyes. "His lawyer has nothing to do and they're always on retainer. This won't cost them anything. If it does, Cam's got it."

"Adri—"

She holds up a hand. "It's already done. Cam is asking if you need someone to go into the meeting with you."

"Are you sure you didn't tell him? How is he volunteering his lawyers without knowing for what?"

Lauren laughs. "Make no mistake, they're not married but this woman is his wife. Cam knows better than anyone that happy Adri equals happy life."

Adri chuckles. "He also knows that whatever you need a lawyer for is not as complex as when I needed one." Her voice drops in the end.

Her story still breaks my heart. Her mom shot her dad because he'd taken them hostage. We all have one shitty parent in common. I don't know who my dad is but he's probably shitty, too.

I put my hand over hers. "Thank you. I really appreciate it. If he has a lawyer there, I'll call Cam's."

9

_____

Winter

The elevator door opens and the first thing that hits me is the wave of cold. I didn't imagine it the first time I was here. I wrap my sweater tighter around me and make my way toward the reception desk.

"Miss Alexander?"

I whip about to find Grayson's secretary at the door to the suites. "Hello."

"I've been expecting you. Mr. Grayson's in a brief meeting but he asked me to take you into his office. I'll let him know you're here." Her smile is warm and just the right kind of inviting, like the banana nut muffins I used to enjoy until the last few weeks.

I can almost smell them and my stomach pangs. *Don't think about the muffins, Winter.*

I follow her into Grayson's office. She points at one of the seats and promises she'll be back with some tea for me. I pull out my cell and there are already messages from the girls. Adri wants me to know she's thinking about me and to call her if I need her.

Lauren's a little more candid. *I'm a hop, a skip, and a jump away. And I'm not afraid to be the bitchy friend who's there to protect you.*

When I first met them, I thought it was kind of odd that they were so nice. They barely knew me. I still laugh at Lauren's baffled face when I tried to give her money for driving me around when my car broke down.

I text her back.

Where were you when I was growing up? I could have used your help with some bullies who used to make my life miserable.

Lauren's reply is swift with a side of snark.

It's not too late. Where do those bitches live?

I laugh so loud it echoes in the empty office and I turn around to make sure I'm not disturbing anyone. That's when I see him. Grayson's standing at the door. He's wearing gray slacks, a white shirt, suspenders, and a smile that should make the buttons of my shirt pop off.

"I startled you."

My cheeks are burning. "Oh, a little. I'm sorry, I didn't mean to be loud."

"Don't be. It's great to hear you laugh…" he trails off as if he didn't mean to say that. Then he moves closer, with his hand stretched out and those eyes bearing deep into mine.

His scent reaches me first and wraps around me like plush blanket that makes me so very wet. He closes his hand over mine and I have to swallow because my pussy clenches at the pressure of his warm skin. I go hot all over.

Oh no. No, no, no, Winter. You need to stop.

I yank my hand away and fan my face.

He blinks a couple of times. "Are you okay?"

"Yeah," I say louder than I meant. I'm making a fool of myself. "I think the pregnancy hormones are getting to me."

Oh fuck. Please don't ask.

He frowns and then he asks. "How so?"

You're such an idiot. What the hell are you going to tell him?

"Hot flashes or cold flashes, at times." I fan my face as fast as my hands let me.

"Oh. I haven't come across those symptoms in my reading yet."

Well, duh. I made them up 'cause I can't tell you how hot you make me. Oh shit. Shut up. Wait a second, did he just say...

"You're reading about pregnancy?"

He nods. "I started when Alice first shared the positive test. I plan to continue because I want to understand what you're going through and how my baby is growing inside you."

His baby? Inside me.

The tingling wave of heat that sweeps through me is so intense I'm glad I'm sitting down. I wish I could say I'm nauseous or appalled at the baby thing. But all my mind can repeat is part of him is inside me and I wish something else were inside me.

And now I'm horrified. *Good God. What is wrong with me today?*

"We should probably get started. I'm sure you have a lot to do—"

"No, I cleared my schedule. I'm all yours this afternoon."

Is he doing this on purpose or am I just so horny that his every word sounds suggestive? Everything he's saying is normal. He's trying to get this situation ironed out in the name of his child and here I am, staring at his stubble and wondering how it would feel against my nipples.

Oh, for fuck's sake.

I exhale so fast. "Good. That way we can work everything out. Do you think I could have some water?"

He nods and moves to the wooden wall on the opposite end of the windows. He pulls at a handle and it opens into a custom fridge. He grabs a bottle. And hands it over to me. I welcome the coolness of the glass bottle against my damp palms. It's VOSS. Of course. Did I really expect King Midas to drink Poland Spring like the rest of us?

"You drink fancy water."

He shrugs. "I get it for free, actually. The company owner owes me big, so I get free water for life. If you like it, I can have some delivered to you."

I'm about to tell him I don't need this kind of uppity water but I take a sip and holy crap. It's good. It has a little sweetness and I bet this is what angels drink. But I can't allow him to give me anything. It would feel like payment and I can't accept payments for this.

"I'm assuming you'll want to go with me to the doctor. I want to tell you up front, I don't plan to ever step back into Better Maryland. Not after what they did."

He leans back in his chair. "You won't ever have to. I have to talk to you about them but let's get our arrangement out of the way. I have a doctor in mind. My physician recommended her. She's also a midwife, which I thought may be better for you. He says she might be easier for you to talk to. I want to take you to her and if you like her, we can move forward."

I frown. "If I like her?"

"Yes, you would have to be comfortable with her. You are the one she'll examine."

"Oh." I was not expecting that kind of consideration from him.

"I'll be paying for all the health care costs. It's my baby." His tone is final.

I want to say no but I am not stupid. There's no way my insurance will cover any doctor he wants. "Fine, I'll see your doctor. I'm assuming she's ritzy and fancy."

"Of course. What other kind of doctor would I have but a fancy one?" His mouth twitches and there's that teasing expression from last night.

I wish he hadn't done this kind of switch. That he would always be like that guy I'd first met. I wish this seemed more like business, and I didn't see how important this is to him. I don't want to have that in my head. I don't need to deal with those thoughts.

"Why are you frowning like that?"

"What? Um. Nothing. I'm surprised you don't have your lawyer here and a twenty-page contract demanding I become a vegan or go through hypnotherapy or buy my groceries from Whole Foods only."

The smile breaks his face wide open and my insides quiver. "What crazy ideas do you have about me? First, I'm not a vegan. I love meat, all kinds of it. If my kid is a vegan, it will be his own choice in life. To me, there's nothing better in life than a thick, juicy, well-seasoned steak cooked slowly to the point where the meat melts in your mouth leaving your taste buds infused with its flavors."

My throat goes painfully dry and I have to take another sip of my water. I think I read somewhere there's a horny stage to pregnancy. This has to be it. I'll have to ask the doctor if my *Pleasurizer* is harmful to the baby. Not while Grayson's there, of course.

Why is he smiling like that? Oh my God. Are my thoughts so obvious?

"To answer your question about the lawyer, I thought it would be best if it's just you and me for this conversation. I think I owe it to you to make this as easy as possible. We can work out contracts later on. But if you want to call lawyers, we can. I will pay for yours since, again, that's my baby and you are doing me a favor."

I shake my head. "I don't think we need lawyers right now."

"I'll have to warn you. You'll have to let me know when I'm being too intense. I tend to get carried away with things. I don't want to annoy you but I'll want reports and to check on you. I'll want to make sure you have the best care."

I stare at his hands and can only nod. "I would expect you to be."

"You'll have to let me know if it becomes too much," he says and I get a feeling that it's like a dare, a taunt. Something that causes stiffening in my spine.

"I will. I'm not shy with my opinions," I shoot back.

"Then we'll be getting to know each other well, Winter. I don't want to upset you but you'll have to let me know if you change your mind and there is something, anything, I can do for you." He holds out his hand again.

Yeah, there is something.

I backhand the thought and shake my head. "I won't change my mind."

Because I'm going to let his baby grow inside me, birth him, and hand him over to Grayson. Then I'll go back to my normal life of non-hormonal quivering or wanting to jump a man based on his scent, his sinful smile, or those big manly hands.

10

Winter

My brush skids on the canvas, making the red paint smear across the circle outline.

I groan. "Come on, man. This is really not fair. I feel like you keep setting me up—"

The burning in my chest intensifies and doubles me over. The paintbrush slips from my fingers. I try to grab it, but I'm not fast enough. It lands between my feet, splotching the floor. *Shit*. I need to clean it before it stains the hardwood. I grab a paper towel and drop to my knees. I wipe in furious circles. I can't believe how clumsy I've been lately. I swear this pregnancy is stealing some of my motor and cognitive skills. Thank God the paint wipes off.

I straighten up and the blood rushes straight to my head. I hold on to the windowsill and try to catch my breath. I moved too fast and now I need to sit down.

I make it to the couch in four uncertain steps. I sit, slouching and lay a hand on my stomach. *Here we go with the nausea.* I massage circles, starting under my breast and making my way down.

"You make me crave avocados and now you make me pay for eating them. We talked about this, little dude. I gave you what you wanted to eat and you're supposed to let me paint. Ever since you appeared in my body—uninvited, if I say so—I haven't been able to get back in a groove. Because you won't let me."

My only answer is buzzing in my chest and the shallowing of my breath. I sit up and push a cushion to my side and try again. "It's a series, you know? The White Tara is the first and then comes this one, the Green Tara. She's all about compassion and mercy, none of which you seem to have for me."

I close my eyes and press perfect circles around my belly button. "I know it's not your fault but we need to compromise here. I thought we were long past these tantrums you seem to pitch on my body."

A tremor starts at my mid-thigh and I brace myself for the charley horse that's about to rock my leg with pain. These are happening way too often lately but it's usually when I'm lying down in bed. But the pain doesn't come. Instead, there's another wave of vibration. I had put my phone on vibrate, as I do whenever I'm painting. I reach for the pocket of my yoga pants and pull out my iPhone.

It's Grayson.

Fluttering breaks all over my stomach. *Damn this heartburn.* At least I've stopped worrying that it's a heart attack. Thanks, Adri, for explaining about the awful heartburn pregnancy brings.

I answer as the melody peaks and don't let him say hello.

"Yes, I took all my vitamins, even the disgusting ones."

He chuckles. "I didn't call to ask that."

Yeah, right.

"Okay, not only for that. How are you feeling today?" he asks.

"I don't know how to answer that. I mean, the day started well but then your child's hatred for me kind of manifested."

"Hatred is a strong word. I don't think it's personal…"

"Hmm. Probably because it's not your body turning into a mine-field and a tiny evil lord inside you blocking you from what you love the most."

"Is it too early for me to come and have a fatherly talk with my child?" he asks.

I'm no longer shocked by his odd brand of humor.

I shake my head like he's beside me and not on the other line. "It won't work. I've tried talking and even succumbed to his blackmail. I ate three avocados for lunch. He won't listen."

"Hmm…well, you know, it's different with fathers. Kids do listen to them."

"Oh, yay. The patriarchy shows up with its traditional and stereo-typical roles. I feel much better already, knowing a man who's never been pregnant is going to mansplain to a fetus."

He laughs out loud this time. It's rich and my smile is instant.

"I'm sorry," he says. "There has to be something I can do for you."

There are some things. My mouth drifts open but I trash the thought before it can come out of it. One, I'm not in the mood for what my brain is conjuring. Two, I am not in the physical condition with this heartburn, and third, just no. That is the biggest no in the history of *No.*

"I've been reading a lot about it. Music is supposed to soothe while helping the brain develop."

"I know. That's why I have *Invasion of Privacy* playing on a loop. Seems apropos for the occasion."

The silence is deafening and I want to giggle so badly. He's so shocked.

"As long as you also listen to Mozart, I guess it's okay to play some trap music, too. The baby will be more well-rounded for it."

What the hell. "Hold on, what do *you* know about trap music?"

"It's my business to learn a little of everything, Winter. I wouldn't be a good business man if I only stayed in my lane."

I love that my name sounds like velvet rustling in the dark when it comes out of his mouth. "I guess that makes sense."

"Plus, Cardi's beats and lyrics are sick. Did you eat dinner yet?"

I frown. Did he just admit he listens to Cardi B? "No. Food is not something I've been wanting any part of after the avocado salad incident."

"You have to eat something. Do you even have anything in your cabinets or your fridge?"

I roll my eyes and try to sound casual because he's working on a nerve right now. *Stay out of my cabinets.* "I'll be fine. Don't worry. I'll order some soup from The Broth or something."

The long pause is a little unnerving. "You know, like I said before, you don't have to take care of menial things like cooking or cleaning. You can come stay here for the rest of the pregnancy. It wouldn't be me paying you. It would be something I'm doing because the baby is causing inconveniences. I have someone who cleans and does the cooking..."

Heat breaks over my neck. "No."

It's forceful and firm as it comes out of my mouth. I'm not a complainer and I'm not looking for sympathy or charity. Besides, there's no way in hell I'm giving up my privacy by moving to his place. This is already weird enough as it is.

"I could also hire someone to help you deal with all these awful symptoms and make you more comfortable."

"The answer is no. I'm fine here, at my place. And it's really not that bad. I can handle this."

His sigh fills the space and silence. "Okay. But—"

"I'm not changing my mind, Grayson."

"There's another reason I called. I need you to come into the office tomorrow. I am meeting with the Better Maryland Clinic director. It's an official meeting with lawyers and everything. They want to discuss a settlement."

My blood turns into lava, as it always does when I remember everything that's happened since I went in for that procedure. How didn't I figure out something was wrong?

Maybe because you turned chicken-shit and she had to give you a Xanax? Combined with the anesthetic, it had you flying high like a red kite.

"Are you there?" Grayson asks.

"Yeah, sorry. Does this mean they heard from the doctor or found the nurse practitioner?"

"No. But my lawyers are putting on enough pressure and the clinic wants to avoid leaking this to the press, as do I. But whatever happened with Alice, the doctor, and the nurse practitioner doesn't excuse them hiding this for so long and not contacting you."

It's true. We should have been informed when this happened, not six weeks later. "I'll be there."

"Okay," he says.

We both go silent. This is really not a good topic. Neither of us wants to talk about it and it's weird because we both should have plenty to say. This is one of the two things that ties us. It's how we got to our current predicament.

"Have you had a chance to paint anything?"

"I was trying earlier but the heartburn…" This is touchy because I've finally been able to have juices to paint what I really want to. I haven't told anyone, not even the girls, that I've been painting something and it's almost involuntary.

"I'm sorry for that, too. I'm assuming that is frustrating. What is it that's blocking you? Is it only all the symptoms?"

I hate that he can ask the right questions time and time again. "No. I am able to finish paintings, just not the things I want. I need to get on this series for ArtScape but it's just not coming organically."

"So why don't you just paint what's coming to you? Wouldn't that help with the block?"

"No, it won't help."

Because there's only one thing I paint without even thinking and I don't want to let that in. At all.

"Oh."

"I should go and keep trying. I'm feeling a tad better." It's the truth. He took my mind off the heartburn.

"I'll see you tomorrow, Winter."

We hang up and I place the phone on the sit beside me. I pat my belly and issue a warning. "Listen, we're going to try this again and you're going to let me finish this time."

I need to stop talking to this kid.

An hour later, I have to stop because I'm so hungry I could gag. I examine my painting and smile at the progress. The head is done and the Tara is so beautiful. She's coming right through the canvas. I look down into my growing belly. "This is so what I needed. Thank you."

Oh God. I really need to stop talking to him. Her. It.

The knock on the door is a welcome reprieve. I'm not expecting anyone, so I'm cautious looking through the peephole. It's the delivery guy from The Broth.

I open the door and he's smiling. "I got a delivery for you. Same variety. Same guy."

I grab the bag and reach for my pocket but he stops me with a hand in the air. "He took care of that, too. Enjoy."

I walk back inside the apartment. Freaking Grayson needs to stop sending me food. The man is so annoying with all the reminders on the vitamins, the music, and the stupid food that smells like heaven. I should blast him, but I'm starving. I pick up my phone and settle for a meek snap.

I can order my own soup, you know?

His reply is quick. *Those are not for you. They're for Baby Grayson. It's not my fault they have to go through you to get to him.*

I burst into laughter. This really needs to stop.

Winter

Fuck this day to hell and beyond.

It's not even ten and I could eat my weight in chicken, followed by egg rolls and peanut-butter-banana sandwiches. My stomach grumbles because I haven't fed it anything today. I can only imagine the lecture I would get from the Food Nazi if he found out I haven't eaten anything yet.

I haven't seen Grayson in a while, since our meeting with the clinic got canceled, but he calls every night. Sometimes he calls to nag. Sometimes we end up shooting the breeze. He's actually not unpleasant at all. I ask myself if that's because he feels he owes me for carrying his kid. As much as I'm grumbling, truth is, I would kill for one of the soups he sent me the other night. Broccoli cheddar would be my damage of choice, even if I had to thank him after.

I force my thoughts away from Grayson and food, moving it back to my students. If I concentrate, I can make the next two hours go faster and then it's lunch. I love the creativity and diversity represented in my kids' projects for the Maryland-wide art competition. Last year's winner and runner-up both came from my class and are currently giggling and critiquing each other's pieces.

"Miss Alexander, can you please ask Bronwyn and Ayla to be quiet? They're really disruptive and I am trying to concentrate," Suzie says, her eyes flashing a green-monster-induced kind of light. The complaint earns her chilly looks from the other two girls.

I had hoped by putting the three of them close to each other the rivalry would die down. Nope. It may take a bigger effort, like making them collaborate together on a project. All three girls would hate it but I think their parents would approve.

For now, because the three are staring at each other in the kind of open and dramatic hostility seen in elementary school, I'll let it go.

"Ladies, please keep it down. Your fellow classmates are trying to work, too."

"Sorry, Miss Alexander," Ayla says and Bron nods.

There's a banana in my bag. Maybe I can sneak some bites from it. Would the kids notice? I can't believe I forgot my breakfast on the counter. Actually, I can fully believe that. My brain is nothing, if not a fuzzy mass of different-colored Silly Putty balled up together. I can't concentrate on a particular thing without forgetting all others.

This morning I had to go back inside the house three times. I forgot my purse. Then I left my phone on the counter. Then I had to go back a third time to get eye drops because my eyes were so dry. *Damned allergies.*

I was halfway to LaSalle when I remembered my breakfast. I grabbed a muffin at Dunkin Donuts, only to drop it as I was getting out of the car. I couldn't go back. I made it inside the school just as the bell rang.

I need to do better. I'll have to take out my clothes at night and plan outfits so I don't start another morning in tears because I can't button my pants. I need bigger clothes. I also need to start carrying granola bars or something wrapped that won't spoil when I drop it.

God, I want that banana. There's also the individual Nutella pack in my drawer. I love Nutella. I can use it as a dip.

My phone vibrates in my pocket and I pretend to go check for something in the teacher's closet so I can answer it. It's Grayson.

I need to talk to you when you get a chance.

I type a discreet reply. *Okay. Call you when I'm done here.*

Please do. It's important.

I roll my eyes. He's so dramatic. Probably wants to know about my fiber intake. That makes me giggle and I get inquisitive looks from the children. I draw an air circle with my index fingers, indicating they should all turn back to their canvases.

I get pulled into a faculty meeting for the next hour, followed by an informal chat with our school director.

"Winter, the staff has come to me with some concerns which I share. We are wondering if everything's okay with you. You've missed quite a couple of days. Is there something going on? Is this a permanent situation?" Ms. Walker asks. Her gaze drifts down slightly.

Ah. The nosy bunch has an inkling I'm pregnant.

"I'm fine, Ms. Walker." I'm careful to keep my voice neutral.

She puts her pen down. "We're just concerned. Is there anything we can help with?"

I unclench my teeth and force my lips to curve up. I'm not required to divulge, so I won't. I need to avoid this conversation for as long as I can. "Thank you for your concern. I assure you I'm well."

"Okay, then. Let me know if that changes. In the meantime, we'll all be praying for you."

I return the smile, making sure mine is extra bright. "Thank you. I can always use the prayers."

I grit my teeth on the way back to the classroom. This is not over and I need to figure it out. Some Catholic schools have been known for firing pregnant, out-of-wedlock teachers. I really should have thought about this before. Ms. Walker is a good person who cares about the faculty and students. She may not fire me but she may be forced to ask me to take a leave of absence if the board puts enough pressure on her.

Shit. "You're really messing with my life," I say, glaring down and then forcing my gaze away. *Stop talking to this kid.*

The rest of the day is a blur of bickering students, classes and end of quarter reports. I have to eat my banana in between class breaks and I don't get to have a full meal until I grab Chick-Fil-A on the drive back home after school. It's not ideal but it's my usual life. I trade the spicy chicken for the traditional one, since, apparently, someone is not keen on anything spicy. I side-eye my belly.

"You have some nerve, you know?" I say between large bites. Traffic is awful and I'm basically parked on the interstate. "You act like this is your body and I have to eat what you want and lay the way you want me to. It's my body and I'm just letting you squat in it for a few months."

Ugh, stop talking to the kid, Winter. I turn on the radio for traffic information. Traffic news is depressing at best. There's an accident and construction on I-95, which is causing a thirty-minute delay.

Great. Just great.

"Howard County Police Department is investigating what is being described as the 'apparent suicide' of a doctor in the upscale neighborhood of Dyson in Laurel. According to a department statement, officers responded to a reported possible death in the Four Hundred block of Montvale Avenue after neighbors complained of a foul odor coming from the townhouse. They found the lifeless body of Doctor Maxine Lawrence. The cause of death is undetermined but there are no preliminary signs of foul play."

Doctor Lawrence. Dead?

My pulse sets off and my hands grip the steering wheel. Doctor Lawrence is dead. The same doctor that did my procedure. I shake my head. "Oh God."

I never called Grayson back. Is that what he needed to talk about?

My hands are shaking so badly I can barely pull my purse closer. I move things around, looking for my phone and struggling to keep my eyes on the road. The honking behind me almost makes me jump out of my skin. My breath comes in and out in violent bursts. I swallow and force myself to concentrate on the road, on moving the car at the traffic's pace.

I concentrate on taking deep breaths, one after the other. I'll call him when I get home. For now, I just need to make it there.

The familiar queasiness breaks in the pit of my stomach and I rub circles into the skin of my belly. "It's going to be okay. We're going to be okay. We're going to drive ourselves home. Don't worry, it's going to be okay."

Grayson

My scalp is still tingling and my heart racing. The doctor is dead. Winter has not returned my calls. The police are not releasing any information but something deep tells me there are no coincidences. This has something to do with the embryo being implanted and Alice going missing. *Could she be dead too?*

"Are you going to at least pretend to be part of this meeting, Grayson? Everyone here's very busy, but we made time to come and take part of this. The least you could do is pay some attention."

I pull myself away from my thoughts to stare at Stephen Miller. I would rather be doing anything, even getting a tooth pulled or judging a company pie-eating contest, anything but sharing the same space with him.

"I believe the last thing said was that dividends for our novelty fashion have grown earnings at an average thirty-three percent pace over the last four months. Projections are that we'll have similar growth for the next quarters. If we go by those estimates, and my own hunch to sign that exclusive agreement to carry and distribute Lash N' Gloss domestic and internationally, our advantage will be solidified." I lean forward. "So where exactly was my attention lag? Did I miss something else?"

No one else is looking at me. All the other representatives and action holders are pretending to read a report none of them ever browses through. All they care about is the last page, where it states the chunk of money they'll be getting, for doing nothing but sit around this table once a month after having invested pocket change.

"My mistake," Stephen bites out. "You seem distracted."

And to be fair I am. It doesn't mean I'm not listening. My father always said a smart man's head needs to be able to be in several places at once when it comes to business and work. In the moment, on where you need to be, on where you want to be, and what's most important.

My gaze drifts to my phone on the table. Still no call from Winter. Sandra has explicit instructions to come grab me out of the meeting if Winter calls my office phone. *Shit.* I need to find her before she finds out. It's better she hears it from me. I don't want her to think she's in any kind of danger. But first, I need to get the fuck out of here.

"As you can see," I say for everyone else's benefit. "Your investment is still safe and Grayson Global continues to solidify itself. That other company may be the world leader in delivering products but they are still mostly importing and allowing people to sell. We are growing a community of vendors to interact with our own. This symbiotic relationship allows us to offer our clients access to exclusive products and vendors. Does anyone have any questions? If not, I really must cut this meeting short and I'll see you next month."

Everyone shakes their head and gets up. I do the same but don't make it halfway out of the room.

"I need a word with you, Grayson."

There's a slight pause by everyone in the room but they exit quickly afterward. Everyone knows of Stephen's dislike for me and the endless ways in which he pushes my buttons. I'm not in the mood today. I'm way over his sense of entitlement. Not to mention how he feels I need to be at his beck and call because I was married to his sister, and his father gave us the starting capital for my company. It doesn't matter that I paid dividends and gave them stock in the company. It's never enough.

"I'm busy today. Make an appointment with my secretary." I move past him but he grabs on to my arm.

"I said I need to talk to you."

Adrenaline barrels into my limbs. My hand balls into a fist and I lift my gaze from his grip on my arm to his face. It's a pointed signal before I knock him out like I've wanted to for years now. He releases my arm and takes a step back. His neck breaks out in blotched spots, visible despite his buttoned-up shirt and tie.

"It's important." His voice drops along with his bravado.

He's one of those word giants. He shoots from his mouth but at any sign of confrontation he turns into a sniveling chihuahua. It's what Astrid used to say about him and I continue to confirm it in my every interaction with him.

"What is it?"

He waits until the last person has left the office. "I was wondering what happened to what you came to report the other day. About the embryos."

"When there's news, you will know."

"This is not about you and your ego, Grayson. Those are my sister's eggs, too, you know? My father and I have a right to know to what's going to happen to her legacy."

I scoff. "You couldn't stand Astrid while she was alive. Now, I'm supposed to believe you're worried about her legacy?"

His nose flares. "I loved her, even if we didn't see eye to eye. I wish I had a chance to tell her that."

Right. Now that she's dead.

I don't believe a word he says but I don't want him to go snooping either. I don't want anyone to know about Winter until I'm ready. "When there is something to know, I will let your father know. Tell him that if he has any questions, he can call me directly. I'm never too busy to speak to him."

His face goes red like he's about to go into convulsions. I don't care, though. His father and I will never be close, but I will always show him respect because he's Astrid's father and he loved her. This little shit will never get anything from me.

I stalk out of the conference room and make my way into my office. I hit the green call button and close my door.

"I was about to call you." Winter's voice is low and without its usual raspy richness.

Shit. "You heard about the doctor. I wanted to tell you—"

"Grayson, I...I'm driving to the hospital right now."

"What? Why?"

"I wasn't feeling well after hearing the news on my drive home. When I got home, I got sick to my stomach and had to lie down for a bit. When I woke up, I went to the bathroom…and I'm spotting."

My blood runs cold like an icy slush. *Spotting? Blood. She's losing the baby. Jesus, no. It can't be.*

I clear my throat. "Are you in pain?"

"No," she says.

I storm out of my office and signal to Sandra that I'm leaving. Elias calls out my name and I wave him away.

I punch the elevator buttons and struggle for what to say.

"Grayson?"

I can barely hear her voice over the thudding in my chest. "I'm here. Why didn't you call me or an ambulance?"

"I don't know. I panicked. I just wanted to get there. I hate hospitals but I didn't want to wait…" Her voice is hoarse and pained.

"Okay. What hospital are you going to?"

"St. Raymond's. It's the closest," she says.

"I'll call Doctor Sahiner and have us meet there."

"Okay…I don't like being alone in hospitals." Her voice drops to a whisper.

"I'm on my way to you. Just breathe and hang on. Okay?"

12

Winter

"I'm going to be strong for you." The words wheeze out of my mouth. I cradle my belly with my right hand and breathe like Grayson asked me to. It's funny how fast I've snatched that same hand when I wake up with it over my small bump. My throat swells. "You're so sensitive. I don't know why you take all my talk seriously. I was just being grumpy. I didn't mean any of it."

I must look like a crazy person as I make it through the doors of the Emergency Room at St. Raymond's. The reception desk is in sight and I beeline for it, ignoring my surroundings, avoiding the white walls and the antiseptic smells trying to stab their way through my nose.

The receptionist raises her head. "How can I help you?"

I take a deep breath and vomit the words. "I'm pregnant and I'm bleeding. I may be losing the baby."

The purging doesn't ease the tightness in my chest or the grip of my hands on my belly. I'm praying to God to help me hold on to this little lime-sized being inside me. I'm pleading with him to hang in there.

The receptionist signals to someone and a young man comes almost flying toward me with a wheelchair. "Is someone coming? Your partner or a family member?"

"Yes, he should be here soon." And again, like I conjure him just by referring to him, Grayson rushes through the doors.

My breath gushes out. "Thank you, God."

He sees me right away and heads my way, kneeling in front of the chair.

"Are you okay?"

I shake my head. Because I'm not. Fear is clawing its way through my insides.

"Come on, let's get you to examination." The orderly pushes the chair and Grayson is right beside me. All I can hear is my own heart-beat and the faint voices as Grayson answers questions.

They bring us into a room and a nurse comes to help me while Grayson is filling out paperwork.

How many times have I told this baby he doesn't belong in my body because I couldn't get into my pants? How many times have I yelled and grumbled because I couldn't lay the way I wanted? I've raged because I couldn't paint or because I couldn't have a glass of wine. *What the actual fuck?* How does that measure to a human life?

I make silent promises. I will eat every day and on time. *I won't yell at you anymore. Just please stay.*

My throat swells, and the tears burn my eyes. But nothing can come out of my mouth and the sound that breaks through my chest is something I've never heard before.

Grayson drops the applications on the chair and rushes to my side. "Are you in pain?"

All I can do is shake my head and grasp his hand. "I'm so sorry. I didn't want this to happen. I've been so mean to the baby, just thinking about myself. But I didn't want this to happen."

"Winter, it's okay. Just breathe. This is normal. At this stage, anything can happen."

His voice is soft and assured and I should be comforted by it, but his eyes are strained. His face is ashen and not rugged and arrogant like the day I met him. This is not the guy who came to my house to convince me. I remember thinking that guy had never been afraid of anything. But this guy, the one who's squeezing my hand so tight and trying to convince me—and probably himself—that this is just life, this guy is afraid.

I force a breath and try to get a hold of myself. Grayson's trying to be strong, when he has so much more to lose than me. I owe it to him and myself to do the same.

A nurse comes in the room but we don't pull apart. My hand tightens around his.

"Hi. I'm Mary. Your doctor should be here momentarily. In the meantime, I need to check your vitals."

She takes my blood pressure and my temperature but when a second attendant steps in with the cart, the needles, and the vials, I almost fly off the bed.

"No needles."

Grayson's hand presses on my shoulders. "It's okay."

"It won't hurt," Mary cajoles in the same voice I use on the second graders.

"They can never find my veins. It's always horrible."

She shakes her head. "Not with me. I swear. Now, I want you to stare into your handsome husband's eyes and trust me."

Husband? My gaze flies to Grayson, who manages a small smile. I'm about to correct her when her hand wraps around my wrist. Gray places a hand on my face and keeps me from turning.

"You're supposed to stare into my handsome face and my gorgeous eyes."

"She didn't say you have gorgeous eyes."

"But that's what you're thinking." He winks at me and I don't know where he's getting this from. I'm dying inside right now. How can he joke?

Mary flicks the inside of my forearm hard enough to make me gasp. "There she is. A nice, fat vein for me to draw from. Now, I want you to stare into those gorgeous eyes again and think beautiful, healthy thoughts. Send that baby all the good energy."

"The baby won't need good energy. Not with his father's handsome face and gorgeous eyes, right?" Grayson says and I'm so caught up in my awe of him that even the small prick in my arm can't make me break eye contact.

He's been so nice and warm and he could be losing his only chance to have his wife's baby. And I want to cry again. But I breathe. Crying is not going to solve anything. What I need is to be strong and make it through.

"All done," Nurse Mary announces and I turn my head just in time for her to slip the needle out and put a Band-Aid over the gauze.

I blink a few times and she chuckles. "I have the magic touch."

Grayson pulls the blanket over my shoulders with his free hand. His other hand is still firmly linked with mine.

Doctor Sahiner steps inside the room and reality crashes in. The examination is coming and she's probably going to have bad news for us. Why else would I be bleeding? Maybe because my body recognizes how wrong it is for me to be pregnant. All my life, I've known this would never happen. Not with my history. No one deserves that. This little baby doesn't belong to me and should be spared the curse.

"We don't know anything yet, sweetheart. I don't want you to throw in the towel just yet," Doctor says in her usual sweet tone.

Grayson's hand flexes around mine and I use my other to rub his forearm up and down. I need to keep reminding myself I'm not the only one scared here.

I'm forced to let go so the doctor can feel her way around. I'm prodded in all sorts of different ways and I should be embarrassed, but I'm too busy praying and staring into Gray's eyes. The doctor lifts my shirt and squirts the cold gel over my belly.

"Isn't it great that your first sonogram gets to be external? My patients normally hate the wand."

She's babbling, which she can sometimes do through exams. It's all to make me more comfortable but nothing can make me feel at ease right now. I'm trembling because the room is freezing like a meat locker and I'm so afraid of what she's going to find. I have to look away from the one thing that has been a comfort up to now, Gray's eyes. Because there's a look of resignation, like a cold mask that's come over him. I can't stand that feeling. It's like she's already told us that the baby is—

Whomp-whomp-whomp-Whomp-whomp-whomp.

The blood rushes in my ears as the sound fills the room and my gaze goes back to meet his. We don't need to be told what that is. It's the weirdest sound I've ever heard in my life but it's comforting. And I think Grayson agrees because the color floods his face. His eyes are warm and a little wet.

"Steady and strong, just as I suspected. This baby is a tough one. He or she is hanging in there, Mom and Dad."

I can't find the words at first. I clear my throat. "But why am I bleeding?"

"We are going to test the blood but I believe it has to do with the fibroids. It should go away in a few days. I want you to rest and stay off your feet for a week, sitting or lying down. Keep the stress level low and just rest."

"But I have to work."

"Not for the next week, you don't. You have to rest for that baby," Nurse Mary chimes in. "Your handsome husband will wait on you hand and foot. Right?" She winks at Grayson.

Gray continues to play the part and smiles.

"If I rest, the baby's going to be okay?" I ask the doctor and if that's what it takes, it doesn't matter.

She smiles. "Baby's going to be okay."

We're left alone and I exhale again. I turn to him. "Baby's going to be okay, Gray."

He blows out a big breath and his shoulders sag forward.

We stare at each other and smile and then chuckle. As if we've done this a million times, his head lowers and our foreheads touch and then our noses, and I can smell him, his cologne, his sweat, all of him. His breath washes over my lips and I don't know why I do it, because I know it's totally wrong.

I pucker up until our mouths are touching. His lips are warm and moist as they move over mine. His hand is warm over my cheek and I open my mouth. His taste is so strong, so, so strong, I need to lap it up with my tongue. He hums and his fingers drift to the back of my neck, pulling me closer. I flick my tongue again and this time I'm rewarded with his. It sends a chill that resonates through my body all the way to my deepest place.

"One more thing—" Nurse Mary says from the door and we both jump back. "I'm sorry. I didn't mean to interrupt."

My heart is hammering my chest as painfully as before, but this time it's not from fear. My cheeks are not bloodless.

Nurse Mary has the impish smile of someone who's not sorry at all. "Doctor Sahiner wants you to know that she has a list of things she wants you to put on hold, and action between the sheets is one of them. Her words, not mine."

Yeah, because kissing wasn't awkward enough. I can't even look at him. What the hell is wrong with me?

"I'm sorry," he says and my gaze flies to meet his.

I want to die right now. Of course, he's sorry. We shouldn't have done that. *Stupid Winter.*

"Yeah, me too. Um. You probably can go now. I should be okay to drive home and I promise to stay off my feet."

His forehead creases. "Yes, you'll stay off your feet and I'll be there to make sure. I'm taking you home with me."

Oh no. No, no, no, no. Not after what just happened.

"Look, you don't have to do that. I can ask my friend, Lauren, to come stay a few days with me."

He crosses his arms. "Oh, I see. Lauren doesn't have a job, or anywhere else to be and can be there to tend to you all the time? Also, what if you need to get back here as soon as possible? Can she make that twenty-four-hour commitment?"

My gut twists into a knot. What if this happens again and I'm alone? I've never been that scared in my life.

Yes, you have. But now it's not just you. You have someone else you're responsible for. Grayson's baby. And that's who he's looking out for. It's not like he's trying to jump your bones.

"You'll have a room and all the space you need. Whenever I'm home, I'm mostly working in my home office. I'm not here to invade your privacy or impose. I just want you to be safe. Both of you." He's staring pointedly at my belly.

"Okay, but this is only for the baby."

And because I don't ever want to be scared for him and all alone.

13

Grayson

Miss Alexander doesn't like to be told what to do and she can get quite the attitude about it. She's barely said two words since we left the hospital and her eyes have been torching the side of my head.

I get it. She doesn't want to come stay with a guy she barely knows, and who's part of her living nightmare. And yet, this is the only compromise. I want her to be comfortable and minimize her stress levels. She's scared of a repeat of today. I'll never forget her ashen face or the way she almost came off the bed when she saw the needles.

We step out of the elevator and she turns to me. "You live in a hotel?"

I shake my head. "I own the penthouse. The hotel stops at floor twenty-four and you use a different elevator to get to my place."

"Oh," she says.

"You sound disappointed."

She shoots me an are-you-kidding-me look. "This is just so different than my Patterson Park place, it even smells…expensive."

At least she didn't say pretentious.

"It's just a place, Winter. The only difference is that there will be someone here to help you when you need it. It's only temporary. And just think about this, I'm even more indebted to you now."

She snorts. "I have to call my boss as soon as we get in. She will need to find a sub for me now that I need to be on bedrest..." She trails off and looks away.

"I'm sorry." I truly am and I hope she knows that.

Aunt Millie is waiting for us inside.

"Good evening, you must be Winter." She steps closer with her blinding smile to shake Winter's hand. "Welcome. I'm Grayson's Aunt Millie. The maid is working on putting fresh linens on your bed. It should be ready soon. Would you like something to drink or eat? There's some of that tomato basil soup I hear you like."

Winter smiles at her and the apprehension is momentarily gone from her face. "Yes, please."

I show Winter to the living room and leave her to make her phone call. Aunt Millie is waiting for me, exactly where I left her. "She needs to be comfortable and on bedrest for a few days. I would like for you to be around."

She nods. "We're going to take care of our baby."

Our baby. It does something weird to my chest.

Aunt Millie dabs at her eyes. "I wish your dad were here. Desi would be so happy to be a grandpa."

I hug her. "He would be. Winter's not happy about staying here. I just want her to stay healthy and comfortable. So, whatever you think she needs, we need to be on the lookout."

She brims. "Say no more. I will make sure she is fed and rested."

I know she will. I don't trust anyone else with this. "Thank you."

"I'll go get her soup and bread. I'll bring you both dinner in the family room," she says.

I raise a brow. Aunt Millie is a stickler for eating at the table. I constantly earn a scolding when she finds crumbs on the couch.

"In the interest of keeping her from moving too much." Her tone carries a don't-get-used-to-it hint.

I chuckle and head into my home office. Winter's still on the phone and though her voice is low, some of her sentences reach my ears.

"Yes, I'll have the doctor send you the note. I know it's a delicate situation. Do you think the board is going to have a big issue with this? Should I call human resources?"

My chest tightens like a belt. I never stopped to think this could affect her job. She could be let go and it's my fault because she's having this baby for me. It's messing with her life now and could mess with her future.

Shit.

I'm not letting that happen. If they try to fire her, I will sue their asses so hard they will have to change LaSalle's name to the Winter Mercedes Alexander Academy because she will own it by the end.

I'll give this to one of my lawyers to handle.

The conversation is over and she's placed the phone next to her on the couch. She's staring out into the view. I come out of the office and sit on the opposite end.

"Did it go okay?"

She doesn't look at me but nods. "This view is spectacular."

"It's one of the reasons I moved here. It's beautiful in the day and even better at night. Winter?" I wait until she looks at me, and I'm caught by the sadness in her gaze. "I can send one of my lawyers to help with the school."

Fast as lightning, her eyes grow cold and her arms cross before her. "I didn't ask you to do that. I can work this out on my own."

"This is happening because you are carrying my child. Shouldn't that be enough for you to let me help?"

"No. I don't want your creepy lawyer in my business."

Anger flares through me because this woman is so stubborn. She could let me help. This is nothing. It's not like I would expect anything in return. She's already giving me the biggest thing anyone could ask for, but she refuses to take anything from me. I'll just have to find another way to work this out for her.

Or you could leave it alone like she asked. The fuck I will. This is my fault and I'll solve it.

"As you wish. I'm here if you change your mind." The lie flows easily from my mouth and my expression remains schooled even as her eyes narrow.

"Thank you," she says and goes back to staring out the window.

Her pride is going to make it hard to take care of her while she's here but that's what I'm going to do. She will not lose her job because of my baby and I will find ways to repay her.

"I didn't know you lived with your aunt. She's nice."

I smile. "She came to live with me right after college. She's the best and I don't know what I would do without her."

Thirty minutes later, I've already finished my dinner but Winter has only pushed hers around the bowl.

"If you don't like it—"

"Winter's friend is here," Aunt Millie says and heads in the direction of the door.

Winter straightens up and pushes her dish a little farther away. Her eyes alight and a few minutes later she smiles as the short, curvy brunette marches into the room. The woman is definitely Winter's friend. Because her gaze lasers around the room, stumbling over me and then over Winter. Her shoulders sag a little and she exhales.

Winter stands. "Hey, thank you for coming."

The woman crosses the distance and comes to hug her. "How are you feeling? You should have called me to take you to the hospital. Is Lemony Cricket okay?" She places a hand on Winter's belly, making her smile.

I've never gotten to feel her belly. The thought is fast and I squelch it just as quick.

Winter's flustered. "I was going to fill you in when you got here. Thank you so much for this."

She points at the bag in her hand.

"Oh, shut up," her friend says and she's still smiling when she turns to me. "I'm Lauren and that's Chase over there."

A tall man walks in the room just in time.

"I'm Grayson." I stand up and shake her hand and then Chase's.

"I was putting the bags in the room, uh, Aunt Miss Millie indicated," he says.

"Oh, I'm sorry for not introducing you. Lauren's one of my closest friends," Winter says.

Lauren waves her away. "I'm her best friend. She just has to share me with Adri."

Winter blushes a little. "I thought she was coming."

"Adri's not feeling well but she sent you something." She reaches out for one of the bags Chase is holding and takes out a food container, which she waves in front of Winter's face.

"Is that Adri's mom's *sopa*?"

Lauren smiles. "She sent you some frozen ones, too." She turns to me. "Can you warm up some of this soup? I'm going to help Winter get to her room and comfortable. She can eat it in bed."

"Let me show you both to the room and I'll come back to warm up the soup," Aunt Millie says.

Winter and Lauren follow Aunt Millie out. I'm left to stare after them with the food container in my hand.

"Lauren's just taking care of her Winter. Don't take it personal," Chase says. "She's worried because none of us knows you."

Lauren's worried but he says *us*.

"Please sit down." I motion to the spot Winter left vacant. "Can I get you anything to drink?"

"No, thanks."

I head to the kitchen to place the food on the microwave. I come back and take my place on the other side of the couch.

The guy's huge. NFL-huge.

"Winter is here because of complications but this house is always open to whoever wants to come visit her. I just want to make sure she is okay." I don't know how much he knows. How much has Winter told her friends? But if the roles were reversed, I probably would act the same way.

He holds my gaze. "That's good to know. She's a special friend to us and she's not alone."

The comment is like a jab to my side. What does he think I'm trying to do to her? Is something going on between him and Winter? Is he a boyfriend I didn't know about? "That's good to know but you don't need to worry about her with me. I have the best of intentions to protect her."

"I hope so. She's good people." Then he smiles. It's cold and challenging. "Lauren and Adri will keep a close eye on you and keep me informed."

Is this guy threatening me?

"Chase?" Aunt Millie comes back in the room. "Your boss is upset because you left a bag in the backseat of the car."

He rolls his eyes but stands up. "I better go get that. Be right back."

He hurries out and Aunt Millie chuckles. "Lauren's not even his girlfriend. Look at how she's got him running."

I frown. How does she know that already? They haven't been gone that long.

She shrugs. "I needed to know if he was interested in Winter but you have no worries."

"I wasn't worried," I say.

"Hmm." She looks around. "Where's the food?"

I tilt my head to the kitchen.

She nods. "She has good friends. They really care about her."

"I think Chase just threatened me."

Aunt Millie gives me one of her sweet, kind smiles. Smiles that turn me back to the ten-year-old boy she used to watch after school. "He doesn't know what a good man you are, Grayson."

Good man? Me? But I don't laugh. Aunt Millie sees me as she wants to.

"Winter will see it, too. It's good to see her smile, though. She was so sad earlier on but that Lauren is something. She has our girl in stitches." She heads to the kitchen.

Our girl.

Winter's carrying my child and all I'm doing for her is messing up her world. First thing I need to do is make sure she keeps her job. I shoot a text to Simone; she's the only one who can handle this for me. I ask her to keep it confidential. While Elias is my primary lawyer,

Simone oversees and does second sign-offs for all my transactions. She's my version of discreet quality control. I briefly explain the situation and ask her to meet with me.

If you're going to overstuff the sandwich, make sure the bread can hold it.

Dad had the funniest sayings. All which I find useful at some point or another.

Had you been alive, you would've been my main adviser and my company would have probably been way further than it is now.

He made the best with little money. We had enough to make ends meet, yet I never lacked for anything and he provided for me until I became an adult. He had a life insurance policy, which had fed and clothed me all the way through college. I still took out student loans so I can keep the capital. The rest, along with Bryce Miller's investment, is what helped me start my company.

And just like that, another idea forms.

I fire another text to Simone, telling her to expect another workload tomorrow, the negotiations with the Better Maryland Clinic. If I have her work with Winter on that, then it will be seamless for her to help with her work issues.

I switch to email and explain my plan. I'm just about finished when Lauren comes back in the room.

She's wringing one hand over the other. "She fell asleep before I finished accommodating her stuff. I sent her a text, letting her know where everything is. I offered to stay but she told me she is going to be okay…"

You don't believe her.

"She will be okay. I'll make sure of it."

"She's not alone." Her tone is sharp and the warning loud.

I think of what Aunt Millie said. "You don't know me and you have all the reason in the world to be skeptical, but I promise you, I will take care of Winter. There's no way I can repay what she is doing for me and she won't even let me compensate her in any way. You have my word. I will take care of her."

She twirls her bracelet around. "And you'll call me if she needs

81

anything?"

"I will call you. I promise, Lauren."

She nods. "Sometimes she tries to be too strong and solve everything on her own, but she's scared and out of her league. We can't leave her alone with this stuff."

We? There's a we now.

I roll with it. "We won't. Tell me what I can do for her."

"The first lesson in all things Winter is that she's a giver, not a taker. I force gifts on her but you can't do that yet. If I were you, I'd make this place more comfortable for her. Painting is her escape."

"She can't paint. She needs to be in bed."

"Which, knowing her, it's bound to depress her." She chews on her knuckles for a second. "Wait, I can borrow Bron or Cam's electronic sketchpad and bring it by in the morning."

"Like a Wacom? One of my companies has developed a better device. She can have as many of those as she wants."

She claps her hands together. "But you can't straight out give it to her. She won't take it."

"I'll work something out."

"Hmm. You should probably call me when in doubt with her."

She just wants to keep an eye on me.

"I will," I say anyway, because I have a feeling Miss Winter is going to be a difficult egg to crack.

Winter

I don't want to open my eyes. I don't want to face the day. I don't want to be in a place that is not mine and where it's freezing.

I don't want a repeat of yesterday. But there's so much more to this. I can't work. Right now I'm okay, but what if LaSalle fires me? What then? It will be hard to find another job. I'm sure my savings can get me through a few months, and they would have to give me severance pay, but it will be hard finding another teaching job while pregnant.

You can't worry about this right now. You've got to stay stress-free for the baby.

This is not me. I don't let fear paralyze me. It's not the first or last time I've been broke. I always find a way.

I open my eyes and find myself staring into deep-gray eyes, not human, but animal eyes. The face is all angles and darker than the body. The triangular ears are pointed up but it's the attitude that gets me. I swear it's like this cat is asking, "what the hell are you doing here?"

"Hi," I say but the cat doesn't blink or move.

I sit up and it still stays where it is, staring at me.

"I'm Winter and I didn't know you live here. Don't worry, I'm only staying for a while."

One of her ears flexes around and two seconds later I hear the soft tapping of shoes. *Oh no.* I smooth my hair back to no avail. Grayson's at the door in my next breath.

"Good morning."

For him it is. He looks straight out of an expensive scotch ad, with his European-cut, navy-blue suit and hair just a little mused. It's sink-your-fingers worthy, as is his stubble. No one should look that good in the morning.

I clear my throat. "Morning. Um. I'm getting to know your other tenant." Thank you, God for letting me sound semi-normal.

The cat jumps onto all fours as Grayson steps into the room and trots to him over my feet on the bed. Her tail and ears are pointing straight up.

"I'm sorry. This teeny, tiny terror is Nin and she knows no boundaries." His fingers scratch the cat's head between her ears and she bobs her head against his knuckles. Her purrs are loud and I'm glad because they fill the silence.

He has a cat.

"You don't look like a cat person," I blurt out. *Damn my mouth.*

"No? What kind of person do I look like?"

83

I shrug. "I don't know."

He chuckles. "I'm not a cat person. I'm a Nin person. Actually, she made me hers."

Hers.

"How long have you had her?"

"About a year. She strayed from her mom and I found her in a property I was negotiating near Fells. She kept following me around that day, so I took her with me. Since then, she's taken over the house."

My heart flexes a little. He's a big man who talks about being at the mercy of a tiny, little creature. I can't help but smile. "So, you're the boss in the office but she's the boss of you?"

He shrugs and then laughs. "She has a way of taking over everything."

Nin drops herself to the side and bares her belly to him, but her eyes are firmly planted on me as if saying, "Don't you get any ideas."

"No, we are not going to do that here. This is Winter's bed."

Nin meows but it's more like a snappy order.

"I said no." But his hands are rubbing up and down her belly.

I'm mesmerized and frankly, a little jealous. I want him to rub my belly like that.

Jesus, Winter.

He shoots me an apologetic look and tries to nudge her off the bed. After a few times, he reaches inside his pocket, pulls out a small paper and balls it in his fist. The cat is up on all fours, her gaze flipping back and forth between him and the door. Then he flings the paper down the hallway and she jumps off the bed and goes after it.

"Cats play fetch?"

"Mine does." The amount of pride in his voice is adorable. So is the flush of red on his cheeks. "How are you feeling this morning?"

"Good. I didn't think I would be able to sleep but I guess I was super tired. I don't even know what time Lauren left. I need to call her and apologize for falling asleep on her."

He leans against the door frame. "I'm sure she understands. She said she sent you a text message, letting you know where she put everything. She didn't want to wake you up."

"That was nice of her."

"Your friends care a lot about you. They were very concerned."

I try to shrug it off. "They shouldn't be. The doctor says I'm fine..."

We fall silent. He's staring at me like he's trying to make sure. I am fidgety as hell under his gaze.

He clears his throat. "I have to go into the office for a couple of hours. Aunt Millie is here for anything you need. She has breakfast for you, which the maid can bring here or she can help set you up in the family room."

"Oh. If it's not a bother, I can sit out there."

"Of course it's not. Think of it as your home. I'm mostly in my office these days."

"I don't want you to feel like you have to leave because of me."

"I'm not. I just work a lot, even at night. I have to get it out of my system before you-know-who arrives." He's staring at my belly and it grows warm under his gaze. "I'm sorry I have to leave today but I can't miss this meeting. Is there something you need me to bring on the way back?"

I shake my head.

"When you feel up to it, one of my lawyers wants to meet with you about the litigation with Better Maryland."

I sigh. "Okay."

"I know you can't paint but my company is working with Z-sketch. We are creating better and improved models of tablets, like Wacom. It's this company that makes—"

"I know who they are. They make drawing and sketching instruments."

His smile is wide and deep enough to rattle my insides. "Yes. We are collaborating with them. We came up with a new sketchpad. It does the same thing that the software on Wacom does, but it's a separate device that's still adaptable to both Mac and PC computers. It's a wider screen but lighter. I'm supposed to get the newest prototype today. Would you like to test it and tell me what you think about it?"

What is he crazy? Of course I would.

85

"Unless that's not your thing. I would totally understand. I didn't even ask if you sketch before painting…"

"I want to try it."

He smiles again. "Oh, good. I'll bring it home with me."

"Thank you."

He shakes his head. "No, thank you. You'll be doing us a favor." He lingers at the door. "I'll see you in a couple of hours."

I nod because for some reason my stomach starts to churn and though I rub circles into it, I can't get it to calm down.

Breathe.

I get off the bed and head to the bathroom. Last night, I hadn't really appreciated it but it's bigger than the bedroom in my apartment. I love the white tiling and the glass shower. I can't wait to get in there. I use the bathroom and I'm relieved that the spotting is mostly gone. I pat my belly and stand.

"You're just trying to scare the crap out of us. You should stop doing that." I think back on those horrible hours yesterday. Grayson's hand in mine so tight. He'd been as scared as me. We'd been relieved when the doctor said the baby was okay. *And then we kissed.*

My belly flops and warmth floods over my skin. His lips were so soft and firm. Nope, not going there. "Yeah kid, you should definitely stop messing with my hormones."

I shower and change into yoga pants and a sweatshirt. Miss Millie is in the bedroom, smoothing the edges of the covers.

"You don't have to do that, Miss Millie. I can make the bed."

She straightens up and smooths her salt-and-pepper hair. "Aunt Millie and no, all you're going to do in the next week or so is rest. Any bleeding today?"

"It's almost gone."

Her smile is warm and bright, like the summer morning sun. "Of course it is. That one's a Grayson. They're strong." She comes closer and loops her arm through mine. "Come on, let's get you to the living room."

I want to tell her that I can walk on my own but she's so sweet, and even though she's way shorter than me, I let her guide me.

86

"I'm not weak, you know?"

She laughs. "I know. But I promised Grayson I would take care of you and it's been a while since I had someone to fuss over." She stops and looks at me. "At least until Baby comes."

My heart leaps and I return the smile. This baby will have someone other than Grayson to love him and care for him. I made the right decision.

14

Grayson

The letters on my screen are starting to blend together and I don't know what I'm reading anymore. That's what happens when you keep going over and over a report, expecting it to change. I need tomorrow's meeting with the board to go fast and smooth. After, I'm finally going to tell Astrid's father about the baby.

I want to keep this baby all to myself longer, but it's time. Winter's stronger and not in danger of miscarrying.

You promised, Grayson. I can almost hear Astrid's voice reminding me I need to let her father be part of the baby's life.

"I don't want to yell at you, but you need to cut me a break here."

Winter's voice comes through loud and clear. *Is she on the phone?* I stand and pad to my office door but I hesitate. I should give her some privacy to move around the house as she wants, but I'm curious as to why she's up at this time. She was practically falling asleep at the dinner table.

I poke my head out the door just to catch her form disappearing into the kitchen. I follow her.

"You are so inconsiderate. You're breaking all my life rules. I never eat anything past midnight. Well, that's not technically true. A night of drinking always leaves me wanting something warm and greasy."

She's talking to the baby. For some reason, that makes me smile.

"Is that really appropriate conversation for a fetus?"

She spins around, her hands bracing on the counter. "You scared me."

"I'm sorry. I couldn't help but overhear."

She flushes and her gaze drops to her feet. "I don't know why I do it. It's not like Lemony can hear me yet."

"I think he can and I think it's nice that you do. Wait, Lemony?"

She laughs. "He's the size of a lemon according to Google."

"Oh." I don't know what else to say. "So, why are you and Lemony up at this hour?"

"He's hungry, therefore I'm hungry. We came to get a sandwich and some hot chocolate."

We. "Sandwiches and hot cocoa don't go together."

"Don't be silly. Of course they do." She moves to the cupboards and grabs the bread and a plate. She's goes into the fridge, pulls out the deli meat, cheese, and a metal carafe. Then, she closes the door.

She places the carafe on the stove. "Aunt Millie left me some hot chocolate ready in case I wanted it. You were right. She's the absolute best."

"She likes you."

"She's way too kind to me. I'm going to miss her when I'm gone. No one's ever brought me breakfast in bed before."

What? How's that possible?

"Your past boyfriends didn't bring you breakfast in bed?"

Shit. I shouldn't have asked that. It's none of my business.

She shrugs. "I don't do that kind of thing."

Let it go. "What kind of thing?" *Jesus, Grayson.*

"The playing house kind of thing. I'm not into those kinds of relationships."

"What kind of relationships are you into?" She's going to tell me to go to hell and I deserve it.

She answers, "The simple kind. We see each other, we enjoy each other's company, we go home to our own space."

I nod. "I can see that. I'm the same way."

She is fidgeting with the bread bag. "Is it because you haven't found someone like Astrid—" She stops to look at me with wide eyes and her hand covers her mouth. "I'm sorry. I shouldn't have asked that."

We may be getting a little too comfortable tonight.

"I felt that way before I met Astrid but we ended up getting married anyway. She didn't know how to take no for an answer and whatever she wanted, she got. Now I have no desire to go down that path again."

"Oh," she says and places the bread on the plate, then reaches for the meat.

She's going to do this all wrong. "Stop. You need to butter that bread. It's all dry. Here, let me."

She frowns at me and I move past her into the fridge and take out the butter.

"You know how to make sandwiches? Does Warren Buffett know that? It wasn't in the article." She presses her lips tight together.

I laugh. "It's okay. I Googled you too, third-time ArtScape artist."

"That's invasive." She cracks up and turns to the cupboard. "Would you like some hot chocolate?"

I shake my head. "No, I'll have coffee."

"It's two in the morning."

I spread the butter over the bread. "I'm still working."

"Do you do that every day?" she asks.

I look up at the shock in her voice. "Yes."

"Are you sure you'll be able to stop when"—she points at her belly —"is born?"

"I'll have to."

I finish making her sandwich and cut a diagonal line, splitting it into two perfect triangles.

She smiles. "Are you going to cut the edges, too?"

"Do you want me to?"

She shakes her head. "I'm too hungry. I need those edges."

Her smile is churning something inside my chest. I need to go back to my office. "I haven't seen you this excited about food since you came here. Aunt Millie was worried just a few days ago about your low appetite."

"I've woken up hungry the past couple of days. It's Lemony's fault because I think I stopped worrying about him not staying put."

I push the plate toward her and she grabs one of the triangles and takes a bite. "Mhmm. So good." She moans. "I'll have to call Warren Buffet to tell him."

I chuckle. "I make a mean sandwich, but you're probably just really hungry."

She pours her hot chocolate into the mug. I can't help but notice how creamy it is. I move to the drawer by the coffee brewer. "Why is your hot chocolate so thick?"

"It's made with evaporated milk and a little water. Adri's mom's recipe. It has cinnamon, too. I told Aunt Millie how to make it and now she keeps it on tap for me. And before you yell, it's actually the only dairy I drink all day."

"It's fine. You can have it in moderation. Have you been able to work on your art project?"

The smile slips from her lips and she sighs. "No. The Taras are not cooperating."

I've come to know what that means. Her muse is giving her nothing. "Why do you think that is? Is it the sketchpad? Do you need a paper one?"

"No." She puts the sandwich down. "The sketchpad is freaking perfect and that's coming from a purist. But I've tried on paper and I just keep sketching something different."

"Like what?"

She looks down for a breath and then back at me. "It's nothing. It will be okay. Maybe all I need is to get in front of a canvas."

"You'll be able to soon. It's been a week and you're not bleeding anymore. I'm sure if you do it in moderation, it will be okay."

"You think so? That would be great. I can set up a canvas in my room and don't worry, I'll put something under it."

"You won't have to. Come with me. I want to show you something."

I move down the hallway, past her room to the one next to mine and she follows close behind me. I open the door for her and she goes in.

"I didn't know you had another bedroom."

"Oh, yes, this one is the baby's room. But what I want you to see is through that door." I point at the door on the far end.

I rush to open the door. I let her go in first and her mouth falls open.

"A sunroom," she gasps.

"I think you'll get plenty of light here. That door on the far end goes to my bedroom. It will stay locked so you can have privacy."

She spins around to stare at me. "You're going to let me use your baby's sunroom?"

"It's not like he's using it right now, and after you've agreed to carrying him for nine months and bringing him into the world, the least he can do is let you play in his room."

She keeps staring at me like she can't figure out what I'm saying. Then her chin trembles and tears well in her eyes. She presses a hand to her mouth and starts to blink fast.

An ache breaks in the back of my throat. I take a step and place my hands on her shoulders. "Don't cry."

"It's the nicest thing." Her voice breaks and it's so natural for me to pull her against me. She stiffens as our bodies make contact, standing straighter and pushing her breasts into my chest. I push her back softly but tighter against me. Her head drifts back and I get to look into her wet eyes, but there's something new in there. A curiosity. Maybe the same hunger brewing inside my chest that I'm really tired of denying.

Her mouth drifts open and I lean towards it.

"We shouldn't kiss," she says. "It's going to complicate things more."

But she doesn't move.

I swallow. "You're right."

I don't move either. I'm going to have to let go of her but I'm not ready yet.

"Winter, can I touch your belly?"

She nods and takes a step back. I'm almost reluctant to let her go but I do and place my hands on her stomach.

Electricity breaks through my skin. I stretch and I flex my fingers over her roundness. It's softer than I expected. And I'm in awe because my baby's in there, growing strong. And I can't help but sink to my knees as if I can get closer to him. I also can't help when my face gets closer and I get caught in the moment. I place on the belly the kiss I can't place on his mother's lips.

Mother? *Oh shit.*

I spring to my feet. "I'm sorry. I shouldn't have done that."

Her eyes are wide and she looks around as if trying to find an escape route. "I'll just go get my food and go back to my room. I need to get under the covers. It's always really cold here."

"Yeah, you know the reason for that. It keeps my heart cold."

I'm an idiot and my stupid joke falls flat because of everything that happened just seconds ago. She knows it and I know it.

15

Grayson

"Grayson, Simone De Castro is here to see you." Sandra announces through the intercom.

I'm happy to hear it. I'm even happier to tear my gaze from this report on the cost of the new plant and distribution center. I know my accountants and lawyers have gone through every single detail of it but since I'll be explaining it to the board, I like to know what I'm talking about so I'll be able to answer their questions.

"Send her in."

"Will do. Oh, Grayson, Stephen's office called, asking to reschedule the meeting today. His father was ill earlier and is resting. He's asking for the day after tomorrow."

"Did his secretary say if it's serious?" I ask.

"No but she mentioned he is home resting already. Do you want me to send flowers or anything?"

"Yes, call for a box of macaroons from *Citlali's*."

"Consider it done, boss."

"Sandra, can you have two boxes sent to my house, too? One with Aunt Millie's favorites and the other hazelnut."

"Sure can."

Simone strolls through the door of my office and shuts it behind her. Her wavy black hair is so glossy it catches the light in the room. She should look like a socialite in her slender figure and demure dress, but she has the eyes of a coroner. "You beckoned, Overlord?"

"Overlord?" I ask.

"My kids are playing *God of the Underworld* and they keep using the lingo. The top boss is called Overlord. He's built an empire and has the power to destroy."

She places her jacket and purse in one of the chairs in front of my desk and takes the other.

"Would you like some coffee or tea?"

She shakes her head. "No, I want to know why you took me out of the tower where you keep me hidden to bring me here."

"I don't hide you…" I say

"Not, literally," she counters.

"…just your true job."

She bobs her head. "Exactly. Don't want the area's top shark to get his panties in a bunch over a woman looking over his shoulder."

I shrug. I couldn't care less what Elias thinks and Simone gets a big kick out of that. "It's not a matter of trust, it's a matter of—"

"No, of course not. You're just a control freak and I appreciate it. Thanks to you, I have triple the work and less stress than I had before. I can also afford my three expensive kids and my trophy stay-at-home wife."

I laugh. "I'm sure Richard loves that you call him that."

"He loves it. He gets to drive our boys around, spend hours in our home gym, and work on growing his YouTube channel. Anyway, to the reason why I'm here. I read the paperwork that you sent me. What a nightmare for that poor woman."

My pulse skips when I think about the woman in question, about the kiss we had in the hospital, the kiss that almost was, and the kiss I placed on her belly.

While thinking of her as the mother of your kid. *Get a fucking grip already.*

"Yes. That's part of the story. The rest is here." I open the drawer above my legs on the desk. I pull out a black folder and hand it to her.

She frowns. "The rest?"

"Yes. Before you read it, I need to warn you. This is the most personal and confidential thing you've done for me. It's probably going to cause issues because I'm removing this workload from Elias and re-assigning him to overseeing the acquisition for the land in Colorado."

"I was looking forward to visiting Colorado and taking Richard and the kids," she says, but digs in and starts reading.

Her gaze is scanning fast over the pages and her mouth widens by the second. It's almost comical. "Oh God. You did it. That baby? The one that woman got inseminated with? That baby is...yours? This is your child?"

"Yes."

She points an accusatory finger. "You're having a kid?"

"Yes."

"I don't understand...I mean, I do. Astrid, the promise, and this whole clusterfuck happened with the hospital...and now...I need a minute." She closes the folder.

"I understand. In the meantime, and for the sake of speeding things up, I'll fill you in on what's been happening."

I explain everything I know, what Elias has done, the doctor's suicide, and finally the issue of the settlement. "I've decided to take the settlement because the last thing I need is this getting out into the world. I don't need the world knowing there's a woman pregnant with my child, or her name. I want to make this as painless as possible for her."

"How can it be painless in any way? This woman went for an everyday procedure, something as routine as a cavity filling, and came out with a life-altering experience. How the hell does that happen? This morning when I woke up, I thought I dreamt it and swore to myself I would stop reading suspense novels before bed. But no, it's true and not only that but my super-rich, boss-slash-best friend is the father. Shonda Rhimes couldn't come up with this shit."

I shrug. "Pretty much. Now she is doing me a favor and I want to do whatever I can for her. She won't take compensation but her job is at risk. She won't talk to me about it but I know she's worried. She works for a Catholic school and the board of directors is a strict one. She already had to divulge her pregnancy. I want to make sure she is not fired for it. So, on top of negotiating on our behalf in this settlement, I want you to find a way to litigate for her with the school."

He face twists like something bitter settled in her tongue. "Leave that to me. I have no patience for these puritanical institutions. If they fire her, she'll own it...what school is that?"

"LaSalle."

"Oh, I'm familiar with them. They'll know all about me when this is over. Is that it?"

That, I count on. "One more thing, when we reach a settlement, I want all the money to go to Winter."

Her mouth quirks into a smile. "Of course, that's chump change for you."

"What lawyer says chump change?"

She laughs. "One that was raised in the hood."

"Point taken. I don't want you conferring with any of the other lawyers, if you can swing it." I still want to keep control on the number of eyes on this.

"Fine by me. Your litigating wonder will probably pitch a fit. I don't want to be there when he finds out. Now, I'm going to go see Winter. After, I'm going to stop by Better Maryland with my assistant. I want to look at the paperwork and make sure all is in order."

"Elias did all that."

She points at the folder. "Yeah, but there's a discrepancy in your paperwork and Winter's."

"What is it?" Elias didn't mention a discrepancy.

"Well, the descriptions of what happened are nearly identical but there's differing language. In her report they keep calling it insemination, while yours says implant. I want them to correct this before we move forward." She places the folders in her purse. "We won't tell the president of your lawyers' boys club that there was an error. He would probably fire his assistant and all the interns."

"Is it simple to fix?" I ask.

"Yes, and to catch, too. But as I've always said, Grayson, it takes a woman to make sure all is done correctly." She stands up. Simone never waits for me to dismiss her. When we get to the root of the matter and what I want done, it's that's-all-folks for her. "Okay, I have a long day ahead of me. Call me if you need anything. I should have an update for you tomorrow. We'll also talk about why you didn't call me in the first place."

16

Winter

The room is covered in darkness and I pad around until I find my phone next to my pillow and flip it over. It's one in the morning. I stretch and my bladder gives me a pressure warning. Ugh, I have to get up.

Yesterday, for the first time since the scare, I painted. *I really, really, really painted.* It's not what I wanted or what I needed, the Taras, but it's what came in a burst of creativity and emotion. Simone came by to discuss the settlement and to tell me she was going to represent me now and somehow, we ended up talking about work. She said since I was in her retainer anyway and this had to do with the settlement, it was her job to call LaSalle and make sure I'm not adversely affected. I told her I don't want problems with Ms. Walker.

Stop thinking like a woman, Winter. You need to worry about yourself. You were the victim of this whole fiasco. You can't let it continue to victimize you and mess up your whole life.

I agreed and chuckled a few times, thinking of the two women butting heads. Loraine is not a pushover and Simone doesn't look like she ever budges.

I was so anxious after our meeting that I had to take it out on something. When I'm that full of pent-up emotion, I punish the canvas, even if it's just with garbage strokes. So, I purged, poured it all out, and was both horrified and touched by what I created. It was pure and raw. I'll need to go over some of the colors but it's there in vibrant colors and undeniable.

I wolfed down a sandwich Aunt Millie left on the table for me and headed to my room.

I used the bathroom, laid on the bed and passed out at five o'clock. Now I am wide awake and my stomach still feels so full.

I'm never going back to sleep.

My bladder warns again. I sigh and kick off the bed sheets. I skooch to the edge of bed and lower one leg and then the next one. I'm still in my paint-stained pants and tank top. When I finish, I grab the soft cotton robe and shrug it on. I put my phone in my pocket and head to the kitchen.

I'm forgoing the hot chocolate after eating a full box of macaroons, but a cup of hot tea should help warm me up and relax me to enough to go back to sleep.

That's how I keep my heart cold.

I could have believed Grayson, if he had not been so gentle when he said it. If I had not seen the fear that night in the hospital when he'd held onto my hand and stroked my hair as we both thought we were losing the baby. How could someone with a cold heart kiss me so gently?

How could someone with a cold heart stroke my sides with his fingers like he did last night? How could someone with a cold heart place the softest of kisses on my belly?

Heat spirals down my spine. I shouldn't have allowed that. Maybe I could have slept the night before without dreaming about his mouth sliding everywhere.

I woke up in the middle of the night, sweating and with my fingers stroking between my legs. I resisted, to no avail. I had to rub circles around my clit and pull on my nipples until I came with my eyes closed so I could still see his face. My lips tightened so I wouldn't moan his name.

I'm so glad I didn't see him last night. The whole day, when a thought of him came, or when Aunt Millie mentioned him, the walls of my stomach would collapse into a wobbly mess. Not to mention the arrival of the macaroons. He'd sent me Nutella ones.

Thank God the talk with Simone helped put things into perspective. She brought it back to business, to our arrangement.

"I'm carrying you and that's it. Stop playing with my hormones because that is so not going to happen." I whisper this time because I don't want Grayson to hear me.

I pass through the living room. His office door is open and the light is on. I frown but then remember it's Grayson. He would still be working at this time.

I make my way to the kitchen and tinker around until I find the decaffeinated tea. *What an abomination.* I don't mind because I'm giddy. I've exorcised the feeling trapped in my chest and though I worry about what I was able to put on the canvas, I can't help but think how at peace I feel.

"Why is that?" I ask out loud and turn my gaze away when I notice that I'm looking at my belly.

It would be really swell if I could stop talking to this kid. My eyes wander to the coffee maker and it's almost empty. Grayson doesn't seem to be going to bed anytime soon. Before I can question myself, I take out one of his coffee pods and brew him some more.

I want to thank him for letting me use the sunroom. I've never had a better place to paint. The light filters and makes it warmer than the rest of the house. I love the view of the city, too.

"You're so lucky." I say and I can almost picture a baby getting the morning sun in there while Grayson reads the paper a few feet away. *Okay, I'm bugging.*

I pour my tea and his mug of black coffee—no sugar, no cream, and super gross—then, head to his office. I pause at the door. *Go back to your room, Winter. You don't know that he wants coffee. It's just stupid.*

I go in anyway and almost drop both mugs. He's at his desk in sweats and an undershirt. He doesn't look like the type to wear these kinds of casual clothes. Honestly, though, I kind of expected him to work out in a suit. *I would give anything to be that undershirt.*

Where did that come from?

You know where it came from, Winter. Get the fuck out of here.

I take a step back but he glances up and smiles like it's normal for me to be standing here by his office door, with my big, growing belly and two mugs.

"I thought you were sleeping."

Say something. Stop staring. I clear my throat. "Routine middle-of-the-night wake-up." Good, I still can talk and I'm pretty sure I'm not drooling. "I needed a hot drink."

"Two mugs? You're living the wild life, Miss Winter."

I laugh. "Actually, this one is for you."

His eyes round a little but the smile spreads wider across his lips. "Gimme."

I pass him the mug. He inclines his head to the chair across from him.

"I don't want to interrupt your work."

"Says the woman who judges me for working too hard."

"Am I wrong? It's one in the morning."

Grayson's eyes narrow and he leans a little closer. "No one likes a know-it-all."

"I'm a teacher. Know-it-all is my DNA code."

His mouth spreads into that perfect smile. The one that turns my world into a hazy riot of shades and tones. Does he know how mouth-watering he is when he smiles like that? The familiar tingle stirs in my chest, between my legs, through the mush pile that is my brain. *Grab your hot chocolate and run back to your room where it's safe.*

Safe? Yeah, right? Not anywhere near him.

"You painted today."

I frown. "How do you know?"

"Aunt Millie told me when I got home. She said you were sleeping."

"Oh. Yeah, I was spent. I think that week I spent laying around made me lazy. I'm sleeping a lot these days."

"Or maybe, just maybe, you're tired because you're carrying another person around?" His gaze drops down to my belly. "It's getting bigger."

His gaze makes my flesh tingle but I try to laugh it off. "Yeah, soon you'll have to roll me to my room."

"Did I make you uncomfortable last night?"

The instant rush of lust blindsides me and leaves me stupefied. Uncomfortable? *You made me so horny I had to rub myself to sleep last night and had dreams about you all night.* "No."

"Are you sure?"

"I'm positive." *Trust me.*

"I don't believe you." There's a teasing smile on his lips.

I recognize a dare when I see it. "Why? Could it be you who got uncomfortable? You seemed pretty embarrassed."

He shrugs. "You told me not to kiss you."

"You kissed me anyway...on the belly. Are you saying you wanted to kiss my mouth?" I blurt without thinking. *What the hell am I doing? Nothing good can come of this.*

His head jerks back. He wasn't expecting that.

He leans forward on the desk. "Yes. I wanted nothing more than to kiss your mouth. Would you let me tonight?"

My heart slams into the walls of my chest and I want to get up and go but I can't. *Shit.* We're still staring at each other.

Say no.

I nod instead.

And he moves, without breaking eye contact. He comes around the desk to kneel in front of me. He takes the mug from my hand and puts it on the desk. I'm transfixed. I can't believe I just gave him permission, even as he cups my face in his warm hands and I'm leaning into him.

"You're so beautiful," he says, like he doesn't see my messy hair or paint-stained pants.

"I'm not."

He pulls my head down and presses a soft kiss on my lips. "You're right. You're not beautiful. You're breathtaking." He kisses me again, this time lingering, running his tongue over my lips. I open my mouth and catch it, flicking it with my own.

My hands roam up his arm and settle at his shoulder. My legs drift open and he settles between them, deepening our kiss until we're a mess of lips and tongues. His hands trail down my neck and all my nerve endings begin to tingle. He follows with his mouth, kissing up my jaw all the way around to my ear. He licks under my lobe. I'm so wet I may slide right off this chair, but his hands are now at my ribs, holding me steady so his mouth can continue wrecking my skin.

My breasts are heavy, painfully straining against my tank top. "Touch me, Gray."

He pulls back to stare into my eyes. His eyes are cloudy and dark like the sky before snow. "Where?"

I swear my body answers for me. My chest pushing forward, my hips bucking up.

He looks from my eyes to my breasts and swipes his tongue over his lower lip. My pussy clenches hard, near violent.

Grayson unties my robe and pushes it down my shoulders. Then, he slides the spaghetti straps, his knuckles brushing against my skin, sending chills down my body.

My breasts spring free and he cups each in his hands. "I only got a hint but they're so much more…"

He kisses one and then the other, like he can't make up his mind or his mouth is set on fair treatment. The first flick of his tongue is like a flash of heat that makes my hips rock. But his mouth settles over me, and he sucks hard enough to rip a gasp from me. I let myself drift back against the chair and open my legs wider. Because I need more. This has set me off and I need more. So much more. I take his hand and press it to my crotch.

"Fuck me."

He pulls his mouth from my tits to stare at me.

"I need your cock," I say like he can't understand me.

He swallows. "Remember what the doctor said."

No sex. Fuck me. Ugh.

But Gray smiles and pulls me to my feet. "I happen to be pretty good with my mouth." He crushes his lips to mine and pushes my pants down my legs until they're pooling at my feet. He bends down and helps me out of them, then guides me back to the couch in the back of his office. He sits me down and kneels between my legs, running his hands up my calves and kissing my thighs.

I need him to hurry and just as I'm about to voice it, he hooks his fingers under my knee and hangs my legs on his shoulders. His hands reach under my ass and pull me to him.

"I want you to promise me something…"

"Anything," I moan. *Any fucking thing you want, just eat me.*

"When you can, we'll do it in bed and you're going to let me play, fuck, and feel all of you."

I could come just from hearing him talk but he needs to give me more. "Yes, I promise. Make me come."

The first flick of his tongue makes me almost come off the chair. The next one leaves me flailing. The third has my hand lost in his hair. And then I lose count because he's swirling and twisting a nipple around with his fingers, and I'm pushing my pussy tighter against his mouth. His mouth latches on to my clit and he sucks it so hard, he yanks an orgasm out of me and sends me straight back against the chair. I'm helpless and don't know words except one and I whisper it in one long rush.

"Gray."

17

Grayson

Winter messed with my head, with my day, with my comprehension skills. I haven't focused all day. If I hadn't kissed her...

That fucking kiss. It fucked me. It fucked my head. It had me fucking her with my tongue.

Now, I can't get her out of my thoughts or get her smell out of my nose. And I don't get it. We kissed before, in the hospital and it was deep and I still was okay. Why was this kiss so different?

Because it was on purpose and it was coming a long time and why did she have to open her legs like that? Why did she have to ask me to eat her pussy? If she hadn't done that...I still would have coaxed her with my tongue and my fingers until she did. I would have rolled her nipples between my index and thumb. I would have licked whatever she wanted me to.

Shit, I'm hard again. I beat off to her this morning just remembering her little moans, those little gasps when I licked anywhere the first time, how tight she'd grabbed on my hair.

My hand feels rough on my dick. I wish it were her mouth.

"Grayson, Simone's here to see you." Sandra's voice blares on the intercom and my back stiffens into a straight position.

Shit. I'm rubbing my dick at work with the door open. Get a grip, Grayson.

"Give me a minute." I adjust my pants and take a swig of water.

My heart's pounding. My dick's a lead pipe on my pants. She's a Catholic school teacher for God's sake. I shouldn't be twisted up like this.

I take a couple of breaths and by the time Simone strolls through the door, I feel in enough control to hold a conversation.

"Good morning, all mighty guardian Setu," she says.

"What?"

She rolls her eyes. "It's the overlord's name."

She's such a complete geek. "Good morning. What you have got for me?"

"Someone's mighty short today. Who peed on your bran muffin?"

I ignore her. "I'm having a hard time with the report accounting sent this morning. It seems like a simple concept when they explain it but it reads like gibberish."

"Like everything accounting does. Do you want me to take a look?"

I shake my head. "Not yet but I'll pass it on to you when I am done with it. You know..."

"Second sign off?"

I really hate her and her humor today.

"Yes." My tone is brusque to my own ears. "I'm sorry. I'm a little distracted this morning."

She snorts. "I bet."

"What is that supposed to mean?"

"You got a hot baby mama at home in that second trimester glow. Richard got the same way with each of my pregnancies."

"It's not the same thing. We are no—"

She chuckles. "Oh. You two are doing *that thing.*"

She's working my nerves. "Doing *what thing?*"

"That whole, 'This is not a thing. We are just having a baby,' thing."

"*That thing* is the actual thing, Simone. We are just having a baby."

"And the hots for each other."

"No—"

"Cut the crap, Grayson. I know you. You're a good guy but you're going way out of your way for her."

"She's having my baby and won't take compensation. It's the least I can do."

Her chin juts out. "That's true but you have to recognize that something's going on between you and this woman. You're both going out of your way for each other. She's living up in your house and you're trying to give her a fortune on the down low."

"It's the—"

She cuts me off. "—least you can do. Got it the first one hundred and fifty times you said it."

"You're being unprofessional."

"No, I'm being your friend," she counters.

"But we're in the office right now." God, will this conversation end?

She rolls her eyes. "You need the friend more than the lawyer right now."

Unfortunately for me, it's true. "What do you want from me?"

"I want you to go into this clear. Since Astrid, you don't do relationships. Yet, you have a woman installed at your house. She has a painting room and you send her macaroons in the middle of the afternoon…"

"She's pregnant and living in a house that is not hers. I just want her to be—"

"Happy?" she offers.

"Stop interrupting me. I was going to say comfortable. Anyway, did you get that paperwork all straightened out."

She nods. "Yes and no, but don't change the subject. You both like each other and you're having a kid together."

THE WINTER OF MY LOVE

"It's my child. She's only carrying it. Besides, she doesn't want kids and she doesn't do relationships."

She chuckles. "Neither do you. And don't look at me like that."

"Let's talk about work. It's everything all set?"

Her eyes narrow. She doesn't like to be put off. "I went there and that paperwork is all wrong. They have it registered as an insemination in her paperwork but implantation on the clinic log. They're going through the doctor files and they're going to get back to me today. Which is code for, they don't have a damned clue."

"How could they not have a clue?"

"How can someone go in for a routine procedure and come out with a bun in her oven?" She waves a hand. "Apparently, anything can happen at the Better Maryland Clinic. They should consider closing the clinic until this stuff is sorted out. The death of the doctor has the staff shaken. The director is so wracked trying to keep this under wraps, making sure the employees get the support they need, and trying to settle this."

"Is that going to affect Winter's payoff?"

"Not with me as a lawyer. So, I have to ask. Is there a possibility that there was only sperm frozen for you?"

"No. We had both. Doctor Cooper at the Mencia Clinic oversaw the whole thing."

She jots down his name. "I'm asking because that's a big error. Something that doesn't happen in a medical community."

An uneasy feeling sits on the pit of my stomach. "But as you said, this kind of thing doesn't usually happen either."

She presses her lips together and she's staring at a point behind me on the wall. It's her thinking look.

"Spit it out, Simone."

She hums low. "You know I don't like messy and this is a messy onion. There're too many layers to this. I wish you had come to me from the beginning. This is something I should've handled for you."

I can't ignore her rebuke or the hurt behind it. "I thought I could keep this strictly professional, like any other transaction. I pay someone. She carries the baby. The baby is delivered and we all go on our ways."

"It was never going to be that simple. First, you chose someone that worked for you, which is crazy. I don't know what you were thinking. Second, why would you ask your male lawyer to advise you on having a child when you have me? I have children. We've been friends for over twenty years. I could have found you a better suited surrogate."

Damn, I hurt her. "I know that now. This wasn't easy for me. I thought you would talk me out of it. We once had a conversation about my promise to Astrid and you said that wasn't fair or legally binding. I couldn't break that promise and you kept saying I didn't have to do it."

She rolls her eyes. "Men are so dumb. I said you didn't have to. I never said that I wouldn't support you. Of course, I would have done everything to make this work seamlessly for you. Well, as seamlessly as having a baby can be, which is not seamless at all. Working with me all these years should have taught you that I do what you need me to do even when I personally disagree."

I fucked up. I did. I let my pride get in the way of this. "I'm sorry. I should have come to you."

"Yeah, I could have told you the little social climber you chose to carry the baby was wrong for the job. Did you not notice the way she made herself essential around here?"

"Alice was the perfect employee." She went above and beyond all the critical categories and I was able to trust her even with some personal items. It seemed like a win-win.

"Of course, she was perfect. She was trying to ingratiate herself to you, Grayson."

"Elias agreed with my assessment."

She scoffs. "Because, like you, he was also thinking with his dick."

"I wasn't sleeping with her."

"I know you weren't, Grayson. You never shit where you eat. It's admirable but you fell for that pretty face, those big eyes, and that come-get-a-piece smile."

"Simone, you're a lawyer for God's sake."

She scoffs. "But I'm a woman first, honey. I know her type and I know you. You like to surround yourself with capable people but love pretty faces. Not to mention a nice set of boobs and sturdy legs. Like your baby mama."

"This conversation is not helping. It's not going to change anything."

She sighs. "You're right. It's the proverbial water under the bridge. Do you know what you want to do with her yet, once your private investigator finds Alice? Are you pressing charges?"

"I can't have this getting out."

She nods. "It would be a PR mess and it would drag your teacher down with it."

"I can't do that to Winter. She doesn't deserve this and I don't want her to suffer because of it. We'll deal with Alice. She is going to tell me who she was working with, return my money, and sign another non-disclosure agreement. Then, I'm going to fire her and she's going to move far away from here. If she even hints at this to anyone, I'll go after her, her whole family, future children, and grandchildren."

She smiles a little. "That's what I like to hear. That part is going to be fun. But for now, we are going to do the sucky parts—" She looks down at her phone. "Wait, I just got an email from the clinic. They need to see me immediately. It's about the paperwork. I'll be in touch."

"Okay, I'm heading home soon. Call me on my cell."

She stands up. "Will do. And by the way…" She rummages through her bag, pulls out a small wrapped box, and puts it on my desk. "Happy birthday, Grayson."

1 8

_____

Winter

"This outer shade is almost perfect." I go over the edge once, smiling at my precision. I won't have to clean anything. I step back and admire the whole vegetable garden that seemed to come alive this morning. The purples in the blueberry, the grape, and the plum are as contrasting as the size between them. The lime and the lemon next to the plum and the peach. In the middle, the luscious apple sliced in the quarter to show the pit, which glows golden and bright.

It's not what I wanted to paint. It never is anymore.

"You had to have it your way," I say, looking down at my belly. I swear it's bigger this morning. All of me feels bigger after last night. I woke up stretching on the bed with my insides still like jelly.

I closed my door after last night, pushed my conscious away, and went to sleep. It's been a long time since I've been touched like that and God knows I've never been eaten like that. A pang sets off in my belly. I wonder if Gray can roll his Rs because, oh my God, his tongue moves fast and slow and his tempo is just…

"Winter?"

112

I whip around. Aunt Millie is standing by the door. "Come in."

She smiles and steps inside the sunroom. She comes to stand by me, her gaze on the painting. "The girls are on their way up." She points to my canvas. "This is beautiful. God has blessed you with amazing talent."

Her voice is above a whisper. Her eyes shine in a way that reminds me of when I went to see the Pre-Raphaelite Legacy at MOMA. I had tears in my eyes when I stepped in front of *Lady Lilith*.

Is that how she feels with my painting? My chest swells with pride.

"You're going to show this to Grayson, right?"

My face heats at the mention of his name. I hope nothing's out of sorts in his office. I don't want Aunt Millie to know what we were doing there. "Maybe?"

She bites her lips, which she usually does when she's trying not to smile. "He would love it. It's something you both share. And besides, it's his birthday today."

"Oh. I didn't know, but I was contemplating giving this to him anyway."

She lets the smile shine. "Desiderio, his dad, used to make a big deal out of Grayson's day. I try as much as he lets me but with you here, I'm going overboard. I'm baking a cake for tonight's special dinner."

"Hello?" Lauren calls from the adjacent room and then she and Adri walk through the door wearing fall coats.

Adri rushes to me and hugs me. I haven't seen her in a while. Her hands immediately go to my belly. "Look at how much it's grown. I'm so sorry I haven't come to see you."

"It's okay. You call and text and you look gorgeous, Adri." And happy. Her face is glowing and her eyes sparkling.

"I have a lot to share," she laughs. "Well, two *big, big, big* things."

Aunt Millie lets go of Lauren, excuses herself and promises to send cookies.

"Well?" I say to Adri.

She pushes her hand toward me in the universal sign for he-put-a-ring-on-it. My mouth falls open and Lauren is clapping. I grab my friend and hug her so tight but something in her middle pushes against my belly. I jump back.

Adri is smiling so hard, it fills her whole face. "That's my other news."

She unbuttons her coat and there's an unmistakable baby bump. One that's bigger than mine.

I freeze. "You're pregnant?"

"I am," she gushes. "I'm sorry I didn't tell you earlier. I found out a couple of weeks after you did and you were so worried with the scare, not to mention I was sick myself. For a couple of weeks I could barely go into the bistro because of the food smell. I've also been a little tired, but I think that's over and I'm through the first trimester, though looking at me you would think I'm like five months."

I smile. "It's okay. I understand. Congratulations." I hug her tight because Adri deserves this. She and Cam went through a lot to get here. "Cam has to be dying of happiness. Weeks ago, he talked about having five kids."

She giggles. "He's not getting five. I told him that he has to go and fulfill his dreams of an infield of his own children in other ways. But we're so happy. I was wracking my brain on how to tell him. Then, he took me away to NY for the weekend and proposed. It was the perfect time to tell him."

"Wow. That's great."

"And bad," Lauren adds. "He's already started thinking of ideas for the baby's room and smothering Bron with love so she doesn't feel jealous.'"

"Not to mention overprotective. I can't even move the big pots on the stove without him having a cow. He wants to lift everything for me and keeps making sure that I'm comfortable. Don't get me started on him calling to check on me all day long. It's crazy."

But her voice rings with happiness. If I had to paint her, I would use yellows and sparkling gold because she's brimming with joy. It's seeping through her pores, shining a light so bright it heats my face, my whole body.

That baby is hers. That happiness is all hers. I woke up smiling, to a bliss of something that was physical and not real. *It was a lie and the baby in my belly, which I painted all over my canvas, is not even mine.*

My vision blurs and I take an unsure step back. Adri rushes forward to grab my arm.

"Are you okay?" Lauren is also next to me and both guide me to the small couch Grayson had brought into the room for me.

"I'm okay," I say, pressing a hand to my chest. My breath is quick and choppy. "I just got winded. It's hot in here."

I shrug off my sweater.

"Get her some juice," Adri tells Lauren. She turns back to me, her happiness veiled by the cloud of worry in her eyes.

God, I'm a shitty person. I've ruined her happy moment. I should be celebrating with her because I'm happy for my friend. I just can't help but compare. She has Cam, and Bron and this new baby. At the end of this pregnancy, Grayson will have the baby he wants and I will have the same thing I walked into this with…nothing.

I wish I had that kind of happiness. I wish I could feel that joyful and hopeful about this baby. But I can't say that. I can't ruin her time. *And besides, this baby will bring happiness to Grayson.* There's satisfaction in that.

I force a smile on my face but the lump in my throat is almost too big to swallow.

"I'm fine, Adri. You know how this baby loves to mess with me. I'm happy for you. There's so much planning to do. Do you know when you'll get married?"

The smile brightens her eyes again. "We're trying to figure it out. It may just be something quick at City Hall. Cam wants to do it before the baby is born and he's obsessed with making sure Bron is okay with every decision."

"He's a sweet dad."

"And a crazy one. He's happy the baby won't be born near Bron's birthday. She, on the other hand, would be delighted. She's so happy. She's recruited you and Ayla to help her and Cam paint a scenery in the baby's room."

It warms my whole heart. "I would be honored."

115

Adri looks around and then down at my stomach. "This is part of the baby's room, right?"

I remove my hands from it fast. "How did you know?"

"It's next to a big room with a bathroom. The baby can take naps here and play and everything is conveniently close. It's the perfect space. I'm going home to have Cam call a designer to add a sunroom like this in our house."

Lauren comes back with a glass of orange juice. "Aunt Millie said to make sure you drink it all. She also wants you to stay off your feet. She says you've been at this all day."

I shake my head. "I'm fine."

Lauren pushes the ottoman to sit next to me. "I know but I'm not messing with her. She's like Adri's mom. I am obeying everything she says."

"How did things go in Acacia Falls? You didn't call me when you got back." I ask Lauren, anxious to move on from my hater moment. I'm a horrible friend.

Adri shakes her head.

Lo looks out into the city. "My sister is a fuck up and my mom insists on backing everything she does. She went to hang out with a boyfriend she has in Connecticut and left her kids with one of his relatives. Last night I had to go get my nephews, take them back to Acacia, and come home. I got in at one in the morning."

"I'm sorry," I say. "You drove all that way by yourself?"

She nods.

"Oh man, I wish I could have gone with you. Why didn't you take Chase?"

She sighs and looks away. "You do know he's not my man, right?"

I press my lips together and Adri turns her face to hide her smile.

"I can see your reflection in the glass," she snaps.

I touch her shoulder. "We know he's not your man. Because you don't let him be, by the way, but he's still your friend. You guys hang out a lot and you shouldn't have gone alone."

"That's what I said," Adri adds. "I wish your mom would stop dragging you into Connie's messes but I can understand her worry about the kids. Your sister needs to get her act together. You don't leave your kids at the mercy of strangers."

Her words slice over my flesh and I swallow the gasp. But Lauren's hand shoots to cover mine over her shoulder.

Adri gets up and excuses herself to go to the bathroom.

The second she is out of the room, Lauren leans toward me. "She didn't mean it like that. She's got prego brain. She forgets everything. Yesterday she texted me twice to ask where I was."

I push a smile onto my lips. God, my face is going to hurt from me forcing it so much today. "I know. It's hard to hear it but it's the truth. Your sister and my mother shouldn't have had children."

"But then we wouldn't have you. And you're pretty awesome," she says with a big smile and now I'm jealous of Adri again. Because she has had this kickass friend all her life. And I'm jealous of Connie, though I think she's a fuck up, too. "Thank you."

"How's Lemony Cricket doing?"

I point at my belly. "No longer a lemon but an apple this week."

Lauren chuckles. "Granny Smith it is."

I laugh. Then she does.

"Speaking of, did you bring me the floating frame I asked you for? It's okay if you didn't. Had I known you had a such a long day yesterday I wouldn't have asked."

She ughs. "Oh, please. You asked me to pick up a frame from your living room not build you one. And yes, I brought it. It's in the other room."

"Thank you."

Adri steps back in the room. "I freaking love that bathroom. The tub is perfect for bathing kids. Cam has a lot of work to do. Well, hire someone to do. Everything in there is bound to make things a little more comfortable for you."

Lauren shoots me a mortified look and I want to laugh because Adri's in a cloud. She's so happy she's forgotten that I won't be here for those things. She's acting like we'll be going through this at the same time, like this baby is actually mine.

I wish that were true. The thought hits me with force and makes my stomach drop.

They leave an hour later to pick up Bron and Ayla from school.

"Bring the girls next week. We can do lessons here. Grayson would have no issues with that," I say hugging Adri and then Lauren.

I wait for the sound of the door closing and then head to my room. The warmth of the sunroom has become too much and I can't look at my painting right now. I'll let it dry and come back later to frame it.

The closer I get to my room, the more the knot tightens in my throat. The first tear drops the minute I step inside. I climb into bed as another follows and then the next. I'm crying for everything and nothing. Because that's the difference between Adri and me.

She has it all and I'm living a borrowed life in a gorgeous penthouse that's not mine, with a baby inside me that doesn't belong to me. And, like always, having casual sex that won't mean anything in the grand scheme of things.

I wish it were real. It felt real when he kissed me goodbye in front of my room last night. That makes the tears drop faster and I have to swallow the sob.

Aunt Millie knocks on the door but I pretend to be asleep.

My crying, like the things I now desire, will have to be kept on the down low.

19

Grayson

I've been parked in bumper-to-bumper traffic for the past forty-five minutes. I should have been home thirty minutes ago. Today has been a circus of what can fuck up my day more. The accident blocking the road is the latest, but the winner is the twenty-minute call with Stephen *Fucking* Miller. His father rescheduled our last meeting and he was irate because I couldn't fit in him today.

How I ended the call without telling him to go fuck himself, is nothing short of a miracle.

All I've wanted all day was to get home. It's a feeling I was unfamiliar with until recently. Since Winter moved into my house. I look forward to going home to her smiles and sassy mouth.

I'm also hoping for a repeat of last night. My conscience screams it's not wise but I don't care. I want to make her moan again, in my bed or hers, I don't care. And I want the doctor to clear her so I can stuff her with my cock like she asked me to. I'll give her every single inch she wants.

If only this traffic on Light Street would move. My phone goes off and I hit the pick-up call button.

"Grayson," Simone's voice blares from the speakers. "Are you alone?"

"Yes…"

"I need to tell you something about my meeting with Better Maryland but I need to know that you're alone."

What fucking now? "Are they refusing to do the settlement? If so, I don't give a fuck about anything, we are suing their asses for every cent they have and forcing NDAs up their asses."

"No. They're going to pay and you're going to want more money after this."

"What is it?"

"The reason the director called me this afternoon is to tell me that they went through the archives and the registries for the times around the procedure. They were trying to straighten out the information in Winter's file. The reason for the discrepancy is because the specimen they received from Doctor Cooper's clinic was labeled with a specific code for sperm."

I slam on the brakes right after the car in front of me. "What the hell does that mean?"

"I needed to make sure, so the director and I went to Doctor Cooper's office and demanded to see him. We showed him the scan on entry and he confirmed it. I'm sickened and I don't know how to tell you this. But somewhere along the way, your embryos never made it on the transport to Better Maryland."

"What are you talking about? Winter is pregnant. She's carrying those embryos."

"Grayson…" She pauses. "…Winter was inseminated. Better Maryland never received embryos from Doctor Cooper's office. They received only the sperm vials in the container."

I can't hear Simone anymore. My whole body goes cold and everything around me fades out.

It was only my sperm. The embryos have gone missing. That can only mean one thing.

The baby is not Astrid's. He's mine...and Winter's.

Blood rushes my ears. My fingers tighten around the steering wheel. Horns are blaring and Simone is yelling my name. I'm trying to find my breath but I can't.

"Grayson? Are you okay? Answer me."

"I'm here, Simone." God knows I wish I wasn't.

"Jesus, don't scare me like that. I thought you crashed or something, with all that fucking noise in the background."

"How the fuck is this happening, Simone? No. Why the hell is this happening? Where the hell are the embryos?"

"I don't know, but Doctor Cooper is going through his father's files. There's something bigger than Better Maryland and Alice behind this, Grayson. We may need to talk to the police."

"Why?"

"Because this was well-planned and executed. I don't know if they have the embryos somewhere, planning to ask for ransom or if the plan was to use the sperm all along. Only Alice, the missing worker, and Doctor Lawrence know what happened, but maybe Doctor Cooper can find out something with his staff."

My stomach coils up. Dr. Cooper's father had been Astrid's doctor since she was a child. "I need to think about all this. Let's talk in the morning."

"Are you going to be okay?"

Probably never. "Yeah...I'll be fine."

I make the decision to concentrate on the road or I'll crash. I make my way to Silo Point in record time after getting past the traffic, but I sit in the parking lot for twenty minutes.

On my way up the elevator, I let it all in. What am I going to tell Winter? It's her baby, too. *Jesus, it's her baby.* Her flesh and her blood and the one thing she's never wanted.

I love children in general. I don't want any of my own.

What if she wants to terminate? My stomach pitches forward. No, she wouldn't do that. I'll just have to convince her nothing has changed.

Except, this changes everything. Because if our situation was an incongruent and jumbled cluster-fuck before, now it's off the charts. I want to turn around and head back downstairs. Maybe head to a bar somewhere, have some drinks, and hope Winter's asleep when I get back. That's the coward's way out. I can almost hear my dad's voice.

Graysons are not cowards. We tell the truth, even if it hurts us.

I hold my breath and turn the key. The hallway is dark and I exhale long and hard. Winter is probably asleep. I'll just take my briefcase up to my office and then go lock myself in my room until the morning. I may not be a coward but I'm not stupid. If the universe is giving me a reprieve until tomorrow, I'm going to take it.

I make it to my office without turning on the lights and throw my briefcase on the desk chair. The desk chair where I got to touch Winter and extracted those delicious noises from her.

I head out of the office to go to my room.

"Grayson?" Aunt Millie's voice stops me on my tracks.

"I'm going to take a shower. Can we talk later?" I answer without turning around.

"Can you just come here for a second? I need to show you something." Her tone is serious and deep.

Something happened to Winter.

My heart sinks. Are we going to the hospital? Jesus. I cross the room in three steps and she's standing in the door to the formal dining room. "What's happened?"

She smiles. "This."

She moves aside. There is dinner and a cake with candles. Winter's standing by the table. She's smiling, too. "Surprise."

Aunt Millie hugs me first. "Happy birthday, my boy."

I can't say anything. The words won't come.

Winter takes a few steps and climbs onto her toes to kiss my cheek. "Happy birthday, Gray."

She smells like fresh-cut flowers. I can't place the scent but it's delicate and teasing. It lingers around me as she steps back and takes a chair. She pats the head of the table. I wait for Aunt Millie and her to sit to my left and take my assigned place.

The words are still not coming and I have to clear my throat three times. "Thank you."

"He speaks," Winter deadpans.

Aunt Millie chuckles. "He doesn't like birthday surprises but I'm determined to celebrate his every single year, like his dad used to."

"Dad used to make my birthday special every year," I say to Winter. "Aunt Millie picked it up after his death."

My voice goes hoarse. I don't know if it's everything I've learned in the past hour or because I still miss Dad or because Aunt Millie loves me in so many ways. I don't deserve it, not when I'm lying to the woman next to me.

"I bet he's watching and smiling." Winter's gaze is so warm and it twists everything inside my chest.

"Let's eat." Aunt Millie uncovers the plate and she has all my favorites. Spaghetti Bolognese, Caesar salad, and the cake, topped with her famous peanut butter mousse.

I have to force the words out of my mouth. "I can't wait to get to the cake. Dad used to always ask Aunt Millie to make the cake. He tried one year and it was awful. He said, 'Son, I think I found my flaw,' and then took us out for ice cream after." The memory is playing before me. I can almost feel the warmth of his bashful smile.

"Your father was a smart and talented man but baking was not one of those talents. You would have liked him, Winter, and he would have loved you. He would've been the best grandpa any kid would ever want." Her eyes grow misty and she looks down at her plate, as if she's searching for something in her salad.

As if she hadn't dropped a bomb insinuating that Winter's more than the surrogate. She knows me like no other human and I'm sure, though she doesn't say it, she's picked up on my feelings for Winter.

Feelings? Good God.

And this is what will make it messier, too. Because I'm not the only one invested in Winter. Now Aunt Millie is, too. I should have seen this coming.

My gaze drifts over to Winter and I'm surprised to find her dabbing at her eyes. She shakes her head at me. "I'm sorry. It's this baby. I never cry."

"That baby didn't do anything. He just loves his Grandma Millie already and if I cry, he cries. Grayson was the same way when he was about one, but it's a happy occasion. Let's get through dinner so we can get to this cake. I want to know if Winter likes it."

They chit chat around me and I can barely hear them because my thoughts are too loud and I just know that when I tell her, this peace will vanish. And maybe she'll go away, too.

2 0

Winter

I'm pacing outside his door and this is the most stalkerish thing I've ever done. I step forward, lift my hand to knock, but take a step right back out. It's been the same insane pattern for the last five minutes. Nin is watching me from a few feet away. Apparently, she's been left out of the room too.

"I'm sure if you were scratching at the door, Grayson would let you in," I say to her.

All through dinner he'd been distant, absent. Aunt Millie and I made the most of the conversation and he was polite and engaging, but he wasn't there. The little voice in my head whispered that this was not uncommon. People regret sexual encounters all the time and this one was probably the least ideal of all.

When he excused himself to go shower and never came back, Aunt Millie said it was probably about missing his dad, but I didn't buy it.

Maybe he's missing Astrid. That's the thought that sent me to my room for the last hour and brought on full force that same hot feeling I got when I found out Adri's pregnant and happy.

Jesus, I'm jealous. Jealous of my friend. Jealous of a dead woman whom he has all the right in the world to miss. It's not me. I don't feel these things. I've never wanted what Adri has but I want him and I do have feelings for him. And even if he doesn't feel the same way, I want to give him this gift.

The painting is all his. Because the subject is all his. It always has been. It's his birthday and he should have it. He's given me a room to paint and has tried to make me comfortable.

I square my shoulders and knock on the door. His footsteps tap against the hardwood floor and stop on the other side of the door. I start counting and if I get to ten, I will head back to my room and won't bother him again about this.

One...two...three...four...five...

The knob turns and the door opens. All I see is naked torso at first and my gaze drifts down to his black pajama pants. Then I force myself to look up to a face I barely recognize because there's no emotion, no surprise, nothing but gray-blue in his eyes.

And it stokes something angry and cold of my own. "Forget it."

I spin on my heel and stalk away.

You're a dumbass, Winter. You had no reason or right to be there knocking on his door when it's clear he doesn't want to be bothered. All you did was embarrass yourself.

A hand closes around my elbow right in front of my bedroom door, bringing me to a full stop and turning me around until I'm face to face with him again.

"I'm sorry," he says.

"About what?"

He runs his free hand over his face. "It's been a long day, a stressful one."

"I get that. That's why I should let you rest." I try for accommodating but all I could hear is the anger, coated in politeness.

"Tell me what you need."

"I don't fucking need anything from you." *And oh my God, what the fuck is wrong with me?*

He flinches. I bet he was so not expecting that. I sure wasn't. His mouth opens but he doesn't say anything and that only makes me feel worse. I'm an idiot and now I look like a crazy one, too.

"Winter, I'm sorry for whatever I did to upset you."

I sigh. "You didn't do anything. I forgot how brush-offs work, but I remember well now. I apologize for swearing at you and being angry."

His face scrunches up. "What the fuck are you talking about? I'm not brushing you off, I just had a fucked-up day, and I didn't know how to handle the birthday dinner…" He stops and breathes.

There was no emotion in his eyes before but he's weighed down now. *Fix it, dummy.*

I take his hand in mine and push a smile on my lips. "It's okay, Gray. Go back to resting. We can talk another time. It can wait."

He covers my hand with his. "No, please tell me. Take my mind off…everything."

I'm torn. He says it's not a brush-off but he's never been like this before. And here he is, not comfortable but still standing here and asking me to spend time with him. When things get this kind of real and stop being fun, I tip my hat to the orgasm and walk away. But this is not like other times. There are those new things I want and maybe this is a step closer, even if it goes nowhere.

"Okay. I have something for you, but it's that way." I point in the direction we just came from, to the bedroom that separates his and mine. The baby's room.

He steps back and lets me lead the way. We walk through the empty room until we make it to the entrance to the sunroom. I stop and turn to face him.

"I have a present for you. It's not much and to be honest, I planned on giving it to you anyway. I didn't know today was your birthday. So, it works out perfectly."

I move aside and his gaze moves past me, and I'm gifted with the exact time he sees it. His eyes widen and light up. He moves toward the easel, where the frame's image is propped on it. His fingers ghost over the surface and he takes it all in.

"It's him…" His head snaps around to look at me.

I nod. "Or her…"

"…or her," he repeats. "I don't know what to say. It's beautiful. It's like the inside of a fruit bowl but it's a baby, all of it, even the rice grains, right?"

"From the beginning to now." I pat my belly and smile at him.

"Did you do this today?"

I move closer. "Mostly yesterday. The colors came alive this morning. This place is pretty perfect, you know? It dried quickly and I had time to come back and nitpick at it."

"Your talent is amazing." His hand rests on my cheek. "Is this what you didn't want to paint but kept sketching?"

I look away, beyond the glass panels to the city lights, and nod. "I kept trying for the Taras but landing on fruits and veggies."

"It's so much more than that." His voice drops to a whisper and his hand slides down my arm, but he's not looking at anything but the painting. "There's the womb and there's the walls and look at the glowing heart. Loud and strong like the sonogram."

His fingers slide between mine and tighten. His gaze is back on me and I'm like the apple in the painting, up close and centered. Like he's zooming me in.

My pulse quickens and I try to swallow but my mouth is so dry. He's going to kiss me and my whole body's buzzing in anticipation. Our lips touch and it's different than the hospital, and the other night in this room, even than last night in his office. There's a different feeling to this kiss. One that I've never had before because it's slow and we're still holding hands but he's using the other to glide up my back. He cups my neck and opens his mouth over mine and I open up to him. I press my body to his and let go.

His tongue swoops inside my mouth to caress, tease, and retreat, and we break away panting.

"Thank you," he breathes into my ear. "It's the best gift. You keep giving me things I can't ever repay."

"Maybe some gifts are not meant to be repaid, because someone does them from the heart—" I clamp my mouth shut.

Shit. Why did you say that?

I place my forehead on his shoulder and pray he forgets what I just said.

He stiffens. "Is this a gift from your heart or is this only a gift because this baby doesn't carry your blood?"

Nope, he's not going to let that go.

"I hope I'm not offending you but artists are very territorial with their pieces. They don't just give them away," he says to my ear. We're tightly bound but looking in opposite directions.

"We are."

"So, answer my question, Winter."

It's not fair that he whispers it like a delicacy and that his question puts me on the spot for feelings I shouldn't have.

I pull away and go sit back on the couch. He stays in place but he's looking down at me, waiting for my answer. I consider all I can say.

"I just thought of you first. Somehow, I knew the painting was going to be yours. As soon as I finished the heart it was yours. Even before I admitted it to myself." I smile. "Why else would it want to come out this badly? Why else would you be the first person I thought about? I can't control what my heart wants me to give to you."

He sits next to me on the couch and pulls me into his lap, burying his face on my neck. "I can't control myself with you either."

And that should take the weight off my chest but it doesn't and I have to ask. "Were you upset today because of your dad or because of Astrid? Do you miss her on your birthdays?"

He pulls back and stares into my eyes. "No."

There's such clarity there. He's not lying. That makes me heart sing.

"One day, if you let me, I'll tell you all about my relationship with Astrid."

I nod, despite the tremor of fear that courses through me. He loved the woman enough to father a child with her after her death. I am not sure if I want to know how deep his love for her was. Could he ever feel that again, with someone else?

"I thought the baby was the size of an avocado this week," he says.

"That's next, after Monday. Right now, I'm at fifteen-and-a-half weeks so Johnny or Jahnny Appleseed it is until we go to the doctor's appointment."

He chuckles. "Lauren found a new nickname?"

"Adri, actually."

He shakes his head. "Hey, tomorrow, I have to interview nannies. I want a second person to help out Aunt Millie. I don't want her to have that kind of workload. Would you like to sit in on it? You know, since you're a teacher and you know about these things?"

My heart trembles a little. Of course, I want to sit in the interviews. I want to make sure a competent professional gets to be there for this baby. I can't help but to be sad that the planning has begun for when I'm not here but I put on a brave face. I've always been good at that.

"I would love to."

He smiles at me and I know he sees exactly what I want him to see. I'm a survivor because I've learned how to mask pain. Something this baby will never know. Because he'll have a father who loves him. He will have an Aunt Millie that's already crazy about him. And if I have anything to do with it, he will have a good nanny who will teach him about colors that stimulate his brain. His world will be vibrant with things that make him feel secure, not with a different home every few months and a parent who can't stay out of rehab or jail.

21

Grayson

Aunt Millie walks the last candidate out of the door and I turn to look at Winter's tightened face. "What exactly was wrong with this one?"

She crosses her arms over her chest and turns her gaze upward. "Where do I start? Shall I begin with her beliefs that toddlers need to be disciplined or how about she would burrito wrap your baby for almost nine months?"

"She says it's for his own feeling of security."

"Or"—she scoffs—"because she wants to be fucking lazy and keep the baby immobilized so she can watch reality TV?"

"She didn't even say she watches reality TV. Where do you come up with that stuff?"

She sighs. "Do you just not listen? She asked how productive a person can really be for the first nine months of his or her life. Every woman I've spoken to and all the ones on the forums talk about what a train-wreck some nannies are. The things they do to keep the babies quiet so they can have free time. I can see swaddling a baby for three months but if the baby wants to move, he or she should be able to with no problems."

She's got a point there. "What about the second one, Fiona Green?"

She pffffts. "Fervorizing Fiona? The one who would let a baby cry as long as it takes until he learns to put himself to sleep? That Fiona? You want that despot taking care of this baby? Be serious."

I try to hold my laughter so hard I snort. "Fine. She's out too. What about Miss Gloria? She has a Montessori teaching certification."

"And she doesn't change diapers or bathe babies. And her schedule is not flexible, which means Aunt Millie will end up doing most of the heavy lifting, while she gets to do the singing and story time."

I flip the files on the desk and put my pen on top of them. "I'll ask the agency to send more people."

"Don't be mad. If you want, I'll just stay quiet."

I shake my head. "No, you're making good points but I don't think you liked any of them on sight."

"I didn't get a warm feeling from any of them. I want to know that the person you hire is going to hold him and squeeze him and give him kisses. Montessori degrees are awesome but they don't make anyone feel secure when they're that tiny and defenseless. I don't want him to cry all day because some bitch thinks it's good for his lungs and developing his independence. He's a baby not a Navy SEAL."

She grabs her huge bottle of water and starts to drink from it, oblivious of all the things she's said. My chest is constricted because I want all those things too. I want the baby to be hugged and kissed and to feel secure. I also need to tell her the truth. Every moment that passes, I become more of a rotten asshole who's stealing moments. Moments *I know* she won't give me once she finds out this baby is hers, too.

What will Winter do then?

Last night, she'd spoken about gifts from the heart and alluded to thinking about feelings. But that's because she doesn't know what I know. This is probably a good time to have this conversation.

"Winter, I need to talk to you about the baby."

She raises a hand. "Hold that thought. I got to potty."

She dashes out and I'm left to stare after her with my heart in my throat. I wish she had stayed put now that I've mustered the courage to tell her. Even though she's at fifteen-and-a-half weeks, which means she can still abort if she decided to do so.

I don't think she would but I don't think I can run the risk. Maybe I could wait a few more days. Maybe I could ease her into it. *No, you're telling her when she gets back.*

"Grayson?" Aunt Millie calls from the door. "Simone is here. She has paperwork for you."

Shit. Not now.

Simone strolls in a couple of breaths later. "Holy crap, I just saw Winter running to the bathroom. That belly is getting big."

I start shaking my head but it's like she doesn't even see me.

"I know I know. I'm sorry to show up unannounced, but I need you to sign these papers. It's the new paperwork for the clinic. We'll have to meet with them again but right now I need you to sign that you've acknowledged both forms saying the same thing. I also need Winter to sign hers."

My stomach plummets and I have to get her out of here before Winter comes back. "Simone, this is not a good time. Take the paper-work and go. I'll call you later."

"Grayson, it will only take a couple of minutes."

She pulls out the paperwork and slaps it on my desk.

"Simone, this is not a good time." My voice is so sharp she raises her head and scowls.

"I'm sorry I'm interrupting. I didn't think you would mind because this is so big and important..." She stops and releases a long sigh. "... and you didn't tell Winter yet."

"No."

"Grayson, this is not like you. Winter has the right to know and this is bound to blow up in your face and make you look like a liar. You need to tell her."

"I know that. I was about—"

"What do I need to know?" Winter asks, stepping into my office.

And with a six-word question, my time is up.

She's looking between me and Simone, who is covering her face.

"Simone, can you please excuse us? You can leave the paperwork. We'll take care of it."

Simone nods. "I'm so sorry, Grayson."

Her face is so pale and she looks rattled, something I've only seen a couple of times in my life.

"It's fine. We were just about to have this conversation anyway."

Simone walks out of the office. Winter doesn't come inside all the way. She is standing at the door with her arms crossed.

"Please sit down."

"No. What are you hiding from me?"

I flinch and start to shake my head but I have been hiding this from her since yesterday afternoon. "I didn't mean to hide it from you. I just didn't know how to tell you. To be honest, I was scared to."

Her face scrunches up. "Scared? Of what? Did you meddle in my work life? Because you told me you wouldn't and I took you at your word."

"No." *At least not directly.*

"Then what, Grayson?"

"Please sit."

She takes the chair she left vacant earlier. "Talk."

"You were right. There was something wrong with me yesterday. A few days ago, Simone noticed a discrepancy between your paperwork from Better Maryland and mine. Your paperwork used the terminology 'Intrauterine Insemination' and mine was labeled as an 'Embryo Implantation.' Two very similar, yet different procedures at the same time. She's been going back and forth with the clinic to correct the error and make sure the two sets of paperwork match for the settlement."

"Did she correct it?"

"Yes and no." I mimic Simone's words. "Yesterday, while I was on my way home, she called me to tell me that, indeed, one of the two sets of paperwork was wrong. Mine."

"Yours..." Her eyebrows knit together. "...yours is the one that said..."

"Embryo implantation." I finish for her. "Winter, I had both sperm and embryos frozen. The embryos have gone missing and they used the sperm, which fertilized your egg. The baby is—"

Her skin goes pale and she stares at me for a few seconds and she looks down at her belly. "Half mine?"

Winter

I must be stuck in the worst nightmare of anyone's life. I shake my head and then throw my head back and laugh. The most ridiculous words in the universe just came out of my mouth. "This baby? The one that was supposed to be an implant of your and Astrid's embryos came from my egg? He's half mine? Do you know how crazy that is?"

My voice raises with each word and Grayson winces. "How the hell did this happen?"

His phone goes off but he ignores it and takes two steps toward me. "Winter…"

I take two steps back. "I mean, I know it's a dumb question because on the large scale of how something could happen this is probably way low. How the hell does anyone get pregnant the way I did? But you told me you had embryos. This was your kid and Astrid's love child. How does this baby turn out to be half mine, now?"

And that's when the thought hit me. "Oh my God. How long have you known this? Did you lie to me from the start? Did you even have frozen embryos?"

An emotion flashes before his eyes but he shuts them and breathes. "Of course, I did. I had both frozen sperm and embryos. There were also other eggs from Astrid. I honestly just found out yesterday. I wouldn't lie to you about that."

He reaches out again and I move even farther away.

"Wouldn't you? If it guaranteed that I would have this baby, you would have done anything. You said it."

"I wouldn't do this. You have to believe me, Winter. I didn't lie to you."

She waves me away. "You did. You knew this and I didn't. You may want to make it sound like an omission but it's not. You lied to me. As always, I'm getting fucked over in this deal. I get pregnant against my will, I have to live in a house that's not mine, and now I'm having a baby with my own DNA. Something I never wanted. You should have told me. You should have let me make the decision knowing the truth."

"I swear to you. I only found out yesterday. That's why I was so out of sorts. I wanted to tell you but—" His phone rings again and this time he glances at it. So do I. Simone's name is on it but he doesn't pick it up.

"But you didn't. Oh my God. I'm a fool. I'm giving you gifts from my heart and almost confessing my feelings. You let me interview women to be the baby's nanny today. All the while my heart was breaking because I was helping you choose a substitute for me. And you were lying to me the whole time."

He hangs his head. "I was trying to figure out how to tell you. I was going to do it right after the interviews but then you went to the bathroom. Simone just beat you to it. I was trying to get her to leave so I could tell you myself. I didn't want you to find out that way. Not another day would have gone by."

My legs start to go out from under me and I have to sit down. He takes two steps toward me but I halt him with my hand in the air. "Don't touch me. I don't believe you. You used me. This whole arrangement, I've been honest with you every step of the way but you—"

"Don't say it. It's not true. Look into my eyes and you'll see the truth."

I cover my face with my hands. I need to breathe. I need to not talk. I need to figure out a way to absorb this and not work myself up. It's not healthy for the... "*Fuuuuuck.*"

The baby. Our baby. Jesus, why is this happening?

This is what I don't want. I shouldn't procreate. I can't have a baby.

My breathing quickens but I can't take good breaths because my chest is so tight.

Grayson clears his throat. I don't look at him. I can't.

"Winter, I swear I was going to tell you. Last night, I panicked. I was scared of what you would do when you found out. I know you're angry, but this doesn't have to change anything if you don't want it to. We can proceed as planned..."

A flash of heat floods over my body and my pulse is jackhammering in my ears. My next breath I'm in front of him. We are face to face and all I can see is red. "Are you fucking kidding me, Grayson? Proceed as planned? It's not a building or construction project in my belly. This is not a fucking hiccup that may delay production."

"You don't fucking think I know that?" he screams and I jump in my chair.

I hold on to the armrest.

He holds his hands in front of him. "You made it clear you don't want children and never planned to have any. I am telling you that doesn't have to change, unless you want it to, because I'll still want and love that baby. There's no shame in admitting you don't want to be a mom and giving him up for adoption. It's actually brave. I respect you. You know what you want. There are people out there who bring children into this world when they have no business doing so. Those who get tired of them when they get in the middle of the life they want to live."

My face tingles and I straighten so fast my back hits the back of the chair. It hits me harder than a blow to the jaw or the chest. He hit me in the heart and broke something I didn't know was still whole. I should be KO'd and unconscious. That's how devastating his words are.

I'm too familiar with a woman like who he mentioned. If you Google them, my mother's name should come up. Those words should be the first sentence on Denise Alexander's Wikipedia. "You can go to hell."

I storm out of the office but don't get far. He stops me. "What is this all about? I'm trying not to burden you any more than I have. I'm trying to let you get back to life as you want when this is over. I know that this is hard, I'm telling you it doesn't have to be the end of the things you want."

"Thank you for your kindness. But you think it would be that easy? It's my fucking blood and my flesh too. It's no longer your baby. It's mine, too."

The second the last words are out, I wish I could chew and swallow them. The silence is deafening and he's stunned. I want to take advantage and head to my room, but Aunt Millie is standing a few feet away and Simone is next to her.

Both are frozen and red faced. *Great, they heard everything.* I need to go to my room and get away from all these people.

"I…I'm so sorry to interrupt again after…I've been trying to call. I made it downstairs to the lobby when I got a call from the private investigator you hired." Simone says to Grayson. "He found Alice."

Alice? It takes a couple of seconds before I place the name. She's the woman who should be in my place right now. *The surrogate.*

2 2

Winter

Aunt Millie almost makes me stay. She's standing outside my door with strained eyes and one hand tightly wound around her other. I feel the squeeze all the way to my belly. I can't keep walking and not say anything. Not when I know she worries. She's been taking care of me for weeks and has shown me love and kindness.

"Please don't look so sad." I throw my arms around her smaller form and whisper in her ear. "I'm just going to hang out with Lauren for a little bit. I need some air and some space."

She softens against me and I linger, breathing in the peony scent that always clings to her clothes.

"I don't want you to do something…"

She means terminate the pregnancy because I'm mad. The pang breaks out in my chest and I pull back.

"I would never do something like that. I know you haven't known me for a long time but you can believe in my word."

Unlike other people's…

Aunt Millie's eyes narrow on me and I love how quick-witted she is. "He's not a liar, you know? But I'll be waiting for you. Make sure you eat."

I nod and head out. Grayson is nowhere to be found and I'm glad. I don't need to see his face when I still don't know where I stand.

Lauren is waiting for me out front, smiling. "You look amazing."

"I do not."

"Girl. Have you looked in the mirror? You may be wanting to kill Grayson and you just might. Did he see you it that outfit? That rack sure has gotten big."

"Yes, and so has my belly."

"Boobs are still bigger." She puts the car on drive and maneuvers past the traffic circle and into the city. "Are you okay?"

"I don't know what I am. All day yesterday and today, I've been pissed. I went to bed mad and got up even more angry. As I was getting dressed, I just kept thinking how tired I am of being mad. It's exhausting. I just want to talk and have a good time outside the house."

She nods. "Wherever we go won't be as fancy as the place you're running from, right?"

"I'm not running. I just need to not be in his presence or on his property for a while."

"Okay. And why couldn't I tell Adri about this? She may have enjoyed girl time, too."

I scratch the back of my neck, trying to ease the kink. "Adri's a mom and the most awesome one I know. She's so loving with Bron... I couldn't handle it if she looked at me different."

Lauren shakes her head. "Adri would never judge you. I know the other day she was a little loose in the mouth but honestly, that was just prego brain."

"I know. I'm not pushing her away. It's just...wait, did you tell her?"

I was so distraught when I called her yesterday. The whole finding out about the baby being mine and dealing with the bullshit with the surrogate who refuses to tell the investigator what she knows was too damned much.

Lauren shakes her head. "Of course not. Adri is my best friend but you are a close second. This is your truth to tell. I wouldn't betray your confidence." She sighs. "I'm kinda tired of telling you that."

She has, way too many times. "Thank you. I'm sorry I'm such a pain."

"Shut up. We're all pains in our own way."

Twenty minutes later, we are sitting at Greenhouse, a restaurant by the lakeside in Columbia.

"So, tell me what you're thinking but first, I have to tell you, I admire you. I don't know how you aren't crying. It would have been too much for me."

If she only knew the time I spent in the fetal position under the covers. "I had my rough moments. The anger was the easiest part. I would just stay mad if it weren't so tiring."

"What else were you feeling?"

I close my eyes for a second and let it out. "Afraid. So afraid. He said that nothing had to change and that pissed me off."

"I think he was just trying to give you an alternative, Win." Her tone is so soft. I wish I could tap into it.

"But that's not his to give. Then he said that women give babies up for adoption all the time and there is no shame in it."

"He said that?" she sputters.

"Not in those words, but I think he meant to reassure me and tell me he would still raise the baby. And that I can live my life as I planned." Heat flushes over my neck. "I wanted to hit him."

"Why?"

I swallow so I can speak. "It reminds me of my mother. I was always an inconvenience to her plans. That's why she left me in people's houses for days at a time or 'forgot' me at restaurants. You know, one time I was at the police station, waiting for Miss Daniels. She was one of my longest social workers. She told the police officer that God had to be protecting me because no one had taken me and something worse had not happened to me."

Lauren's eyes go liquid.

"She had no maternal instincts for me, unless she needed a check and I was the gateway to what the state of New York could give her.

Miss Daniels used to say not all women are born to be mothers. There's a lot of mean people out there, Lauren. People for whom babies are nothing but checks or pawns or the means to something. That's where I come from. A woman who didn't care enough for me and loved her vices. Do you know how much I love to paint?"

"Yes, it's the most important thing to you. But, you're not her. You wouldn't neglect your child to go paint. You'll never be like her. Like I'll never be Connie. They don't care about anyone but themselves. You care about your students and the people in your life. You didn't have many friends before Adri and me, but you kick major ass in the sisterhood department."

We both end up wiping the corners of our eyes. She knows a little of what this is. There were plenty of times she'd had to run to get her nephews from somewhere her sister had left them. The time before last, I went with her to pick them up.

"I know I'm not her but...what if? I'm afraid of what this means now. I'm going to be this baby's mom. Everything I do is going to affect him or her because..."

I need to say the words I haven't dared to even think. I need to make it real.

"...I can't walk away. I can't do to this baby what my mom did to me. I can't be the woman who leaves her baby in the hands of others and doesn't look back. I can't do that to someone else."

I freeze and then my words sink in.

Lauren smiles. "I think you made your decision, Winter. Actually, I think you've known all along."

I let out a shaky breath. "I'm still afraid."

"You won't let it paralyze you. When Adri got pregnant, she was scared about more than just being a mom and it wasn't easy, trust me, but she did it. You're older and you won't have to parent alone. And you have us. We've been through this shit together. We can help."

That's true. I'm not alone. And best of all, I don't have to be my mom. I know the mess she made of my life. I won't do the same to my baby.

23

Grayson

"She says she will take an Uber and meet you at the doctor's office, Grayson." Aunt Millie says and her voice no longer carries the warm, apologetic tone of six days ago. There's laughter in her voice now.

"Are you sure? Maybe she would prefer I didn't come at all." I don't know what pisses me off more, Winter's icing of me or that it's become funny to everyone else.

Aunt Millie laughs. "Hang in there, my boy. I think you'll both figure it out soon." But she's enjoying this too much.

And it would be funny, this Cold War Winter has waged, if only I wasn't on the other end of it.

She doesn't talk to me, doesn't come to sit at the table if I'm there. My flowers and apology gifts all mysteriously end up in my office. The only thing that hasn't found its way there are the edibles Lauren suggested. Nutella cookies from the DC bakery, flan brought from New York. She shares them with Aunt Millie and the maid. The other day, I saw the cleaning lady with the latest box of macaroons from *Citlali's*. I don't even get to see her at night anymore. I don't know how she's getting her hot chocolate, because she's not going to the kitchen. I've been watching out for her.

I signal my driver to go straight to Dr. Sahiner's office. I arrive early and am eye-stalked by two children, while their mom, who has to be like fifty-five weeks pregnant, sleeps with her face against the wall.

I pull out my phone and try to read but the kids are now sitting right in front of me. Winter walks through the door five minutes before our actual appointment time. Her hair is down instead of in a bun and her skin is radiant. She looks beautiful, from her glowing eyes to the long-sleeved, gray dress that's fitted around her body. Her every curve is on beautiful display and so is her belly, which looks only slightly bigger than a week ago. I haven't seen it since the day of our fight. I haven't seen her face since, either.

She doesn't smile when she sees me, like the fifty-five-week pregnant lady had for her husband when he'd come in. Instead, she sighs and takes the chair next to the one next to me.

I bite my tongue so I don't point out the one she missed across the room. Sarcasm wouldn't help and I understand her anger. I just wish she would see I had really tried to tell her the truth.

"How are you feeling?" I ask. I can't help it, I want to know. Even if she's dry and cold, I want to hear her voice.

"I'm fine," she says in that smoky tone of hers. "How about you?"

"I'm okay, too." That's a lie. Unlike her, I feel, and am pretty sure I look, like shit in a suit.

I stare down at my hands. I don't want to annoy her with my questions.

"You look tired," she whispers.

That's an understatement. I haven't slept well since the day at the office, work is the pits of hell, and Alice is refusing to talk. Mostly, this whole issue with her, not knowing where I stand with the baby, and…and her.

"Yeah, I'm a little tired," I admit.

Her phone buzzes and she smiles. Like a real smile, the kind I haven't seen in almost a week. My lip curls and I get caught when she looks up and frowns. "Are you okay?"

"I'm fine."

She types a quick message and then drops her phone on the purse. "Look, I don't know what the doctor is going to say when we go in there today." She stands and moves one chair closer.

We're alone in the waiting room but she leans toward me and I get a whiff of rosemary.

"I'm going to be in this."

I don't have to ask her what. I can see it in her eyes. I just don't know what that's going to mean for us and that makes me edgy but I nod. "We'll figure it out."

She blinks a few times and our gazes hold.

"Miss Alexander," the nurse calls and she jumps to her feet.

We follow the nurse inside, who shows us to a small area where she weighs Winter, takes her temperature and blood pressure, and gives her a cup to fill with a sample, and a gown.

I wait in the room while she changes in the bathroom. When she comes out with her gown tied in the front. I help her into the bed.

Her breaths are paced and she no longer looks as healthy as she did earlier. Her skin has lost most of its rich color.

"What's wrong?"

She shakes her head.

"Come on, Win. Tell me what's wrong."

"You know...I don't like hospitals...or these kinds of places."

I place my arm on her shoulder. "I don't think anyone does. I started hating them after my dad died. What about you?"

She's staring at her hands. "I was five. I fell down the stairs in the building where I lived. I dislocated my shoulder. The neighbors found me and took me to Immaculate Presbyterian. They popped it back in but I was there for hours in the bed, watching the people who came in. They forgot I was in the last room."

Five? She had still been so little. "Where were your mom and dad?"

"I don't know who my dad is and my mom was at her new boyfriend's."

"Wait. Who was taking care of you?"

145

"Her boyfriend, back then, lived in the floor above ours. She didn't know what happened until later that night. It was the second time CPS removed me from her care."

Every hair on my body stands like little soldiers on nerve's end.

"That's why I don't like these places. I spent way too much time in them. People were screaming and the blood and the vomit. I don't want to be alone here, Grayson."

I grab her icy hand in mine and squeeze. "I won't leave you alone."

That seems enough for her. She closes her eyes and breathes, sinking more into the bed. It hurts that no one was there for her to make her comfortable. How didn't I know this about her? It explains her attitude when we first met and how adamant she had been about finding out if I was planning to be there for this child.

"Thank you," she whispers, as if she didn't want anyone but me to hear.

I force away the thoughts of a little girl alone in a hospital, afraid of all the horrible noises, and I smile. "You were pretty brave when you went into St. Raymond's by yourself, too."

She shakes her head. "My insides were shaking I was so afraid."

"But you did it," I insist.

"For the baby. Not for me."

"A baby who was wreaking havoc on your body. You're amazing."

"Stop buttering me up. I'm not."

"Not buttering you up. You faced your fear for a baby you didn't know was yours." I'm almost sorry I said it, but it's the truth, even if she looks away. She can't go anywhere and this is the time for me to tell her what she won't allow me to say after. "You were right. I should have told you that night when I got home. But I was scared. I didn't know how you would react or if you would choose to terminate. It would have been your right. It's always been your right. You didn't have to carry this baby for me but you did it out of the kindness of your heart. And then this happened. I'm sorry."

She nods. "I wouldn't have done that. I don't want to have a child but you do. This baby was already loved and wanted. DNA had

nothing to do with it at first but it has everything to do with it now."
She looks into my eyes. "I can't walk away. I won't be my mother."

"How can you be? You're the anti of what she was. You take care
of kids every day."

She opens her mouth but there's a knock on the door.

"Hello, Hello." Dr. Sahiner comes in. She's wearing a purple
crocus flower in her hair and a smile that fills most of her face. "I'm
excited to see the two of you today. Last time, baby was giving you
both a scare."

Winter squeezes my hand but she's staring at the doctor.

She tsk-tsks and laughs. "Get used to it. Having kids is all about
being worried all the time, because they never stay still. Well, except
for the first seven months. You enjoy those. So, this is what we're
going to do today. I'm going to examine you, measure your uterus, do
some testing for AFP and hCG to make sure our little avocado is developing according to the marks. We are also going to do an ultrasound
like we discussed over the phone. How does that sound?"

Winter squeezes harder. *Yup, we are both nervous as fuck.*

"Don't worry, we will have everything brought here so you don't
have to go anywhere else." She nods to me, and then looks at Winter
again. "Talk to me. How are things going? Have you been keeping the
stress down?"

Winter laughs. "As much as I can. I've been resting and doing the
bare minimum."

"Okay. Is there anything you want to talk about before we start?
Any questions you may have? It can be physical or are you more
emotional than usual?"

"Well, I tear up easily and there's this sense of worry sometimes.
It's like bubbles in my belly."

"The crying is normal and I'm sorry to say it's only going to get
worse. There will be times when you weep for no apparent reason."
She pauses and smiles. "The bubbles are also a good thing. It means
your little avocado is moving around."

Winter gasps and turns to look at me. "Moving," she repeats.

The next twenty minutes go by in a blur of doctor's questions, samples, and an exam of Winter's body. Then, Dr. Sahiner opens the door and a technician comes in, rolling a machine with what looks like a laptop attached.

"This is Rachel and she will be doing your ultrasound. I'm staying for this because I want to answer any questions you may have."

"I read about this appointment, but I didn't think you would stay. Do you do this for all your patients?" Winter asks.

"No. Just for the special ones." The doctor winks at her and then turns to talks to the technician.

Winter side-eyes me. "Your money makes me special."

"Nah. You were born special. My money simply buys some comforts."

She giggles and it's crazy how that sound stirs something in my chest.

"I like it when you laugh like that." I whisper in her ear.

"You should give me more reasons to."

I don't know what she means by that. Does she want something more from me? I thought she was pretty much done after what happened the other day.

The loud pfffffft sound makes us both jump and her hand goes tight around mine.

"Are you ready to get this party started?" Rachel asks. She's all smiley and peppy like a cheerleader that decided at half-time that she needed to become an ultrasound technician. She looks at Winter for permission to open her gown and she nods. "It's going to be a little cold."

Doctor Sahiner turns on a TV directly across from the bed. "All your attention here."

Rachel parts the gown and slathers the gel over her belly. Then she grabs what looks like a supermarket scanner and begins to move it around from one side of the belly to the next. It's like a black hole and the more it moves, the tighter Winter's hold on me gets.

Something's wrong. It has to be. There's nothing there and then he's there and *oh my God.* There's a head there and a little body attached, surrounded by light. My heart climbs in my throat and my

THE WINTER OF MY LOVE

breath is shaky. I try to swallow but I can't. That's my son. I look down at Winter and there are tears on her cheeks.

Winter

My heart is out of control and I can barely breathe. My body is too big under my skin and I can't hold anything in. I'm crying and I can't help it. There's a little person inside me. I knew this baby was there but seeing it, with the lights shining over that little body, like a little angel floating in clouds, floors me.

And it's my baby in there. Not Grayson's and someone else's. Mine. I'm going to paint this so many times but I'll never be able to do it justice.

I look up and Gray is staring at the screen and his expression is everything inside me right now. There's this look, like an utter disbelief, but there are tears in his eyes and his Adam's apple bobs up and down. He doesn't know how tight he's holding onto my hand and I know. I know this feeling.

Our eyes meet and the room fills with that weird and fast noise, like a horse galloping inside a washing machine. Grayson's eyes go wide and I press my head back against the pillow because I know that's my baby's heartbeat. I think I would know it anywhere. "That's our baby, Gray."

He leans down and presses his warm lips to my forehead. One of his tears rolls on to my cheek. And I'm so happy he's here with me, for this moment.

"Right here is the spine. As you can see, it's fully formed. And the head is upright." Rachel moves her pointer around her screen. "You see an arm here and there's the hand."

"He's really muscular. He'll be an athlete for sure."

I frown at him and the other women laugh. "Kidneys are fully formed already and already in use."

149

"In use?" I ask. "He's peeing."

The doctor chuckles. "Yes, there's urine in there."

"Is that sanitary?" Gray asks and we all laugh at him again.

"It's normal," Rachel says. The baby shifts around, flashing fingers and toes and with every move, I'm more obsessed with watching. "Look at you, hamming it up for Mom and Dad. There's some hand and elbow flexing."

I smile, loving how much he moves and I smile because, when he does the big moves, my stomach ripples. Now I know what that is. He's happy inside my belly.

"What did you eat this morning? This baby is all over the place." Rachel shakes her head.

My cheeks are burning. "I had a little coffee with sugar. I don't drink it often but I needed it and—"

I won't tattle that it was Aunt Millie's idea.

You want the baby to move a lot or you won't be able to see her little pearl or his little wand.

It still makes me laugh. I almost broke down and asked her to come with me today but this is Gray's and my moment.

"Coffee is okay once in a while but don't make it a habit," the doctor says. "Not too much dairy, either. I'm surprised the weird cravings haven't started for you."

There's more movement on the screen. Baby moves upside down. He rolls away with his back to us and then he comes back around. The legs part.

"Ooooh," Rachel squeals. "Do you want to know what you're having?"

"Yes," I say and then remember Gray is standing next to me. He has a say in it too. "Do you want to know?"

At first, I don't think he heard me but he nods.

The typing pointer appears on the screen and she types the words, *future queen of the empire* on the screen.

It's a girl.

Joy bubbles in my chest and my hand flies to my mouth. "I always thought of Baby as a boy for some reason. Even if I said girl sometimes."

"Well, she is correcting you. Time to start thinking of names."

Gray's mouth is hanging open and he's frozen for a bit. Then he smiles, first at the screen and then at me. "We're having a girl."

"Yes, and it seems like a big girl." Dr. Sahiner says. "The measurements show that she's growing a little faster than we originally projected. I will look at all the paperwork and compare it to the twenty-week exam and we may have to adjust the due date to a little sooner."

The smile melts off Gray's face and my stomach knots all over again. "Is that normal?"

"It is. Her dad's a pretty tall guy and mom is not a shorty."

Shorty? This woman is too motherly sometimes.

"Well, we are done here." Rachel turns off the machine and wipes my belly. I sent some of these pics to print so you can go home and brag to your family and friends about your gorgeous little queen. It was such a pleasure meeting you both. See you in four weeks."

We thank her and she leaves.

Doctor Sahiner grabs a chair and gives me some instructions. "You need to give us a blood sample before you go. I want you to come back in four weeks for your next appointment. You can go back to work and resume all normal activity, including sex."

I'm so not looking at Grayson.

"Oh, honey, no shame here. Pregnant sex is not only good for Mom and Dad, it's good for all three of you to connect."

I want to die. She's like that old lady who gives sex advice and gets pretty graphic on cable TV.

Gray clears his throat. "Is there anything we should be doing?"

Yes, good. Change the subject.

"Start planning for her. Time flies and you need to be ready. I want you to start taking birthing classes. Whatever you're comfortable with, Lamaze, Bradley, we have a pamphlet that covers them all. Have you been reading on it?"

I shake my head. I watched a sonogram video and closed my browser because it kinda freaked me out.

"Well, you can start discussing it now. Start buying things." She stands. "I'll see you in four weeks and let me warn you, it's different for every woman but I'm pretty sure that belly is about to pop."

We're left alone to stare at each other. Gray's gaze jumps from mine to my belly and he places a hand over it.

"She's there, all solid." His voice carries so much wonder, as if I hadn't been in the room all along with him. "And you can feel her move."

I can't help but smile. "I'm going to go crazy waiting for that bubbly feeling now."

"She's there," he says again, his fingers ghosting as if they were trying to track the baby.

And I was wrong. I don't even have to wait, because the bubbling starts and spreads around. Can babies feel touch? Does she sense that's her daddy, touching mommy so gently, so softly?

Mommy.

"I'm her mom," I say and it's so stupid because, duh, of course I am. But it feels so good to say it and it makes me smile until my face hurts.

"Yes, you're her mom and I'm her dad…"

"And we're both here for her."

Gray offers me his hand. "Let's get out of here."

I take his help off the bed and go into the bathroom to change into my clothes. I put on my dress and smooth the fabric over my belly and then stop to feel it. It's getting harder and bigger. "You are going to be a big girl, aren't you?"

I finish smoothing my hair and put on some lip gloss. I like the way my skin looks right now, all happy and flushed. Because I *am* happy and that's the last thing I expected to be today. I thought I would be mad at Grayson all over again. I thought I would be tense and petrified of this place. I thought I would be stressed by the examination and what the doctor would say.

But no.

I'm excited for this little girl and somewhere between Grayson's hand holding and our talk, I forgot to be afraid of this place. And I'm not mad at him anymore. I still think he should have told me about the baby the minute he found out. But I believe him when he says he meant to tell me. Part of me, oddly enough, understands. He so wants this baby. He has from the beginning. I won't ever forget his smile when he found out she's a girl.

"Are you okay in there?" The concern in his voice makes me laugh. *He's a caring man, Winter. Give him the chance to show you.* It's been Aunt Millie's litany all week.

I open the door and find him right outside. A towering man with strained eyebrows and flattened lips. *Yeah, he cares. I believe it.*

"I'm sorry I took too long. I was reapplying lip gloss and fixing my hair. I didn't notice the time."

His features relax. "It's okay. I just wanted to make sure you were all right. Let's go get our baby pics."

Our baby pictures. I don't squeal but God knows I want to. He turns to open the door but I stop him with a hand to his wrist.

"Gray." I wait until he turns to look at me. "I believe you when you said you didn't mean to keep this from me and I forgive you for not telling me right away."

He exhales so long that I swear he was holding that breath for hours. His shoulders sag like a boulder rolls off them. And that's all it takes for me to throw my arms around his neck and pull him to me. His hands go to my waist and he crushes me against his chest. The only thing between us is my belly, as if he's cradling both of us.

All we do is hug and I get my fill of him. My mind can't help but drift to that day last week when I wished for this to be real. This feels pretty real to me. "Promise me you'll never lie to me again, Gray."

"I promise," he says, staring into my eyes.

I believe.

24

Grayson

"We're on our way home now. We have to show Aunt Millie and there's so much for me to do," Winter says. Her every word is a gush of happiness and she overflows with it. "Isn't she gorgeous?"

She laughs and the sound fills the car. My driver doesn't even turn around, like he's not affected by it. How could he not be? Her joy is embedded in her every word. I couldn't stop looking into her eyes all throughout our lunch. Even the waitresses were fawning over her.

"You better get back to work before Adri yells at you. I'll send her the pic too. I'll call you later tonight." She turns to me. "Lauren says hi and congratulations. She's going to come tomorrow night to talk baby stuff."

I nod. "Thank you."

"I'm going to call LaSalle to say I can come back to work tomorrow."

"Are you sure you want to do that? You can wait a few more days."

Her eyes narrow at me. "You heard the doctor, and plus, as

154

amazing as your place is, I've been cooped up for too long. I miss my kids."

Her kids.

She gets on the phone and I'm left to stare out the window. I could call the office and check on things or answer all the emails that have been piling up all morning. The groundbreaking for the new factory campus is tomorrow and I should check with Simone about what's happening with Better Maryland. There's so much on my list.

But.

I don't want to do any of that. Not today. Today, I want to think of the woman next to me and our baby. I want to savor what I saw on that screen, the smile on Winter's face and her new discovery that she wants this baby like I do. That she could possibly want *me* a percentage of the way I want her.

We kissed again today but our hug at the clinic still makes my heart constrict, and I was not imagining the fuck-me looks she was sending my way all throughout lunch. But I'm not going to fuck this up. I just got out the dog house with her.

Jesus. Is it normal to get this caught up again?

I didn't with Astrid. Not at first. She would tease and nag me and take me away from work. She would get naked in my dorm room and parade around while I was trying to study for finals. I think that's the reason she made sure her father gave us the one-hundred-thousand-dollar wedding gift. She thought that would make me slow down. But I was obsessed, single-minded in making my dad proud. I wanted him, wherever he was, to know that his sacrifice and struggle weren't in vain. I was going to be the successful business man he wanted me to be.

I had been so pissed off at her when her father gave me that check, but I wasn't a fool. I'd always been good at maximizing. I created a separate account, hidden from her, and began putting in the profits of my business ventures. It was a fuck-you to her dad and kind of a fuck-you to her, too, for trying to manipulate me.

I loved Astrid, in my own way. It just wasn't in the way she wanted.

When she got sick, I did everything in my power to find a cure. My next goal became to make her happy in her last days. I couldn't do that either. By the time she died, I was tired of feeling. So, I stopped for a while.

Until I met Winter. Until I found out that she was willing to do something that big without expecting money from me, as long as I was going to do right by my child.

Now I can't stop staring at her. This beautiful glow was made for her. I don't know how she couldn't see that before.

"What are you thinking about? You haven't said much since we left the restaurant." Winter says.

"Oh, you remembered I'm here. You've barely looked at me since we got in the car."

"I can't believe she's inside me. I mean, I can, but look at her." She shows me the photo again.

"It is amazing." I take the photo into my hand.

"Were you thinking about Astrid?"

My gaze flies from the photo of our little girl to her face. My first instinct is to say no. No woman wants to hear you're thinking of another, but I promised her I wouldn't lie. I plan on keeping my word.

"I was but not in the way you think."

She purses her lips. "Which way am I thinking?"

"You're probably thinking that I am regretting or lamenting that this baby is not hers or probably thinking about what if this were her baby and her reaction."

Her gaze drops briefly. "And that's not what you were thinking?"

I shake my head. "I was thinking that she was the first person to force me to have fun. She would go out of her way to distract me from studying in college and get super pissed when I worked late every night."

"Sounds like she loved you and wanted to spend time with you."

"She did. We loved each other but our relationship is complicated." I grab her hand and squeeze it. "I always placated her and went back to work. I wasn't the best husband."

"I'm sure you did your best."

I run the pad of my thumb over her palm. "I couldn't love her like she needed me to."

"Why do you think that was?"

Her expression is unreadable. Am I getting myself in trouble with this conversation?

"I don't know. I was just thinking about how, by the time I met her, part of me had died and by the time she died, I couldn't feel. Until you. Except with you."

Her eyes widen.

"You didn't want anything from me except that I be a good father to this baby. You were willing to carry a baby for me. Do you know how much money you could've had for that?"

She shakes her head.

"Of course you don't. You never wanted to know. You were going through all this shit for a baby that wasn't even yours. I think I started falling in love with you at St. Raymond's when you were pale and scared. You braved it there. When I walked into the room, I was sure nothing good was going to come out of that night. I could see how bad it was for you, but today, with everything you told me, I finally get the whole picture. You amaze me."

"You're in love with me?" she asks. "Oh my God, wait. You're in love with me. And we don't do this kind of thing. We don't fall for other people, or do intimacy, or..."

"Have babies, or live together, or share details about our lives, like my complex marriage and what happened to you as a child," I say, leaning closer to her. "We didn't used to do that but we're doing that now. And I think we are going to keep doing it, because that little girl is coming and since neither of us has a clue what we're doing, we need to stick together."

"So, we're staying together because we don't know anything about babies. You believe that two half parents make one full one?"

I laugh. "No, we're sticking together because I'm in love with you and I think you're falling for me and we should see where this goes."

"I'm definitely more than falling for you," she says. "But this is a little crazy. Did you know I asked Doctor Lawrence to remove my uterus all together?"

"You did?" I can't believe this conversation. "Why?"

She shrugs. "I never thought I would need it and I was in so much pain. The IUD procedure was to control the fibroids that have been torturing me for a few years now."

I'm floored. What do I even say to that?

She shakes her head. "It explains a lot about why she had that look on her face. She kept telling me I was healthy and young. That someday I would change my mind. And she's the one that made the decision for me by implanting this baby. As happy as I am today, I'm still hurt. She violated me. And for what? Money? And now she's not here to answer."

"She's not, but Alice still is and sooner or later, she will talk and tell us why all this happened."

"Maybe she just changed her mind and didn't know how to tell you, Gray."

I shake my head. I've gone over this plenty of times and that wouldn't make sense. "That's not it. There was a clause in our agreement that she could change her mind at any time. There would have been no hard feelings and she could have gone back to her job. Instead, she took the money and left. I have a feeling she has to know where the embryos are."

Her fist presses to her chest. "The embryos. I forgot about them."

"I haven't. I can't. Someone has them and they meant a lot to Astrid. I don't want them to be used for God knows what. I keep wondering if it is ransom but no one has come forward."

"Where exactly is Alice? You didn't tell me. You didn't have her taken, did you?"

I laugh but the thought did cross my mind. God knows I have enough money and connections to do it. "No, she's been arrested in Mexico after she entered the country with a fake passport. She's being held by the authorities, and my private investigator is pretty much her only hope."

"You're breaking the law."

"Not technically. Not U.S. law. My guy is an independent agent and I'm not doing anything but offering my help to an employee who stole from me. I don't want a scandal but if the FBI has to get involved, so be it."

"She will go to jail, right?"

I nod. "She and whoever is helping her. They messed with your life, mine, stole money and did God knows what with the embryos. They're all going to pay."

I expect her to say something like this is wrong and we shouldn't do this. She's a teacher after all and being "good" and law abiding is part of their agenda. But she shakes her head and looks straight into my eyes.

"Good."

Winter

Aunt Millie's tears unhinge my own again and we are both dabbing at our eyes. We're staring at the sonogram photos.

"I can't believe it's finally happening." She dabs some more and steals a look toward Grayson's office. He's on an emergency work conference call. "There are no mistakes. She was meant to be yours and his. You are both good people who will do right by her."

"What about Astrid? Grayson told me she was a really good person."

A sad light, something rooted in yesterday, crosses her face. "Astrid loved Grayson as much as someone raised the way she was could. She was a rich, spoiled girl. She thought she could have him at her mercy. She needed his attention all the time and when she couldn't get it freely, she manipulated her way into it. Don't get me wrong. She was sweet and likeable, not at all like her brother. That's a piece of work right there."

I look at the office door. "I don't think Grayson remembers her that way."

"Oh, honey. Yes, he does. But I told you, he's a good man. You won't catch him bad-mouthing her or saying anything untoward. You know he tried, but we can only do what we're capable of. The more she nagged for his attention and threw temper tantrums, the less responsive he was to her. And then she got sick. He blamed himself for years for not being able to do what she wanted."

"Give her a baby?"

Aunt Millie nods. "Or save her."

"From the cancer?"

She nods. "My boy is a fixer. He did everything he could. He took her to doctors, brought some here, but it was her time."

I don't know what to say to that. I haven't dealt much with death, just shitty factions of life.

"As much as I wanted grandchildren, I dreaded the day she made him promise that. I think the baby was her way of keeping him tethered to her, even after she was gone. Grayson didn't see that. I figured we would raise her like his dad did with him. This one will be different. You both are more suited for each other."

My heart stumbles into an erratic beat. "Why do you say that?"

"Because you're not spoiled or desperate for his attention. You have your own things going. And you have enough life experiences and have gone through enough to make sure she is appreciative and kind." She taps my belly.

"And she'll have you to help us keep her in check."

Aunt Millie presses the photo to her chest. "Oh no, honey. You two will have to do that. I'm going to be in grandma mode."

Her words are like air that expands inside my chest and I feel like bursting. "I wish I had someone like you my whole life." The words fly out of my mouth before I can stop them.

Aunt Millie leans and hugs me. "You do now."

"Are you two still crying?"

She turns a frown on him. "How could you not cry when you see this?" She waves the photo in front of her. "I'm going to make us a very nice dinner tonight. We have to celebrate."

"Oh," he says. "I was going to make reservations."

"Nonsense. You two can go alone another time. Tonight, it's a family night."

She walks away and I want to laugh at Grayson's expression. He's like a kid, intent on something else. "Whatever she's planning for dinner, you know it will be delicious."

"I know but..."

"What?"

"I wanted to take you out somewhere nice and..."

God, he's so cute when he's nervous. It's like he doesn't dare say it.

"...then get romantic?" I can't help but smile.

He laughs. "I didn't want to assume."

I push myself off the couch and go stand in front of him. I climb on my tiptoes to whisper in his ear. "We can always do the romance first and celebrate in your room now. How does that sound?"

I flick my tongue over his earlobe. His hands close around my hips, pulling me against his body. His rock-hard cock nestles between my legs, and he nods.

Raw chills break out on my skin. "Let's go fuck to seal this deal, Gray."

He growls low and strong enough to send an electric current down my spine. He lets go of my hips and grabs my hand and starts dragging me behind him. We get to his door so fast. He opens it and his room is amazing. It's like a hotel luxury suite. It must run the length of the penthouse because there are windows on the opposite ends. It's divided into a sitting area with two plush chairs and the other side of the room, separated by two sliding doors. An enormous bed sits in the center of the section and a wall of windows on the far end. A certain spoiled, gray cat is lying on one like the queen she is.

Nin takes one look at us and it's like she doesn't want to see what's about to happen. She jumps off the chair and heads out of the room. I shake my head.

Gray pulls me in the direction of the bed. We stand in front of it and he draws me closer.

"Wait. I said fuck but we shouldn't fuck because that's what we always do with other people. If we are doing the intimacy thing, we should make love. Right?"

"We are doing the intimacy thing but we don't have to limit ourselves. We can fuck and then make love."

"Good point." I fist my hand into his hair and drag his face to mine.

I kiss him, plunging my tongue into his mouth and caressing his in slow flicks. His hands roam my back and cup my ass against him. I try to inch myself closer but he pushes back.

"Take your clothes off for me." His voice is husky and low.

I get so wet and eager, but I swallow hard because I'm not in stripping shape. *At all.*

Grayson sits on the bed, leaning on his elbows. His eyes slowly roam from my head to my toes. When his gaze comes back to mine, he lets out that small smile. The one that makes me want to rip my panties and spread my legs. "I want to see all of you. Show it to me."

My hands are reaching for the hem of my dress of their own accord. His gaze is setting my skin on fire. I'm so hot, so wanton. I don't know how to strip because that shit is always awkward as hell. I prefer when my partner takes the clothes off me but I don't want to disappoint him. I pull the hem of my skirt slowly up, letting it glide up the skin of my thighs. He follows the move with his gaze and I begin to play with it. If I stop, his gaze stays in place, centered in the patch of skin I've just uncovered. If I pull up again, it follows.

I shimmy a little to get my skirt past my hips and he flexes, his erection pressing against his pants. I think he's enjoying this. I let the fabric brush its way along, just pulling hard enough to make it move, like light feather painting.

The air whisks over my skin and when I pull the dress over my breasts, it fans over my nipples and Grayson sucks in a gasp. I push the dress over my head and discard it on the floor.

He sits up right like he needs to get closer to the action. "Touch yourself."

"Where?"

"Start from your lips and work yourself down."

I do as he says, trailing my three middle fingers over my lips, letting them linger and then slide over my chin and down my neck. I use my fingers to mold my way to my chest and I rake the top of my breast with my nails, outlining soft cups. Grayson's eyes don't miss a thing and I play that to my advantage, squeezing both breasts.

I massage them gently but firmly, sneaking a finger through the fabric. Finding my nipple, I brush it side to side a few times. Sending so many waves straight into my pussy. It would be easy to make myself come. All I would need to do is put my other hand between my legs and massage circles into my...

"Take off the bra." His voice is so rough it makes me jump.

My heart is trying to find its way out of my chest but that's nothing compared to the fluttering in my belly. My hands tremble as they reach for the front clasp. My tits spring free like they're trying to jump him on their own. I shrug the bra from my shoulders and my fingers immediately go back to them. I squeeze them, gently kneading and using my thumbs on the hard pebbles.

"Are you going to make me get myself off, Gray?"

His smile is wicked and has me praying he doesn't say yes. I can do it. I'm more than an expert at it. But I haven't been dreaming for three months of getting myself off. I want him to do it. I want him to fuck me.

"Come here," he finally says. I move forward until I'm standing between his legs. "Do you know how hot you are when you touch yourself?"

I shake my head. "Tell me how hot."

He presses a kiss to the top of my chest and takes my hand. He presses it to his crotch, guiding it over the length of a very hard and very long cock. My mouth waters and my knees begin to sink with the need to put all that in my mouth. I want to suck him, savor him, feel the weight of his hot and heavy meat on my tongue.

I don't get to. The most delicious wetness feathers across my nipple and I find myself arching against his mouth. With his hands at my waist he straightens me up and laves one breast with his very talented mouth. He kisses, nips, and sucks me so hard, it straddles the line between pain and a pleasure that threatens to make me come on my feet.

I love the way he loses himself and I press my tits together for him and he manages to open his mouth and suck on both nipples at the same time.

"Oh God," I scream and I can barely hold myself together. I can't even keep my hand from pressing the front of my panties. "I need more, Gray. I need to come."

He pulls his head from my tits and guides me to lie on the bed. I switch to my side. He unbuttons his shirt and throws it away, along with the T-shirt underneath. He unbuckles his belt and I need air. I hope I looked as hot as he does right now when I was taking my clothes off. He pushes his pants down along with the underwear and his cock is free and on display.

It's so beautiful and fat. I roll one of my nipples, watching him and begging him to come take me.

"Tell me how you want it."

"Inside me," I all but scream. We both laugh.

"I have an idea." He grabs a pillow and places it under my hips. Then he climbs on the bed.

The minute I see him between my legs, all my thoughts fly far, far away and there's only him with his lean and long muscular torso. With that narrow waist and that beautiful trail of faint hair that stops above his belly. With that amazingly thick cock that my pussy keeps beckoning to in throbbing beats.

His hands glide under my legs and he places them on his chest. "You have the most beautiful long legs. I love that I can put them over my shoulders."

And he does just that, hikes them up and then leans forward, aligning himself with me. One hand by my waist and the other holding on to his dick, hovering by my entrance. He slowly guides it past my folds, stretching me, and I bite my lip at the amazing pressure. My walls flex around it, squeezing. It's involuntary but his eyes press shut and he groans.

"So wet, so warm, so tight," he chants.

And I do it again, this time on purpose, holding on tighter.

"Jesus, Winter." He pushes forward, with one hand under my ass. He flicks his hips like a whip, bringing his cock deeper.

I moan and he does it again and again until he picks up a rhythm. A tempo that sends my hands flailing, looking for something to hold on to. My hands won't stick to the satin coverlet and I'm frantic for something to stall the wave of fiery pressure. But I can't and all I can do is press my palms to my side and arch my chest. Cold shivers break out all over my skin. The first explosion rocks my body then, followed by the next and a third. One more time and I'm floating only barely aware that my body still rocks back and forth.

"Gray," I whisper and my eyes fly open to see the beauty of his face going from dark strain to a blissful smile.

And another first in my life, as he comes inside me and then collapses by my side with one hand on my thigh. We lay in silence with our chests heaving.

I can't stay still for long because I can't breathe well. I have to turn on my side.

His fingers trail my spine. "Are you okay?"

"Yeah, I just can't lay on my back for long periods of time. It's like something's sitting on my chest."

"Oh. I'm sorry."

I chuckle. "At this rate, you're going to spend your life apologizing."

"Is that your way of saying you're going to brave it and spend your life with me?"

Air lodges on my chest and I force myself to breathe it out. "Going fast, are we? I'm not committing myself after one orgasm. That's a rookie mistake."

"I believe that's two orgasms. The other night counts, thank you very much. I also believe you don't have to work today and I'm taking the afternoon off to make you come."

"Hmmm... I could be persuaded."

His hand sneaks around my waist and he pulls me close to him. "That's what I like to hear."

"Is it weird that your sperm was inside me before you ever were?"

"Yes. But kinda cool. I claimed you before I even had you."

I elbow him. "You're weird."

"Says the woman who is musing about my sperm when we're pressed together naked."

"That part sounds kind of normal, since I'm knocked up with your kid."

His hand drifts to my belly and he presses a kiss to my ear. "Yes, you are. Very knocked up with my kid. But never more beautiful or sexy."

This time I'm left to wonder about the ripples in my belly. Is it my reaction to his voice, his words, or is it our daughter's?

25

Grayson

"Grayson, Bryce and Stephen Miller are here to see you," Sandra announces.

Fuck everything to hell.

I slam my hand onto the surface of my desk. We couldn't have just a few hours of happiness to enjoy ourselves and the good baby news from yesterday.

Of course not. Where do you get these stupid ideas, Grayson?

Shit had to become convoluted and dramatic. I stare at the words on my screen, the offending article that fucked up my day and ruined Winter's first day back at work.

Midas' Baby. Spencer Grayson's secret is out as he's seen having lunch with his baby mama. The lady in question is artist Winter Alexander, a Maryland school teacher. They've managed to keep their relationship in secret for a while but the cat's out the bag as they're seen canoodling and so in love at a high-end eatery in Baltimore's Harbor East.

Reporters have been calling my office every thirty minutes, looking

167

for an exclusive interview. They're camping outside LaSalle. Simone and my publicist already called and warned me against telling them all to fuck off.

Now I just have to deal with another shit storm, in the form of my former father-in-law, before I can go home to Winter. No doubt he saw the papers and wants to talk about the baby.

And he had to bring the spawn of Satan with him. *Because my day wasn't completely fucked in every way possible.*

I stand to receive them. The father walks in first. There are more wrinkles on his face this year than last, but I can still see Astrid in his face. Both his children inherited his features and those greenish-blue colored eyes. Astrid had a lot of her mother in her, which softened and beautified her. She also had a warmth and natural charm. All of that didn't transfer to the cold weasel that is her brother.

Stephen walks in behind him. His eyes are alight and there's a smirk on his mouth. He's like a happy little rat. I would wonder how he found someone to marry but his wife doesn't have a soul either. And money is a powerful aphrodisiac.

Not for Winter, though.

"Bryce, Stephen." I shake the father's hand and then the son's.

"Grayson." He takes a seat after his father.

"I imagine this impromptu meeting is about the article in the news-paper today."

Bryce nods. "You know I don't care what you do with your personal life but if you were going to use my daughter's embryos, I expected a call from you earlier on letting me know it had been successful."

Stephen crosses one leg over the other. "It's the least you could do. We are that child's relatives after all. Unless you were planning to show up with the birth certificate and the DNA test to claim his portion of the inheritance."

"Son." Bryce's tone is one you wouldn't expect of a man who looks as frail as he does and Stephen's face flares into a tomato shade.

"I know it's hard for both of you to believe, but I'll repeat this again. I don't care about the clause in your father's inheritance, Bryce. I do not want the money for my child or myself. I don't need it."

"Yeah, because my father already bankrolled all of this." He gestures around the room.

My blood shoots into my fist. All my life, I've wanted to punch the fuck out of this little shit. "Your father gave us a gift on our wedding day. One that I accepted only because Astrid insisted and on the condition that I would pay it back. And I have, with three times the interest of the original loan. The stock in Grayson Global alone... Should I pull out the ledger of when I paid your father in full and the amount of interest?"

"That's not necessary, Grayson," Bryce insists.

"I'm tired of your son bringing it up at every meeting. I sold you shares of this company in good faith because you wanted to be part of Astrid's and my lives, but I want to buy those back from you. I'm willing to pay double what they're worth."

Bryce's jaw works but Stephen's eyes gleam with one of the few emotions he's capable of feeling. Greed.

His father clears his throat. "We came here to talk about my grandchild."

"Bryce, I'm sorry to have to tell you this, but the child that Winter is expecting is not from one of Astrid's and my embryos."

The old man shakes his head. "That can't be true."

"I'm sorry."

Stephen comes off the chair. "What? You're lying. You called my father to tell him that you were having those embryos implanted."

His eyes are bulging and his face has turned even redder.

My gaze shoots to the old man, who, in turn, stares at the floor. "I thought that conversation was between us, Bryce."

"He's my son and his inheritance would have been affected," he mumbles.

"And it was about Astrid's and my child. Do you think she would have wanted her brother to know this early? And again, I told you I didn't want the money."

169

"You did, but people's minds change. Explain this nonsense right now. I won't let you keep me from the child."

This is worse than I expected but I need to hurry because I need to get to Winter. "I'm not trying to keep you from anything. The baby Winter is expecting is hers and mine. I had all the intention in the world to use the embryos, but the whole plan went to hell when the embryos disappeared and my surrogate never got impregnated."

"What are you talking about? That kind of stuff doesn't disappear." Stephen scoffs. "You probably have some sort of underhanded plan."

"I don't care what you think but I want to explain to your father what happened. Bryce, I can show you the reports and my litigation with the clinic. But you would have to look at that here, with my attorneys and yours present. I am not giving you copies."

"Because you're lying," his son yells.

"If I'm lying, would I offer to have your attorneys present?" I never take my eyes off Bryce. "I am not releasing those copies because it's not only my private life in there. And I'm only showing them to you out of courtesy. If this were Astrid's child, I would never keep it from you."

Bryce leans back into his chair. "This seems so far-fetched."

"You don't know the half of it. This has been a nightmare in many ways. You've never liked me in your entire life, but you know I'm not a liar. I intended to fulfill my promise to your daughter."

"We can test the fetus," Stephen says.

Red clouds my vision and in a blink I'm on my feet and halfway around the desk with my hands fisted at my sides. *Stop now.* My body somehow obeys and I place a flat palm on the surface of my desk and breathe. "No way in hell will you test my child."

"Why?" Bryce asks. "If you're telling the truth, you have nothing to fear."

Stephen laughs. "He has everything to fear. This is all some bullshit story he's concocted to get our money, dad."

I don't even look at him because if I do, I'm going break his face. But then I would bring more publicity onto myself and by default, Winter. No, I'm not letting this spoiled little shit bait me.

I look at his father and unclench my teeth. "A DNA test in utero is a risk to the baby and I am not risking my child for your son's morbid curiosity."

"We can get a subpoena."

I laugh at him this time. "How, you dumb shit? What judge would grant either of you the right to test my child? Even if it were Astrid's, and I assure you it's not, neither of you is a parent and I already put it in writing that I don't want Astrid's money. Anyway, this is not her child."

Bryce stalls a reply from his son with a hand. "Where are the embryos?"

"We do not know that but are currently looking into it. We'll find them."

"So, you can use them with your new girlfriend and you can both roll in what was rightfully my sister's?"

This motherfucker...

"I can do whatever the hell I want with them because they belong to me." I close my eyes and breathe until the red behind my eyelids goes away. "Why do you keep insisting on this inheritance bullshit? I don't want the money. I'm about to go blue in the face from repeating it."

"It doesn't matter what you said because Astrid was stupid enough to leave the money to you. The children clause was just something our lawyer had the genius idea to add so you couldn't get your hands on what my grandfather worked so hard—"

"Stephen!"

I can barely hear Bryce because his son's words are echoing in my ear. Astrid wanted to leave me the money and her father convinced her to add the clause. Why? She knew I didn't need it. That it would only bring me nothing but grief because she had to know that her brother would be after me for it.

I lift my head and I find the sniveling rat staring at me. The hatred and contempt are blatant in his eyes. He's always hated me and has always had it out for me.

I never got why, but I think I'm beginning to understand a lot of things.

Could he hate me enough to be behind all this?

"Grayson, I'm speaking to you," Bryce says. Is the old man in on all this too? Is this all a dog and pony show?

"Can you repeat that?"

"Are we boring you?" Stephen asks.

This time, I don't stop myself. I go all the way around the desk and stand in front of his chair. He flinches and scoots back. "I'm not going to take your shit anymore. I don't have to. I told you I don't want your money. I told you my child is not related to you. We have nothing else to discuss. Please leave."

Bryce jumps to his feet with more agility than he came in with, but he walks out with drooping shoulders, followed by his son.

I grab my jacket and head out the door. "Sandra, cancel all my appointments. If it's an emergency, I'll be at home."

"Elias is on his way. Do I tell him to call you?" she asks.

"No, whatever it is can wait."

26

Winter

I'm tired of pacing and reassuring my friends that I'm okay. I even ate because Aunt Millie wouldn't have it any other way. Somehow, she knew I hadn't eaten lunch when I walked through the door.

My first day back to work ended in disaster and, somehow, the media has my phone number. I get calls from reporters, asking for comments and interviews.

I'm a freaking artist and teacher. I'm no one famous. I guess I can consider myself lucky because they don't know the juiciest part of the story: *how I got pregnant.*

I grab the still-clean brush, breathe, and try to concentrate again on anything to paint. I can't hear my muse because the comments from my coworkers are still echoing in my ears.

She's set for life now.

Do you know how much money Spencer Grayson is worth?

She snatched herself a real winner.

Ms. Walker advised me to not pay it any mind but it's hard. Especially when for a full meeting everyone is staring at you. I wanted to scream that they should mind their business and stay out of my life. But my little avocado began making waves in my belly, reminding me of what's important.

And shit. Now I don't even want to paint. I fling my brush to the far side of the room.

"It's not the brush's fault. The person you probably want to fling away is me," Grayson says from the door.

I probably should blame him but one look at that gorgeous face and that amazing body and all I could think is how much I missed him.

"You know—"

I don't get to finish because he moves so fast and grabs me in his arms and kisses me until my fingers are digging at his back and my body is pressed hard enough against him, we're about to fuse together.

He pulls me toward the small seat in the sunroom. He sits first and settles me next to him. "Before we get into the bad, let's talk about the good parts of our day."

I frown. "That's so…so relationship-y."

"Is that even a word, madam teacher?"

I laugh. "Not really. My day was really good until the end. Well, actually it started weird and that part I'm almost sure had something to do with you."

"Why? Were your horny?"

I elbow him but smile anyway. "Yes. But the weird part was that Miss Walker went out of her way to welcome me back. She was sweet and warm. I almost called to yell at you, but Simone took responsibility. I still think you had a part in this but you're off the hook."

"Well, thank you. I guess."

I ignore his dry tone. "The kids were amazing. They hugged me and were so excited to see me. I didn't realize how badly I missed them. Hey, you don't mind if I start giving my private classes to the girls here again? It's just Bron and Ayla."

"Of course not, it's your home too."

I smile. "Thank you. I have some ideas for the walls in here and in the nursery."

"Good. I'll have my assistant make an appointment with a designer so they can come help us decorate and get the furniture."

"A designer? Shouldn't we choose that?"

"I don't know anything about design. I mean, you can probably choose the art but I don't know the difference between a crib and a bassinet."

"Choose the art? Oh no. This little girl has too many artists in her life. I'm going to paint a mural over this whole wall behind us. I'm going to ask Ayla and Bron to help me. Adri said Cam is willing to do something. Can you believe that? She can get something on her wall painted by Cameron Blake."

He smiles. "That sounds great but she'll love the stuff by Winter Alexander way more. I will too."

He just knows what to say. "You are so sweet sometimes."

"Sometimes?"

"You can be a jerk, too."

His arms tighten around me. "I'm sorry about today. I hate that part of my life. Just because I have money, people think they have a right to know things about me."

"How did they find out?"

"The photos are from the restaurant, but someone probably tipped them off." His shoulders are stiff and his eyes strained.

He's had a rough day too.

I touch his cheek. "Tell me about your day?"

"Hellish from the minute I walked into my office. There are issues with the new factory campus. There's a plumbing issue in the area and I don't want it to affect the school across the street. Reporters have been calling my office all day about us. Sandra has been fielding and re-routing their calls to my publicist. And worst of all, I had to meet with Astrid's father and brother."

"You had a board meeting today?"

He shakes his head. "They asked for an impromptu meeting because of the headlines."

"Oh."

"Months ago, I told Bryce that I planned to implant the embryos and would tell him when I did. I didn't tell him when Alice first told us she was pregnant because I wanted to make sure the baby would stay...the doctor said the first three months, anything can happen."

I shudder, remembering our scare. "Did you tell him the baby is not Astrid's?

He nods. "I didn't tell them everything. Just that the embryos went missing and my surrogate was never inseminated. I told him this is our baby." His hand strokes my belly but his eyes are far, staring out into the city.

"And he didn't take it well."

"I am not sure he fully believes me. Stephen pitched a fit. I thought I was going to have to deck him. He's such a little shit."

"Maybe he's just worried about his sister's embryos missing, Gray."

He shakes his head. "Not the way you think. Their grandfather left Astrid, her brother, and father a lot of millions. Today, I found out that Astrid left all that money to me as long as I bring one of the embryos to the world."

I blink a few times.

He takes my hand in his. "I don't want the money. I never have. When she mentioned it, I told her not to leave it to me. I have my own money and way more than them. Not to sound like a jerk or anything. Her brother thinks I want to have the baby so I can get that inheritance. He's getting in his father's ear about it. Bryce even suggested we have the baby tested in utero to make sure she's not Astrid's."

I start to move off his lap but he holds me fast to him.

"Don't worry, I told them no. That would never happen. I know what can happen and I wouldn't risk our girl for anyone."

I blow out a breath. "I'm sorry you went through that. That guy sounds like a dick."

"He is even worse than I thought. Because I don't have proof, but I'm willing to bet he's the one behind the missing embryos."

"Why would he do that?"

He shrugs. "Because of money. Because unfortunately, like you once said, I am surrounded by people who would do anything for it."

"I don't understand how people can be like that. Maybe it's because I never had any."

"People who always have would do anything to keep it. Stephen's never had to work a day in his life for anything. He would never be able to build a company from the ground and he's afraid."

"And he feels threatened by you."

He nods. "You should've seen the way he reacted to the news. He was irate. Something like this would have made him happy."

"Because there's no one to stand in his way now."

"Exactly. He walked in smarmy and content. I got the feeling that he came looking for something. I can't explain it well, but everything changed when he heard what happened. He went red in the face and he lashed out more directly than usual."

"What are you going to do?"

He kisses my temple. "I want to dig deeper. Simone told me she's coming by to talk to you later. I want to talk to her first about this...and then I'm going to talk to the person that has the answers I'm looking for. Alice."

"The surrogate?"

"Yes, I'm going to travel across the border to talk to her."

My stomach sinks. He's leaving. "You're going there?"

"I have to. She's the only one who can tell me. I was so stupid at first. I kept thinking she had help in the clinic, but she had to have help from someone else. We need those answers."

"But if someone on your team is capable of doing this to you, aren't you in danger?"

"I'll be safe and back here in a day or so. You don't have to worry about me."

Too late. My gut is twisting. He's so confident, when someone is willing to go through so many steps to hurt him. Why would they hesitate in hiring someone to hurt him? "I'm scared."

"You're going to be okay. This place is secure. You don't see the cameras and the guards, but they're here and after yesterday no one comes close to you that you don't want to." He rubs his hand up and down my back.

I press myself closer to him. "I'm worried about you, Gray. What if this guy is really bad and he sends someone to hurt you?"

"I'll be just fine. I have security and I'll have people there."

I cup his cheeks with my hands. "You have people here, too. This all still happened. If you're right, someone set you up, took those embryos, and somehow chose me to impregnate with your sperm. You say it's because of money, right?"

"Yes, I believe that."

"If he's so threatened by you, he wants to destroy you so badly that he would jeopardize his own sister's embryos. What is stopping him from doing worse?"

His mouth drifts open but he doesn't say anything. His eyes go dark like I've never seen, and I can't protect him from that darkness. *I can't protect him and I want to protect him. I need him to be safe for himself. For Baby. For me.*

What if I lose everything we have? What if I lose him?

My eyes fly open and he's staring at me. "Are you okay?"

I shake my head and tell myself to calm down. I tell myself to stop being dramatic. He'll be fine and back in a day or so like he says. Yet, I still fear and tremble and my eyes fill with tears.

Because people come and go in my life and I've learned never to get attached, but he's different.

Because he's different than any other man I've ever met.

Because I love him.

Because losing him would be the worst thing ever.

"I don't want to lose you." The words just fly out of my mouth and I don't try to take them back. Not this time.

"You're not going to lose me," he says and tilts my mouth to his. His lips settle over mine. His thumb rubs circles into my shoulder and he devours my mouth until I'm kissing him back with the same desperation.

He helps me up and we head through the adjourning door to our bedroom. We make it to the bed and he's already discarding his shirt. I reach for the bow under my breast but he stills my hands.

"Let me do it." He pulls on the cotton belt that holds my dress together. He undoes it and unwraps the garment from my body, shrugging it over my shoulders. "I've been wanting to open this present all day."

Yeah, he said it before I left for work.

He kisses my cheek, my chin, slides his lips down my neck and reaches to unclasp my bra. He discards it and presses his lips to the middle of my chest, palming at my breasts and rubbing my nipples with the back of his fingers until they hurt so good.

I moan and he walks me back until I'm sitting on the bed and he's standing in front of me. I waste no time and reach for his belt, unbuckling and undoing it. He tries to help me but now I push his hands away and pull his pants down. His cock is pressing hard against his boxers and I sketch his outline with my fingers, keeping them light enough. Then I lean forward and brush my tongue over his underwear.

He groans, bucking his hips forward.

I chuckle. "You have to be patient."

I sneak my hand past the elastic and grasp him. He's hot and hard and I wish can rub myself while I stroke him because I'm throbbing just as he is. I free him from the boxers. My mouth waters because there's a white dew drop on his tip. I rub it with my fingers.

"How long have you been hard?" I ask.

"All fucking day," he growls.

"Hmmm. For me."

He nods.

"I like that," I say and rub the pre-come in the center of my chest, the spot he was just kissing.

"Jesus Christ, Winter."

I love the sound of my name on his lips when he's this desperate. I bring my mouth down and lick him slow until he moans. Then I do it again.

"Come on," he snaps.

"What's the magic word?"

"Please."

I smile and close my lips around his cock. I suck him into my mouth, once, twice, a third time. I go deeper every time, hollowing my cheeks, pressing my tongue down his hot length. He's frantic, burying his fingers into my hair and yanking hard. I moan too because my pussy begins to pulsate. I want to give him everything I have. I want him to fuck my mouth.

I lift my gaze up to his and lay my hands flat on my thighs.

He hisses but doesn't stop. Recognition is in his eyes as he begins to take control, moving his hips in expert moves, guiding his cock inside my mouth, toward the back of my throat but never hitting it.

I concentrate on his eyes but I take care of me as I take care of him, tugging at my nipple and circling my clit until I feel the explosion coming. My fingers are working hard and fast and he's moving even faster.

Then, he pulls all the way out of my mouth and presses my back into the mattress, yanking my panties up and placing my ass against his hips. He plunges all the way in, making my eyes roll and pounding me until the world blurs and I arch against the bed.

27

Grayson

The gray walls, courtesy of cement plaster, the old, worn and peeled furniture, and the screaming noises of the inmates outside would make anyone want to run to the end of the earth. But it's the guards, with their impassive demeanors and eyes that seem capable of anything, that should scare the words out of you.

And Alice is scared to death. Her hands tremble so badly she can't drink her water without spilling it. Yet, she refuses to say who she worked with.

"I already told you everything," she says and her lips glue together.

"I recommend you talk," her local lawyer tells her in broken English. "You don't want to see the bad side of this jail."

I try again. "Alice, whoever you are protecting doesn't care enough to make sure you are protected. If you tell me who it was that set this in motion, I will pay off your legal fees and my lawyers won't rest until you're freed."

She looks me in the eye for the first time. "Grayson, I'm so sorry I ran away. I panicked and I didn't think I could face you after I left the clinic, but I don't know anything else."

"Yes, you do. You can give me the name of your associate and help yourself."

Her lip trembles. "I ran because I was scared."

"With a fake passport? How did you get it? You also hopped cities and made it here through Cuba. You took the long way to get here. The expensive route—"

"I had two million dollars. Remember?"

I don't let her taunt get to me. If I lose my patience, there goes objectivity. "—it's also the connected route. Money alone wouldn't have gotten you here."

"Money talks, Grayson."

"In your case, money also sinks, Alice. You're going to spend your life in jail and why? Because greed got the best of you? Because you thought you could scam me for more?"

"I've already said—"

"All you've been doing is bullshitting me." I push the words through my teeth. "There's a lot I already know. All I need you to do is confirm. You do that, I'll help you."

She says nothing.

"I know you were working with Doctor Lawrence, the nurse practitioner and one of the technicians at Better Maryland. Doctor Lawrence is dead but she didn't take it all to the grave. She left a suicide note saying you were all in cahoots and you were the one that set it all up."

She blanches.

"She hung herself out of guilt, Alice. She knew my investigators were getting close." I'm lying through my teeth but her reaction tells me I'm on the right track.

"Or she did it out of desperation. She probably spent all her money gambling and couldn't take it anymore. The woman had a real problem."

I keep talking since she doesn't realize what she just admitted. "One you probably exploited to get her to help you."

She shrugs. "Believe what you want."

She's cold. She doesn't even blink as she says it. Simone was right. I was completely wrong about her. "Tell me who the mastermind of all this is or I'll leave you to your fate here in Mexico."

Her gaze shifts from side to side. "I can't."

"Why can't you? Does he have you threatened? I can protect you, in exchange for the truth."

"Who is 'he?'" Her fingers curve in air quotes.

"You tell me."

"Tell your goons to let me go, Grayson."

I chuckle. "These are not my goons. You broke the law and entered this country with a fake passport." I lean forward and whisper. "I can probably buy your way out, even though you stole from me and you did God knows what with my embryos."

She leans in. "You can't do anything when there *is* nothing."

"What the hell are you talking about?"

"You got taken for a ride." Hands clasp in front of her and she looks at ease for the first time.

Tension snakes up my spine but I shake it off. The woman is a liar. *Don't fall for her bullshit.* "I did. By you. That's why I'm about to leave you here to rot."

"You won't. I know too much. I can go to the press and talk about King Midas paying someone to carry his embryos. Everyone would know the secret you're so ashamed of and made me sign two million papers to keep hidden."

If she were a man, I would leap across this table and choke the life out of her. "How did I get it so wrong with you? If you changed your mind, all you had to do was say so."

She lowers her gaze to the table for a fleeting moment. "I'm telling you the truth and you keep insisting on holding me hostage. You leave me no choice. I'm going to own Grayson Global pretty soon."

This time I laugh.

"So that's what this is about. I hate to break it to you, but that's not going to happen. You were a pawn he used to try to hurt me but you know what? You both did me a favor. I'm better off. And you're going to stay stranded here."

"You don't believe I'll call the press?"

"Oh, I believe you, but you're the dumb one for believing it will do anything. Go ahead and call the press. And I'll go ahead and call the cops. I'll press charges for the two million you owe me and for destroying embryos. I wonder if that's considered murder? And what will Stephen do when he realizes you could put him in jeopardy? He does pretty stupid things when he gets desperate. But you know that."

Her skin goes red. "I have rights. The U.S. government would help me."

"You're about to be wanted in Maryland for stealing, fraud, and possibly as an accessory to murder. As soon as I get back, the authorities will also get an anonymous call alerting them about someone who used a fake passport to get through TSA and on a plane to Cuba and then Mexico. There's no place on earth you will be able to hide. It's life in jail, either here or in the United States for you. Pick your poison."

I stand up and don't look back, not even when her sob fills the room.

Outside, my private investigator is waiting for me. "Don't worry. It won't be long 'til she talks. It's really her only way out. I doubt she would hold out more than a few weeks. It's rough in here, especially for a *gringa*. The other inmates will help her make a quick decision."

"I don't want her hurt. I just want her to talk. Please have someone with her. I will pay for her security."

He shakes his head. "You're a good guy. If she did that to me, I would let nature in a foreign country takes its course."

"She was just a guppy. I'm looking for the bigger fish, the person she's protecting."

He nods. "She'll talk. Go home to your pregnant wife. You'll be hearing from me soon."

Wife. Winter would probably freak at the word. The trip to the airport has me in thought. As frustrated as I am with not getting an answer, I'm happy to get back home. To get me back to the woman Santana called my wife.

What would Winter say to that? I snort. Last night, I got an earful from her about the settlement but it went easier than I expected. She told me Simone had a long talk with her and knowing Simone like I do, she probably put everything in a way that made it impossible for Winter to turn it down.

Don't stay there after tomorrow. Come back. I miss you.

Her words still do funny things to my chest. I've missed her more than I thought I would. I've had trouble falling asleep and it has nothing to do with frustrations over Alice. I miss Winter's raspy voice, that huge smile, that spicy and quick wit, her body, her tongue. *Jesus, that tongue, that uninhibited mouth.*

Grayson

I don't make it home 'til around nine. Winter's half sitting on the bed, very much asleep. Nin, coiled and pressed to her thigh, barely opens her eyes to look at me. The only things moving in this room are the shadows from the TV, tuned to some vampire show.

I go sit by her side, and touch her arm, rubbing it softly up and down. I woke up this morning reaching for this soft skin, looking for this sleepy and floral scent.

She smiles and then her eyes drift open. "You're home."

"I am. You and Nin have gotten close in my absence." I hook a thumb toward the cat.

"I think she was missing you," she mumbles.

"How about you?" I kiss her until she smiles.

"I was definitely missing you."

"How much did you miss me, Winter?"

"Like crazy." She closes her eyes and her head drifts back.

I stand and put my hands by her back. I start to ease her into the bed. Nin is none too happy when I move her. I cover Winter all the way up to her neck, the way she likes it, but when I try to move away from her, she grabs my hand.

185

"Get in the bed."

I'll get in for a bit and then when she's deep in sleep, I'll head to the home office. I'm behind on work. I shrug off my shirt, shoes, and pants and get in on the other side. I gather her close, until her warm breath fans over my neck.

"This feels good."

"Aren't you sleepy? I should probably turn the TV off." I grab the remote.

She snatches it from my hand. "No. We're watching this show."

"Whose we? You and Nin."

"And Pear Bear."

"Pear Bear? You and Lauren need to stop. Better yet, we need a name, so you can stop calling her fruit names."

"I like Pear Bear." Her voice is dreamy but she's more lucid now. "It's the cutest fruit. We do need a name before we get to carrot or artichoke."

I chuckle. "What did you do today? We didn't talk much."

"Because you had some mysterious layover and didn't call me. But Lauren brought Bron and Ayla and we worked on the mural for the sunroom. It's so cute, with crocuses and nymphs. The girls were awesome. Wait 'til you see what they did. Oh, and Ollie came by, I told him about the built-in shelves and he's going to change the nursery bathroom vanity to a farmhouse sink so we can bathe—"

"Don't say Pear Bear."

"—Avelyn."

"Avelyn?" I'm taken aback.

She nods. "After Sister Aveline, who got me into painting. Just make it a little more edgy with a y. What do you think?"

"Avelyn Winter Grayson." I savor it. "I like it."

"You don't mind, do you?"

"That you named our baby without me? Not at all."

She laughs. "No, that I'm changing the vanity. I just think that's more comfor—"

I kiss her. "You can change anything you want in this house."

"Thank you. I'm going to pay for it. Since, you know, I have ten point five million dollars now."

I wince. I should have known she was going to bring this up.

"Winter, you don't need to—"

"I want to buy things for my baby, too. And if this is to be my house, too, it's only normal I invest in it."

I swallow. "Is this going to be your home?"

"We're raising a baby and we're together. I don't want to be away from either of you."

And it all falls into place. I don't have to wait to ask her. This moment is perfect. "Me either. I'm happy you feel this way. Let me get something."

I swing off the bed.

"I'm happy too. It's weird as hell, you know? A few months ago, I would have run for the hills at the idea of this but—"

"You're knocked up and without other prospects?"

She laughs. "You're such an ass. You know that? I'm here, confessing how much I love you and how that's changed the way I view the world and you're just… What?"

There's a rumbling in my chest, something that's loud enough to ring in my ears. "You just said you love me."

She flips her palms up. "Well, duh. We're playing house and planning our baby's life together."

I go sit by her side with my trousers in my hand. "I think there's a problem with that sentence."

She frowns. "What's that?"

"You said we were playing house. I think we need to stop playing."

"What do you mean…"

I grab the box from the pocket of my trousers and hold it in my palm. "It shouldn't be playing. It needs to be real. We are having a real baby. And we love each other for real, right?"

"Right…" She's still not looking down at the box.

I grab her hand and place it on it. "Everything needs to be real. What we have needs to be official."

"There better be a Ring Pop inside this thing."

She flips the top and her eyes go huge. Her gasp is louder than the pummeling of my heart. "Grayson, what the hell did you do? Oh my God."

"I'm asking you to marry me, Winter Mercedes Alexander."

"Why? This is not the thirties. People have kids now without getting married. We can be like Brangelina before the breakup. Look at what happened when they got married."

"We are not Brangelina. I want to marry you and not just because you're having my baby. You were already doing that. I want to marry you because I love you and I like you. Because you're amazing. Can I tell you a story?"

Her mouth is hanging open, so I take advantage.

"Someone told me yesterday that I should go home to my wife and your name immediately came to my head. And I loved it. I even laughed, thinking how shocked you would be and what you would say. I didn't stop thinking about how I wasn't shocked. I should have been. I probably should have said we were not married but I didn't. You make me laugh and I set aside my job to spend time with you. You've become home to me."

"Gray..."

I take her face in my hands. "Tell me you don't feel the same way and I'll leave it alone."

"I can't. I missed you so much I didn't sleep all that well. I've never missed anyone before. But I don't know how to do the family thing. I don't know how to be a wife. I have no clue how to be a mom and you want me to be all these things all at once. You don't even know the whole story about my mother. She's a gambler and a drunk who likes—"

I shake my head. "I don't fucking need to know that right now. I just want to know if you'll be my wife."

"I don't know who my father is," she insists.

"My mother abandoned my father and me to go live in Europe with some guy she met. She only reconnected with me after I made money. I send her money to keep her the hell away."

"Oh my God."

"We're not them, Winter. We don't have to be them. We can be us, however we choose to make it work. I wanted it to be with this ring, official and binding. But I'll take you any way I can have you."

Her eyes are cloudy and her face scrunches up like someone doing heavy arithmetic. She shakes her head a bunch of times but her fingers stay fastened around my hand and she's muttering. Then she stops and goes still and exhales.

"I do. I don't know how to do any of this but I know three things. I love this baby. I love you. I want to be yours."

28

Winter

I run my fingers over the pine branches and the raw aroma of the white fir tickles my nose. I inhale deeply, taking it all in. I'm not a nature person but I love this smell, like I love the rosemary bushes we spread around the house. Everything's vivid, the plants bring the green and the ornaments bring the deep red and the silvery white.

"I wish you could see this, Avy. I think you would love it. Your little eyes would light up at the colored lights. Did you know that I used to draw my Christmas trees on the walls?"

"Probably because you didn't like anything you saw in the stores," Grayson says from behind me.

I shoot him a dirty look over my shoulder. "Or because I didn't have money to spend…"

"You didn't have twenty dollars for a tree?"

I turn around. "I have fancy taste."

"Yes, I know. You're standing next to a white fir that had to be brought in from up north."

I look up the length of our family room tree and smile. I love it, even if I had to use a little white paint to bring out a snowy look. "You did a good job with the top branches."

He snorts. "Oh, wow. A compliment. I guess I got something right."

I go take a seat by his side. "You get a lot of stuff right. Don't be sulky. Look at how pretty our tree is. Don't you just love our white birds? Everyone says they look so natural."

"Of course, they do. We worked ourselves to the bone to make it look like that. When *someone* didn't like anything and insisted, we perfected it."

"You're so dramatic. It's so beautiful." I lay my head on his shoulder and he hooks an arm around my shoulders.

We stare at the tree in silence and my throat starts to close a little. I sigh. "I used to paint big wide trees on my walls. It would take me an entire night but I would work on it and then decide on the ornaments. This one is like a three-dimensional version of it."

"Do you have photos of it?"

I reach for my phone and search back to the pics I used to take. "This is the last one I painted. It was two years ago."

His eyes widen. "That's amazing. Where is it now? It's not on your wall."

"I primed over it when Christmas was over. I used to do that every year." I have to laugh at the astonished look in his face.

"I can't believe you would paint over that."

I kiss his jaw. "It's a rip-off from *The Joy of Painting*. I used to watch that show whenever I could. Even as a teenager. You can imagine what a joy, no pun intended, that was at the group home."

His eyes cloud and he tries to cover the wince.

"Don't do that, Gray. Don't pity me. I survived."

He squeezes my side. "I'm sorry. I don't pity you. I hate to think of what you went through."

"It made me strong and who I am."

"An amazing woman."

Yeah, right. "You didn't think so when I took you away from work and made you carefully paint individual branches. Or during my stroke precision lesson."

He dips his head. "I still thought so. It was just hidden really deep."

That makes me laugh.

He's back staring at the photo on my phone and widening it with his fingers. "Why did you stop two years ago?"

"That's when I started teaching at LaSalle and met Adri and Lauren. I've spent *Noche Buena* and Christmas with them since."

"Oh, that's how you became so close."

I find the photos from that year. "Yes. The first time was so weird because I just didn't know them all that well or what to expect. I came and they were all happy and cheery. I thought I'd hate going there so much, but they made me feel welcome. Adri's mom made scarves for all of us. I didn't know what to get them and I didn't have much money, so I made them mini canvas images. I think you're going to love Christmas Eve at Adri's."

"I'm sure I will. You better make a canvas for me too."

"I'll make a life size one of you. Naked."

He smirks. "Of course, I want nothing more than for the both of us to stare at my naked body all the time."

"I wouldn't mind."

He shakes his head. "We are not doing that."

"You're not posing for me?"

"That's a no, my lady," he says.

"You're no fun. What if I paint you on top of a stallion?"

"Naked?"

"Yes."

"Then, no, ma'am." His fingers massage my belly. His daughter kicks twice under his hand.

"I love how hard your stomach's gotten and that she moves so often. It's like she's there, all proud and showing herself. You know? We need to start thinking about you know what. Christmas is the day after tomorrow and March will be here before you know it."

My heart skips a beat. It's the routine every time he mentions getting married. I stare at the sparkling ring on my finger. "Shouldn't we wait for the Christmas hoopla to be over first?"

"Or we can do it on that day, right there by the tree. I can have the mayor marry us. I'll call in a favor."

I tilt my head to tell him it sounds nice and how touched I am by his romantic views but I get the breath kissed out of me. His lips are sweet and his touch is gentle. How could I ever have thought this man was cold? Everything about him scorches.

"Everyone will be busy for Christmas, but what if we do a New Years' Eve wedding instead? We can have it here and I can invite the girls and you can invite Simone and her family and we'll be good."

"I like that. But then, we'll have to wait 'til they all leave to get the honeymoon started. People are going to linger until the new year."

I shove him. "You're crazy."

My phone starts ringing and I'm padding around looking for it. I find it, unlock the screen and freeze.

It's my mother again. This time it's a text. *I need some more help.*

My head snaps around and I'm fully expecting to find Grayson looking at the text, too, but he pulls himself away and is staring at his own phone. "I'll be right back."

My breath gushes out. I haven't told him my mom has been calling or that I've been sending her more money.

I'm going to send you some more but that's it for now.

I open the cash application and send her my usual Christmas quota. It's just a little more than the usual that's kept her at bay for the last couple of months. I flip the phone onto the seat and use my hands for something more soothing, rubbing my belly.

I'm going to tell Gray, but first, I want to be married and secure in our lives. Not letting her ruin what we have right now.

Winter

. . .

193

It's not freaking working. One hour of breathing, stretching as much as my five-months-pregnant body would let me, and trying to find my center. Still, I wish I were punching something.

"How is this the day before my wedding? I'm tense, angry, and so hungry I could punch someone in the face." I ask out loud.

Adri turns to look at me and giggles. "Come on, I think we've had enough yoga for a while."

We uncoil from the floor and end up laughing again at how hard it is for us to get up. My stomach has ballooned in the past two months, but Adri's bigger than me and she's like five weeks behind.

"How can I be further along than you? Your belly is so much bigger."

The smile on her face can't be described as anything else but proud. "Second kid. The doctor warned me early on. It was crazy because one week the test turned positive, the next, boom, bump. Did the yoga help at all?"

I shrug. "My body feels more relaxed, my mind not so much. But I'm glad we are out and about. I needed to get out and breathe. I'm glad you found a place where we don't have to be running away from photos and people harassing me for an interview."

"It's going to die down. Don't worry. Remember when the press found out Bron was Cam's daughter? They were interested at first but then it all died down. We get mild interest but the security helps."

Avelyn will have to deal with that. She will never be just a little girl playing because her dad has so much money.

"What's wrong?" Adri asks.

"Nothing."

She stares at me until I relent.

"I hate it that our baby has to deal with all this stuff. We're not getting time to get used to the idea of her because we have to worry about people intruding. And what if she finds out how I got pregnant?"

"Do you regret her?"

"Of course not." My tone is harsh and I want to apologize but Adri shakes her head.

"Do you regret what you have with Grayson?"

"No. I've never been more sure of anything."

"Then that's what you'll tell her. She didn't come around like other kids in the beginning, but you and her dad grew to love each other, with her, and because of her."

Warmth explodes over my heart and I look at my friend with a mixture of love and pure envy. "You need to pass all that mommy knowledge on to me. You always have the right words."

"My daughter told me this morning that she needed time away and alone. That her father and I are smothering her." She says it with a straight face but there's a light of hurt reflected in her eyes.

"She's growing up and she says that today, but all during the lesson yesterday she was talking to Ayla and me about taking care of you and helping you out. She adores you guys. I hope my baby comes to think of me that way."

"That you're smothering?"

I laugh. "You know what I mean."

We walk into the changing rooms and head to the spa shower. The yoga may not have worked but I still feel a little sweaty and yucky. After I'm done, I check my phone for messages before we head to the massage lounge. My screen is full of message prompts but I hit on Grayson's name first.

We're getting married tomorrow. Make sure you stretch for the fireworks. #honeymoonvibes

There's a winky face at the end and just like that, my body goes hot. The man is insane but God I'm so in love with him. I send him back an eggplant emoji and a tongue out.

There's another text message from my mom. She needs more money. My chest threatens to close and I break the rules. I send her more because nothing's going to ruin this day. I hit send on the usual amount and go through the rest of my messages. Simone will come early, in case I need any help. The Millers secretary sent me an email asking me for an interview. I need to tell Grayson but I can do that later.

Hell no. I can almost hear him.

There are more messages, like every day, from newspapers, magazines and blogs. Can't people just leave me alone? I throw the phone back in my bag and start walking. The room has grown warm or maybe the water in the shower was too hot. I fan my face. Adri is waiting for me outside.

"Are you okay?" Adri's frowning and staring at me. She places a hand on my forehead. "Your skin has gotten darker and flushed."

"Messages. All over my phone and email."

"Winter, pregnancy is difficult enough. You need to swipe every-thing away and just concentrate on you, Avelyn, and Grayson. You don't need added stress. Today is about you. Forget everything else."

"Tell that to my mom," I blurt out.

"Your mom? What about her?"

Damn, my mouth. "Forget I said anything. It's stupid."

"No. Tell me. I know I've been involved with my pregnancy a lot but we are still friends and Lauren won't tell me things. I would like to think you trust me, too."

"I do. It's just I didn't want to bother you. It's easier to tell Lauren because my mom is just like Connie. They operate the same way."

She grimaces and I loved the shock in her eyes. She's such a good mom she can't even picture it. "What does she want?"

"What she always wants. Money. I've been sending her small amounts but it's becoming more and more frequent. Lo said not to send her any more but I just want to be happy and at peace."

"I get that but it's only a temporary cure. She'll be back for more. But I probably would have done the same thing if I were in your posi-tion. You may have to start thinking of something more permanent."

"I know. I just want this time to pass. I don't want to face her. She's everything I don't want to be. What if she scares me away?" I hate how insecure I sound to my own ears.

"She won't. You have all the things she didn't. You're a strong woman and you made a choice for this baby. Yeah, she was implanted without your will but you are choosing to love her and raise her and be there for her. You're going to be a great mom."

"Were you always this sure of yourself?"

She laughs. "I was panicking so bad when I found out I was preg-

THE WINTER OF MY LOVE

nant. I was barely eighteen and Cam had left town. He didn't know I was pregnant and you know all that happened with his dad."

I nod. His father kept Cam away from Adri and blackmailed her not to tell him about the baby.

There's water waiting for us at the lounge and the attendant tells us our masseuses will be right out.

"How did you deal with the panic?" I ask.

"I talked it out with Lo, a lot. We used to cry together and she was my rock. You have both of us and Grayson. You can let us be your rocks through this."

"I haven't told him about my mom and the money I've been sending her."

"You should. I am sure he will understand." Then she sighs. "Now that you're going to be married, you also need to come clean. You don't want to keep this a secret. It's only a matter of time before your mom finds out. Your face is in the papers."

She's right. "When I make up my mind to start telling him, it's like my throat shuts down. What is he going to think about me? He already knows part of my history and her neglect. I don't want him to hate her. I don't even hate her. I just don't want her around me. That's horrible, right?"

She shakes her head. "Of course not. Why would you have warm feelings about someone who didn't show them to you? You know the story about my dad and you know I did what I thought was right to protect my mom and Bron, but sometimes I wish I hadn't let Cam's dad intimidate me. That I'd contacted Cam and told him the truth. Things would have been so different. At the same time, I did what I had to do to survive. You've done that all your life. But there comes a point when we stop running and face our fears."

I nod and swallow the lump in my throat.

"It doesn't have to be tonight, though. Because you're having a relaxing day, an awesome brunch, and you're getting married tonight." She smiles at the end.

It warms my heart. I can't wait. I love Grayson, way too much.

Our masseuses come in to get us. I've had massages before but not

197

after getting pregnant and I was assured and reassured that this is okay and encouraged. She works with me until we find a comfortable position. Then she works on my back, relieving pressure from my shoulders, and finishes with a scalp massage that leaves me limp and undone.

"Gray so needs to learn some of this woman's moves," I say to Adri in the recovery room.

"Cam does, too. But then we would be too hooked and every time they'd mess up, they would fix it with massages."

I think of all our arguments lately. There are days all he does is breathe and he pisses me off. "Good point."

We get dressed and go in search of the dining room. "How did you even find this place?"

"Lux. This is one of the places she has to review. Can you believe that her job is to test and criticize products and places?"

"That's a good gig."

The waiter takes our name but doesn't sit us in the main dining room. He takes us to the far end of a room and opens a door to a private room. It's a glass-encased terrace. There's a long table set up with flowers going down. In the corner there is a table with gifts. In the far end of the room, Lauren and Aunt Millie are waiting for us with Simone, Adri's sister in law, Lux, Adri's mom, and Bron and Ayla.

"Surprise!"

They yell in unison, their smiles livelier than the sunlight that brightens the room.

I'm speechless as a wave of emotion rushes through me and in my next breath, I can't find air and I'm crying.

Adri side hugs me. "You can't cry. We are taking photos. It's going in the scrapbook."

"It's a bridal shower," I say like an idiot. Like it's not obvious from the delicate and beautiful décor.

Lauren pulls me into her arms. "Yes, it is. I'm so happy we are doing this. Congratulations."

They sit me at the head of the table for lunch. Which I'm glad for, because between the emotions and the botched yoga, I'm starving.

"Thank you for making my day," I manage between chopped breaths.

"We're making your day and tomorrow, it's Grayson's turn to make your night."

It's funny because that's what he said to me this morning before I'd left the house.

I smile all the way home. I can't believe how happy I am and the day is just going to get better. Aunt Millie is chatting about tonight and all that we have to do. We step through the door and the maid is waiting. There's a wrinkle in her forehead and her hands are pressed together.

"Missus Grayson, I'm so glad you are home. There's someone here to see you. Normally, I wouldn't let her in but with all the reporters outside, I thought you may not like her hanging around in the lobby."

I don't bother to correct her on the premature use of the last name because she looks so worked up. "I'm not expecting anyone."

"Ma'am, your mother is here."

29

Winter

She shows up today.

I've been living in Maryland for three years and my mom has never visited. But hours before I marry Grayson and put the past behind me, she's here to ruin my happiness.

I'm not going to let her.

I push down the nausea, take a deep breath, and smile at Aunt Millie. "It's going to be okay. I'll go talk to her."

"But...are you sure?" The worry deepens the lines on her face.

"It's going to be just fine."

My feet are heavy on my way to the living room, like I'm trying to run through quicksand. I rub a hand over my belly and stop right outside the room.

"It's going be okay," I whisper.

Cowards don't get the good things. Only the courageous do because they have gumption to go get it.

Sister Aveline would have been proud of me. I repeat the phrase in my head three times and then I walk in with my shoulders squared and back straight. Denise Alexander is sipping from a tumbler.

The smile spreads across her face when she sees me, and she sets her glass down and stands. "Look at you. You're beautiful, Winter. Pregnancy suits you."

She hasn't aged, still doesn't look a day over forty. Her body is naturally tight and her long hair tumbles down her shoulders. Her looks are something that neither jail nor time have been able to dull. She's my own personal version of Dorian Gray's mirror.

"Mom."

"Yes, *muñeca*."

Doll. I don't know what makes me cringe more, the nickname or the embrace she subjects me to. I have to breathe through my mouth because my nose is not pulling enough air. That's what I've always been, her doll. An object you pick up when you need it and discard when you're done.

I let her linger and even pat her a couple of times on the back. Then, I extricate myself and take a seat across from her. I need this coffee table between us like I need to send her on her way before Grayson comes home. I don't want him to meet her before I have the chance to talk to him.

"You've never visited me before. Why are you here?"

Her shrug is delicate. "Seems to me there's a lot you and I have to catch up on. You're pregnant, set up quite nicely, and I have to find out through the papers."

I try to emulate her casual. "We catch up, mom. You text me when you need money and I send it. The only time you showed up to anything is when I graduated from high school to take me to *dinner*."

I say the word dinner with enough strength, praying, hoping with all my spite that she remembers the day she embarrassed me in front of a whole class. I want her to be ashamed and leave. I want an inkling that she feels something akin to human decency.

"We had fun that day."

"You had fun." *Yes, she did.* She was half drunk and found another trashy mom to sit with.

"*No seas pariguaya*, Winter."

Don't be a chump?

"I'm not a *pariguaya*. It just wasn't a fun time for me—" I blow out a mouthful of air and try to tap into the good in my life. Grayson, Avy, and friends, a real family. "Let's not rehash. How much do you need?"

Her eyes flash with an intense emotion. "Who says I came here looking for money? I could just want to see you now that you're having a baby. I also want to meet your fiancé to make sure he is the right guy for you."

This, coming from the woman who used to leave me alone with strangers.

The look on my face must say everything I'm thinking because she hums. "But now that you mention money, isn't it funny how you send so little when you now live like this?" Her finger circles around the room. "Your husband is so rich he doesn't even know how many millions he has. I kept waiting for your compassion to kick in, but I guess money changes people."

It's up to you the kind of relationship you choose to have with her. The counselor's words ring in my ears. It was the mantra he repeated during our sessions. *It's up to you to set the boundaries and not let her cross them. She will only get away with what you allow.*

She's not going to change, so I will have to. It's time to redefine this relationship again.

"I'm not going to discuss Grayson's money with you. I send you what I have, which comes from my salary." It's true, I've only touched the settlement money to buy stuff for Avelyn. "I'm not adding a cent more, Denise. And I'm going to back to only sending you money once a month. You can take that or you'll get nothing."

She jumps to her feet, making my heart gallop to my chest. She doesn't take another step forward, but she leans in.

"You're loaded now and all you want to send me is a miserable two hundred dollars a month? I'm your mother. You're supposed to honor me."

The blood rushes all the way to my head and I don't even know when I stand up, but I'm the one who takes a step forward.

"Honor you? Because you did such a bang-up job being there for me all my life? All you've done is traumatize me. I've been so afraid of turning into you, I planned never to have a child."

"That sure changed fast when Spencer Grayson came along. You capitalized really quickly on that. Now you won't share with me. After all I went through with you."

I laugh. "You left me to roll around. The system took care of me because not even your family stepped in."

She scoffs. "I was okay before you. I was happy and in school to be a nurse until the day I got pregnant. And then my hell started. I bled every month, threw up every day, was sick through the entire pregnancy. But I was so happy, so hopeful for my baby girl. When I went into labor, the nurses and doctors kept telling me the baby was almost there. It was never ending." Her eyes go glossy, as if she were back in time.

I don't want to hear anymore but she keeps talking like I'm not even here.

"You were born, after thirty-six hours of the worst agony anyone can take and everyone gushed about how beautiful and strong you were and they put you on my chest. And you know what happened when I saw you?"

I shake my head, against my better judgment.

"I felt nothing. I looked at you, I nursed you for days, and I might as well have been washing my hair. There was nothing there, except the pain every time you latched on to my tits. Everyone said it would be fine. They sent me home with you and I still felt nothing. So, I started finding things that made me feel me feel happy, angry, high. The same things you always judged me for."

She points a finger at me. "It was always in those big, accusing eyes. Now, you think you're better than me. You know all about me, since you've judged me to death. But you've never had a kid before. I hope with you it's different. I hope you can feel something for that—"

My skin begins to tingle. The bile tickles my throat and I can't stand to look at her anymore. "Get out."

The smile slips off her face. "What?"

"You need to leave my house. Don't you ever come back here, Denise." I heave and have to rush out of the room. Aunt Millie is standing outside and so is the security person Grayson hired for the floor.

"Please see her out."

I barely make it to the bathroom. I kneel in front of the toilet and throw up. Down the toilet goes my whole afternoon, the loving feeling I got from my friends, and a part of my soul.

What if she's right? What if I don't feel anything? What if Avelyn is coming to the world to a mom just like the one I'd spent my whole life running from?

3 0

Grayson

Come home, Grayson. Her mother showed up and now Winter's really sick.

The car is barely parked before I'm out and hurrying my way to the private elevators.

The elevator is not moving fast enough and the alerts on my phone are going insane. A text from my publicist says I have to call him back immediately. One of his contacts let him know that Winter's mom is already doing an emotional interview with a newspaper. There was also a news crew waiting outside for her. I sigh, text back that I'll call him later, and drop my phone in my pocket.

Aunt Millie is waiting for me at the door.

"Where is she?"

"She's sleeping. I haven't seen her get that sick in a long time."

"Thank you. I'm going to talk to her." I start to move but she stops me with her hand on my wrist.

"Grayson, that woman told her some horrible things. I'm worried about Winter. She was pale and shaky. She was so happy after the shower. She couldn't stop smiling and was really chatty about the wedding. After...she didn't want my help. She locked herself in the bathroom but I could hear her crying."

The pang spreads over my belly and I place a hand on her shoulder to comfort her as much as to quell all that's brewing inside me.

I should've been here. *What the fuck was I doing in the office today?* Tomorrow's my wedding. I should've been home. I could have handled this.

"Why did they let her in?"

"Security was worried she was going to make a scene and we were already on the way home."

I nod. "It's okay. We're just going to have to take better care of her."

She wrings her hands. "The decorators just came in..."

"Can you take care of all that?"

"Yes. Lauren is coming to help out."

"Good. Let me go check on Winter."

She's lying in the middle of the bed. Nin is lying by her feet, not sleeping but staring at her. I wish I could just take care of this for her. Pay off her mom and send her away. But it's not my place. She doesn't even talk that much about her.

I sit by her in the bed and run my fingers through her wet hair. She stirs, staring at me with swollen eyes. "Aunt Millie called you."

I nod.

"I should've told you long ago. I never thought she would show up, not as long as I was sending her money. But she found out about you and the baby and now she wants more. I messed up. Lauren told me not to send her more but she kept texting me and it was just easier that way."

She's getting worked up and that's the last thing I want or she needs.

"It's okay, babe. You did what you had to, but you can't keep dealing with her the same way. For now, I just want to make sure you are going to be okay. We can postpone the wedding, if you want."

She sits on my bed, her hand latched around mine. "No. I wouldn't postpone our day for anything in the world. If you still want to..."

Her voice breaks and so does something inside me. I pull her against my chest and hold her tight. "I want nothing more."

She lifts her face up and I kiss her, trying to convince her with my mouth that I feel the same way, because I don't trust my voice anymore.

She pulls away and lays her head against my neck.

"So, we are getting married tomorrow, then?" I say it to tease her, hoping she laughs or elbows me.

But she just nods against me. "I've been sending her money since I graduated. It was the only way to keep her away from me. I know it's terrible—"

"It's understandable. She disrupted your life, time and time again."

"I told her today that I would keep giving her two hundred dollars once a month like I always have but that's it. She's not getting a penny more from me. It's from my salary at the school, I'm not touching the settlement."

Well, there goes the idea to pay her off to go away.

"I don't come from good stock like you, Grayson. I don't know who my dad is and my mom will probably strike again soon. You'll get to meet her someday."

How to tell her that her mother has already struck again?

"Winter, we all have baggage in our lives. It's most common with parents."

She shakes her head. "Not you. Your dad was amazing."

"My mother isn't. You know that."

"But she doesn't try to get in your way."

I grunt. "Because I won't let her. I keep her far away from me. We have more in common than you think."

She sighs. "Aunt Millie is the only grandma Avelyn will be able to count on."

"But she'll have the best mom."

She smiles but then her face crumples, she buries her head in my chest, and starts to cry.

Winter

"See you in school, Miss Winter." Bron and Ayla rush out to the elevators together, passing Oliver, who is in deep conversation with Bron's aunt, Lux.

I turn to Adri and Cam, whose gazes are on the pair. I hug him first.

"I think they're talking about new repairs to her townhouse before she moves in." He says goodnight and goes to join them.

Adri laughs. "The looks that have been flying between those two have nothing to do with construction."

"You saw that too." I throw my arms around her. "Thank you for everything today and for making sure I'm not the only pregnant woman here tonight. I probably should have thanked Cam for that."

"No, thank you for letting us be part of your day. I'm glad you think of us as family like we do you. You and Grayson will be really happy. And Avelyn, too."

Gray joins us then, Elias by his side. He says his goodbyes and Adri rolls her eyes.

Then her hand flies to cover her face. "I'm sorry, Grayson. I forgot he's your friend."

"He's just one of his lawyers," Simone says, walking from behind. "I'm his only friend. I'm so glad the legal wonder left because your hottie brother-in-law was about to punch him."

We say goodbye to her husband and her two boys. They all head out the door. Lauren and Chase, with tightened faces, are the last of the guests. The look she shoots him should have landed him dead on the spot.

"Thank you for everything you did. You're a godsend with the glam squad, my dress and helping me get everything together."

She curtsies, sending the fringes of her off-the-shoulder top into a sparkling frenzy. "Tell your bougie friends about me."

"I think Adri already knows, and so do all the women from

tonight." We both giggle and I pull her in for a hug. "Seriously, everything was beautiful. Your business is going to be a huge success. You're going to make every occasion feel so special for your customers."

"Thank you. I'm happy for you. You deserve all this happiness. Milk it for all it's worth," she whispers the last part in my ear.

We switch and I have to climb on my toes to hug Chase. "As the president of Team Lauren, I just want you to know you have my full endorsement."

He laughs. It's deep and bodied, with pure mischief sparkling in his eyes. "Thank you. You're a smart woman."

We wave to them from the door and barely close it before Grayson turns to me. "What was that all about?"

"I was letting him know he has my support for winning Lauren from your sleazy lawyer."

"Sleazy? Is that why Elias was talking to her all night? He's interested in her?"

I roll my eyes at him. "Where the hell have your eyes been all night?"

"On my beautiful, sexy wife and her gorgeous breasts and amazing ass."

Warmth flows through my body and all the way between my legs. I bunch my hand on his shirt and bring him down to whisper against his lips. "Great answer."

"Only telling the truth." He pecks my lips, takes my hand, and starts pulling me toward the bedroom.

"Wait, we have to help Aunt Millie pick up everything."

He shakes his head. "No, she already went to bed and a cleaning crew is coming in the morning, so...you will stay in bed with me all day."

"I like the sound of that better than cleaning."

"I thought you would."

We step into our bedroom and everything is clean and organized and the bizarre opposite of the mess I left getting dressed in here. "Thank God you have maids."

"*We* have maids," he corrects and the word *we* makes me a new level of delirious.

"Tonight was just so beautiful. Everything was perfect. Friends and family. I'm not even bothered about the mayor marrying us. How did you swing that?"

He laughs. "Do you know how much I pay the state in taxes? Thank you for not mentioning that you didn't vote for him."

"I don't think anyone in the room did."

"I bet Elias did." He laughs again when my lip curls.

I hook my arms around his neck. "I love that our ceremony was in front of our tree, overlooking the city. The phone photos were amazing. I can't wait to see the professional ones."

He kisses my ear, then my neck. "Yes, everything was great tonight, but you know what I can't wait to see?"

His touch is a lick of flames over my skin.

"What's that?"

His fingers find the zipper of my dress and slide my arms out of it. "All of you. Happiness looks sexy on you, Winter. You've been glowing all night. I could barely contain myself, I wanted to taste you so badly. I was way too happy when the clock hit midnight."

"Me, too. Let's start this year right."

His lips return to mine. I bury my fingers in his hair and give myself into the kiss, into his mouth. His hands are everywhere, on my back, my ass, pulling the dress down my waist, and past my hips.

I melt against him as his hands mold over my ass, his fingers sliding past the folds to caress my pussy. And I grind hard against him.

"You're so fucking wet. I love how wet you get for me, every time."

He moves the fabric of my panties aside and rubs me with the pads of his fingers. My whole body vibrates and I attack his mouth, reveling in the smell of his cologne.

He pulls his fingers out. "You know I'll have to taste this."

"Then do it and stop torturing me."

He freezes.

"Oh, I see. You need encouragement? I thought you couldn't stop thinking about this all night."

He's not saying anything or hugging me or kissing me.

I pull back and his lips have gone white. His eyes are fixed on something over my shoulder.

"Gray?"

His gaze shifts to mine and he swallows. "Babe, I don't want you to panic." His voice is soft and his eyes are shifting around the room.

But my pulse goes off. "What is it?"

He brings his hand around and shows me his fingers. They're bright and wet and red.

My world spins. I take a step back, only to trip on my dress, but he's there, hooking a hand under my shoulder and keeping me steady. *Oh no. Oh God.*

"I'm losing her."

"No," he says and his voice is so strong. He springs to action, going to the closet and grabbing a dress for me. He puts it over my head. "I'll get your shoes."

I can only stand there and watch as fear splinters my body. *I can't lose her.* Then, I feel her. She moves and something bigger than the fear kicks into me. "Grab me some underwear."

I go into the bathroom and wipe. The toilet paper comes back so vivid and red. The sob rocks my whole body but I grab a pad and he hands me my panties.

He's calling the driver and he rushes back in the room. "He's waiting downstairs."

The ride down the elevator is a blur. He's on the phone with the doctor's response line and all I can do is rub my belly. Inside the car, he gives the driver instructions to go to St. Raymond's and continues holding for the operator.

"It's an emergency. She's bleeding really badly and we are headed to the hospital. No, we don't know how long she's been bleeding. We just realized it. I guess not long because it didn't go through her clothes. Look, I don't fucking have all the answers. Tell Doctor Sahiner to meet us at St. Raymond's," he screams, jolting me and the baby, too. She shifts to the other side of my belly. I grab his hand.

I need to be strong for them.

"Let's just breathe and take it one minute at a time, okay?"

He nods. "She has to be okay."

The panic in his voice shatters me. "She's moving."

He looks at me and the light of hope in his eyes threatens to undo me. I want to keep that for him and for me. "She moved in the elevator and when you yelled. I think she responds to you already."

The knot in my throat grows tighter as the building comes into view. Nothing good ever happens in hospitals. I close my eyes and try to find my calm.

"We're here," Grayson says and his voice is accompanied by a gust of cold air. It's frigid as we rush out of the car. There's a wheelchair waiting for me.

Unlike last time, they wheel me past reception and Grayson is answering questions as we head into examination.

They guide us into a room and I have to get undressed again and put on a gown. He helps me into the bed and the nurse comes in. We go into familiar territory with my blood pressure taken and the nurse using a fetal doppler to hear the heartbeat.

"Heartbeat sounds strong. We are just waiting for your doctor now."

She leaves us to wait and Grayson opens the cabinets, searching around. He comes back with thick knit covers and drapes them over my legs and torso.

"Thank you. It's cold here."

"You're always cold." His smile is more like a grimace.

I take his hand in mine. It's icy and I rub it. He stares into my eyes and all my worst fears are written in his gaze. This is just like last time, except something feels horribly wrong right now. Like our happy night may just end in tragedy.

31

Grayson

We're losing her.

Those words keep playing over and over in my head and I have to push them far away, so I don't say them or think about them as I look at Winter. But every second of silence we have, it echoes loud like the rumble of the fireworks we watched at midnight tonight.

Life really knows how to paralyze me. The night I get married for the second time, it reminds me how impotent I am. I couldn't protect Astrid, like I can't protect Winter or keep her from losing our baby.

We were so happy tonight. I didn't tell her about her mom's interview with the papers. No one did. We all turned off our phones, kept it to ourselves, and let her be happy. And she was. I've never seen her smile that much. But it wasn't enough.

"I shouldn't have gotten that worked up. If I hadn't let the whole situation with my mom get to me, this wouldn't be happening."

Her voice jars me out of my thoughts. "You didn't do anything wrong. If anything, I'm to blame because I should have clarified that they should've contacted me in case of visitors."

"You can't protect me from everything, Gray. And I don't want you to. I appreciate what you did tonight but don't hide things from me."

I try for puzzled but her eyes narrow.

"I know about the interview. I have a smartphone, too."

"I'm sorry, I just wanted you to be happy tonight." And I couldn't even do that.

"I was happy tonight. I never imagined getting married, but I don't think my imagination could have done any better. Friends, family, fireworks. It was perfect...." She presses her lips together and breathes. "...now our baby has to be okay."

I want to say that she will, that everything will be okay, but I don't want to lie to her. I say the only thing I can say for certain. "Me, too."

We sit in silence, her hand clasped tightly around mine but I can't do this silence anymore and I need to tell her something. "Winter, no matter what happens tonight..." My throat grows thick and my eyes burn. God, that part is so hard to say. "...I want you to know that I love you and I've never been so happy as I've been in the last months with you."

Her hand grip tightens. "Me, too."

"Even if we lose her—"

She shakes her head and reaches to wipe my cheek. "We won't."

There's a knock on the door and Doctor Sahiner stands at the door, with her bright, sympathetic smile and another bright-purple crocus in her hair. "I hear baby Grayson is up to her antics again."

"I hope they're just antics." Winter says in a barely-there voice.

"Are you in any pain?" The doctor asks,

"No, everything was fine and normal."

Doctor looks over her folder of notes. "Did anything out of the norm happen?"

"I got really upset yesterday and sick to my stomach. Do you think that's why—"

"Winter, I need you to breathe. This is not caused by an emotional reaction. You have been keeping low stress, right?"

Her gaze shoots to mine and then to the side.

"We have been trying, but we've been under tension."

"I saw your names in the paper. The first instinct for parents is to blame themselves. This wasn't caused by a fight, or intimacy, or anything you did wrong, unless you ran a marathon this morning. The heartbeat is strong and that's a good sign. I am going to do an ultrasound today and a transvaginal test. We need to know where this bleeding is coming from. I need you, Mom and Dad, to try to relax and we'll get to the bottom of this."

We go through the ultrasound and we see the baby move on the screen and look at each other. The smile on Winter's face makes the world fade. It takes over her whole face and it makes her eyes sparkle.

I close my eyes and let the breath settle me.

"She's okay, Gray."

I can only nod.

The doctor moves to the end of the bed. "We're going to switch to transvaginal now. I'm going to take some pictures of your uterus and your placenta."

Winter bends her knees and lifts her pelvis. The doctor reaches and removes her underwear.

"There's still a good amount of bleeding going on but I want you to remain calm."

She's careful to fold the underwear and place it in a small basin behind her. Then she returns to her machine and pulls out something that looks like Winter's curling iron.

I'm about to ask if it's an ear thing when she rolls what looks like a condom over it. Then she squirts lubricant and rubs it up and down the shaft in a motion that's been very familiar since I was ten. "What the fuck is about to happen here?"

The doctor pffffts into a laugh and Winter joins along. "I guess you have not explained the different kinds of ultrasounds to your husband."

Winter laughs again and I glare at her.

"Wait, how did you know we got married?"

"You filled out husband on the form. And also…that huge sparkler on her finger. Congratulations."

"Thank you. It happened tonight." Winter's voice is soft, as if we we're still standing in our foyer seeing our wedding guests out.

The doctor rolls the chair toward the middle of the bed and then pulls the machine table closer. She sits and guides the wand in between Winter's legs. "I want you to breathe, drop your butt, and relax your hips."

"Wait. Is there another way to do this? She's bleeding. Is it safe to be inserting that…thing in there?"

The doctor chuckles. "Isn't it funny that when men are uncomfortable, they can't seem to find the right words for things they usually have a million names for?"

I don't appreciate her sarcasm and I'm about to tell her when Winter tugs at my hand.

"She knows what she's doing. She wouldn't do anything unsafe. I've had this done before."

Dr. Sahiner clears her throat. "This wand is called a transducer or ultrasound wand. It can give us better images of her internal organs. In this case, we are going to look at her uterus, cervix, and placenta."

I keep my gaze on the screen in front. I don't want to see this woman and her medical dildo move around. She clicks on the keyboard quite often.

"I'm taking photographs."

Winter squeezes my hand, "That's what the clicking is."

"Exactly, you see? Nothing to worry about. Your wife is an absolute pro at this."

"She is beautiful, smart, and brave," I say, looking into her eyes. The flush makes her cheeks glow.

"You two are so cute," the doctor says. "Oh, mhmm. Just as I suspected. Remember I talked to you that there may be a possibility that your placenta can settle on top of your uterus? That's what's causing your bleeding. You have developed placenta previa."

"That's dangerous, right?"

"In some cases, yes. It can cause you to bleed through the rest of the pregnancy. For some women, if the bleeding gets heavy enough, they require a blood transfusion. I don't think your condition is that severe. We are going to take really good care of you and your little peanut."

"How do we prevent that?"

"Well, you're both going to hate this, but I want you to go back on bedrest for a while. Until the bleeding stops. I don't want you walking for long periods of time, no squatting, no jumping or running…and no penetration of anything other than our little wand here."

"That should take care of it?" I ask.

"I think so, but if it doesn't, we may have to schedule a C-section for you, once we know baby is fully developed. It would be as close to your due date as we can get."

"Oh God." Winter's hand goes clammy on mine.

"I don't want you to worry about that right now. I want you to focus all that beautiful energy on resting and getting better. I know a doula and I want you to make an appointment with her. She does home visits and will talk you through this."

We look at each other but don't say anything.

"I know this is scary stuff but this is not unseen. It happens to fifteen percent of pregnant women and we know what to do for it. So, you two are going to go home. I'm going to take samples and we'll analyze them for anything we may have missed, but remember what I said."

"Rest and relax, however I can make that happen," Winter repeats.

But we will make this happen. Even if I have to buy her mother a mansion in the Caymans.

The doctor leaves us alone. I offer my hand to help her stand but she doesn't take it.

"We will make decisions together on how to deal with my mom."

I rush to answer. "Of course, how else…"

"Don't lie to me. I see it all over your face. I don't want you paying off my mom." Her gaze is so sharp on me I can't even deny it.

Ugh. "How do you know I was thinking about that?"

"I know you."

Well, shit.

217

32

Grayson

I lift my gaze to the sky, which seems so close outside my office's glass panel, and pray. I'm praying for patience and for a divine intervention to keep my mouth shut.

"Did you hear what I said?" Winter asks. Her voice, as always lately, is drenched in the type of tight annoyance I know for a fact she never oozes on her students or her friends.

No, that type of irritation only erupts out of her whenever she speaks to me, the asshole who can never seem to get anything right. Also, the same asshole who can never give it back because the last thing we need is for her to be stressed out. So, I swallow the I'm-not-fucking-deaf at the tip of my tongue and breathe.

"I did hear you." I drop my voice two decibels at the end of the sentence. "I didn't forget about the meeting with the Bradley teacher this morning. It was my understanding that you canceled it. Yesterday, you said you were sick of her tired advice and freaky, primrose-oil, fisting stories."

"I changed my mind. We need her. That's why Doctor Sahiner

recommended her and we need to make the effort, even if what she suggests seems out of this world. We can't just ignore our need for her."

We. We? We are not ignoring anything. You. Only you are. You hate that woman's kooky-ass methods and you think she is batshit crazy for suggesting that I stick my fingers, one by one in inside you until I'm basically open-palm fisting you with both hands and stretching that deliciously tight, almost squeezing, pussy, which I haven't been able to fuck in almost two months.

I don't say any of that, though. Instead, I swallow. "You are correct, sweetheart, but I had no way of knowing you changed your mind. I didn't get a phone call or text message."

"I said never mind right before we fell asleep last night."

Yeah, you also say never mind to a lot of shit. And how could I have remembered what you were saying that about? You had just given me one of the best blow jobs of my life and let me hit the back of your throat and come all over your tits. It literally left me comatose and I passed out on the bed. And I'm so looking forward to that dirty mouth all over again, so I'll gladly take another one for the team today.

"It's my fault. I should have known what you meant. You're just very good with your mouth and honestly, I wasn't thinking straight last night."

Her eyes flash with something akin to murder.

Oh shit. I fucked up again. But how? That's the highest compliment to her skills.

"I'm sorry I can't give you what you really want, Grayson."

What? Okay, now that pisses me off. "I don't know what you're talking about or what kind of shit you're concocting. That was a compliment and I know more than anyone how safe we need to keep things. The last thing I want is to trigger an early labor. It's fucking insulting that you'd insinuate that is why I didn't show up today."

"Stop being sensitive. I didn't insinuate anything."

"The fuck you didn't. Everything I say to you lately, you turn into something else. It's like you're looking for excuses to jump down my throat every chance you get. I don't see how you can be pissed off at me for missing an appointment you didn't tell me you changed your mind about. So, since I know I must have fucked up some other way, tell me what it is so I can apologize."

Her mouth drops open but it lasts less than a second as she flies onto her feet. "What the fuck—"

"Please sit down. You've proven enough that you can scream at me, just as effectively, sitting in a chair." *Damn, that's only going to rile her up some more.* I really need to get the hell out of here for a while.

"Fuck—" She lowers her ass back to the chair and presses all her digits together like the yoga instructor taught her. "No, I'm not going to swear because that won't help. I wouldn't have to scream at you if you'd remember what we have to do. You missed the Bradley class and the meeting with the doctor this afternoon, just like you missed the appointment with the decorator last week."

Shit, I'm a damned asshole.

I open my mouth to apologize but someone clears her throat and Lauren is standing by my office door.

"I'm sorry to interrupt but Aunt Millie said she told you I was coming."

Winter sighs. "She did. I forgot."

Probably in her hurry to come chew my head off.

"It's fine," I say.

"Yeah," Winter agrees and smiles at Lauren. Really smiles at her. "Let me use the bathroom and we can go chat in the baby's room."

I wait until she's out of the room before I speak. "She means far away from me."

Lauren laughs. "This sucks. I came here to get away from this same thing at Adri's but the bickering virus is here, too. Angry fighting couple is the special of the day."

"We're not angry." But I can't make it sound convincing.

"I have an idea. Hold on." She pulls out her phone and turns away from me. "Hey, I'm calling for a favor. I need you to go get your brother and Adri and bring them to Winter's. Then, you and Cam can go out with Grayson. We need to have a girls' night."

I don't need her setting up playdates for me but before I can speak, she puts up a hand.

"Jesus Christ, Chase. Just do it. Why do I have to explain anything —" Her face goes red. "I'm so sorry. I do know we are not in a relationship and I apologize for trying to boss you around, but I just want to give my girls, who are very much pregnant, some relaxing time and their guys a break. Don't do it for me. I'm not your girlfriend and I wouldn't think of asking something this big for me. Do it because you love your brother and sister-in-law."

Jesus. This guy can't be that gullible.

"Thank you so much. I really appreciate you." She hangs up the phone and turns to me. Her dark skin is glowing with tinges of red, her eyes flashing with the same intensity her friend focuses my way.

"Why are you still mad? He's doing your bidding."

"I hate ego massaging."

We can never please them. "Maybe it's not his ego needing massaging. Maybe he's reminding you that you may as well be in a relationship, since you already boss him like my wife does me."

Her face blanks and then she laughs. "Maybe. Our history is convoluted. I'm sorry if I didn't ask you first, but I think you married people need a little break from each other."

"So, Cam and Adrianna…"

"At each other's throats, too. Perfect time for a girls' night out."

"Girls' night out?" Winter appears at the door. She looks so beautiful and her belly is big and ripe, like her Tara paintings.

"More like girls' night in. I want to girl talk and I thought maybe you, Adri, and I could hang. We can have one of our famous orgies."

Her words penetrate the haze and I snap my head from Winter to her and back to Winter. "Orgy?"

Lauren laughs. "Don't get your hopes up. It's a movie night with the two Ryans, Reynolds and Gosling, or the Hemsworths, and adding in Idris Elba."

"Oh."

"Someone sounds disappointed," Winter says and there's a twinkle in her eye. Something that's been missing way too often lately.

"No. I'm considering staying. I don't think I like this orgy idea."

She smiles. "No, go out. It would be good for you. I need this time with Adri and Lo. We can find out what's going on with Lauren and her two men."

"I do not have two men."

I move to the door and lean in to give Winter's lips a quick peck.

She takes my face in her hands and opens her mouth, deepening the kiss. "I'll see you in a little while."

I head to the room to change, putting distance between me, my wife, and her revolving personalities. I don't get far before giggling comes from my office.

An hour later, I am sitting at a bar in Federal Hill, not too far from where I live. There's only about ten people there, including us. Cam and I aren't saying much. He looks dead tired and staring past the screen instead of watching the spring training game.

"Lauren really owes me for this. The two of you are a joy to be around." Chase waves to the bartender. "We'll take shots of whiskey."

"It's going to take more than shots to fix it." Cam's voice holds a resignation I've become way too familiar with.

"It's a start," Chase says.

The bartender sets the drinks before us and walks away. We clink our glasses and throw them back.

"So, your wives hate you..."

"Shut up, Chase. You get bossed around by a woman who is not even your girlfriend."

Chase leans on the bar. "Jesus, Cam. You're nasty when you fight with Adri."

"We're not fighting. Just disagreeing."

"Cut the shit," his brother says. "I'm not Bron. You don't have to reassure me. I know you two weirdos will make it."

Cam scratches his neck. "We're fine. It's just...."

I shrug. "You can't seem to do anything right and she forgets things but blames you for not knowing them."

Cam nods. "Pretty fucking much."

The next round, we drink to that. By the next, we are laughing hard at how incompetent our wives think we are, how much we're yelled at, and how many times Chase rolls his eyes at our issues. He asks for another round and my phone starts ringing. I almost hit ignore but that will only piss off Simone and she would keep calling.

"I'm out having a good time for the first time in forever. Whatever it is, let it wait."

"Grayson, your guy in Mexico has made contact. Alice wants to make a deal with you."

My hand stills on my drink. "Are you serious? This is great."

"I know, right. Apparently, pretty faces do you no good in jail. She wants you to get her out of Mexico."

I side swipe her sarcasm. "What is she willing to give us?"

Simone chuckles. "Everything. She is going to tell you about her accomplice and—"

The words "tell all," on the TV screen ticker, followed by my name, catch my eye.

The Daily to release tell all interview with Spencer Grayson's mother-in-law. Among the revelations is Winter's father's identity, her problems with addiction, and how her daughter continually ignores her desperate calls for help.

"Mother fucker."

In my next breath, I'm running out of the bar.

Winter

"This was a good idea," Adri says, popping a piece of fried chicken in her mouth. "I needed you girls and Royal Farms chicken. So bad. No one tell Cam. What happens tonight stays here."

I shake my head. "Agreed and ditto. I've been getting the feeling lately that Gray can use a vacation from me."

"Please. Both of those guys are too in love with the two of you. I think you're just cooped up here, Win, and it's only normal if you resent him a little."

Resent him?

That does sound possible. I am mostly annoyed when he gets to go anywhere and when he gets back. I wish I could come and go as I pleased. "I miss my independence. You know how I used to be. I hate being trapped anywhere. It brings back bad memories."

My friends stare at me with sad eyes.

"I'm sorry," Adri says, dabbing at her eyes with the same napkin she just wiped her mouth with.

"Don't be. I don't want you to pity me. I turned out okay. It's just not being able to do what I want that brings it all back."

"Have you heard from your mom? Is she back in Massachusetts?" Adri asks.

I shake my head. "I'm sure she'll give another interview to the *Daily Mail* when her money runs out. I'm not giving her shit, not even my attention, while she's still talking about Grayson and me."

"That's the best thing to do." Lauren swipes a cookie and hands it over. "You don't need that shit right now. Avy will be here soon and only good vibes for our princess."

I smile. I pat my big belly. "Six more weeks."

Adri smiles. "And then six more and her future husband will be born."

"What if she's not into boys?" Lauren asks.

"Then Cam will get his wish and I'll have another baby. Wait...that may not be Cam's wish after this one." She giggles and the two of us join in.

"I'm sure Cam will want more kids," I reassure her. "How's the nursery going?"

"That's what caused today's fight. Ollie's already finished the built-ins and is going to start painting but Cam didn't tell Marli, his assistant, to order the paint. He also didn't tell her about the basin for the bathroom and we still don't have furniture for the baby's room. He insisted on using his decorator and then he doesn't have the stuff when we need it."

"I had a similar fight with Gray. Yesterday, I was flip-flopping over Bradley class. You know? I was just thinking out loud and it's like they stop listening when the clothes come off. I clearly said that we were still going to do the class before we fell asleep and then today it's like I canceled life. He didn't show up to anything."

Lauren holds up a hand. "Wait a minute. Clothes come off. I thought you guys couldn't…"

I bite my lip but the smile still breaks through. "We find our ways…"

Adri claps. "Wait. And you expect him to remember stuff after that?"

Lauren laughs. "I'm happy for you. You guys just got married. Something needs to be going down in that bedroom before Avy puts the full brakes on."

"In more ways than one. I'm having a C-section. Six weeks of nada."

"Eh. You'll be too in love with that baby to care. You'll see. The minute you see her, it's like nothing and no one else exists. I spent my whole pregnancy so sad about Cam's and my breakup and his dad's threats but when Bron was born…poof. Remember that, Lo?"

The look they exchange is so warm and familiar. They went through it together.

"Our Bron was so beautiful from day one and our Avelyn will be too. I can't wait to meet her."

The flutter in my chest is strong and I smile. "I can't wait, either. I'm going to kiss her and hug her so much. I'm going to tell her ten thousand times again how much I love her and how much we want her."

"I knew it," Adri gushes. "I knew that baby was going to win you over. You're a natural-born mom. The way you love your students and are there for them. You're so encouraging, and they adore you. Bron and Ayla can't stop talking about you and your talent."

"I'll need all your advice. You and Ollie are raising perfect little girls. I want my Avelyn to be like them, fearless." Every word stomps over the fear looming at bay.

"She will. She will have the best auntie ever. Me." Lauren points at herself.

"I know that." We high-five each other. "I'm a little scared about this whole process. I wish I wasn't so quick to get mad and since I can't paint, my triggers are extra sensitive. I need to stay calm and relaxed. It just doesn't seem to happen all the time."

"You're human. You are doing just fine. We can't control pregnancies. Bron was like two weeks late. It was exhausting. I was so heavy I could barely move. It was still during the school year so my mom wasn't around. Poor Lo got to hear me complain the whole time."

Lauren laughs. "I lost ten pounds from walking with her so she could have a good labor. Everywhere we went. Everyone was nice to Adri because she was super pregnant and to me because I was such a patient saint."

Adri throws a piece of her biscuit at her, which she catches and throws back.

"I don't think I'll get to walk. The doctor is worried too much activity will send me into early labor."

Adri shrugs. "I'll come sit with you during that time. I doubt anyone would want to put up with me then."

"Actually," Lauren says. "I'll come over and we can sort out my new inventory. I'll be putting together styling boards for my clients' summer wardrobes."

"That sounds like fun. You need to start styling pregos and new moms. I'll need help after the baby. We'll have to start walking."

"We'll bring Avy in the stroller."

I can almost see it. The wind blowing by the water and my baby as I push her along like all the moms I see.

The movie we were not watching ends and Adri runs to the bathroom. I grab my phone, looking for messages from Grayson. There are none. But there's a familiar alert with my name on it. I tell myself not to click on it. I really don't need to know, but my finger is already ghosting and pressing over it.

Winter Grayson's mother Denise reveals her father's name.

My pulse sets off and my hand presses against my chest. I click on the article and dig in, skimming through the words "married professor," "one-night stand," and "he didn't want to know about the baby." *He gave me money to go away and I swore to keep his secret but I am done protecting a man that didn't do right by me and a daughter who refuses to help me.*

His name is Julio Alvarez and he lives in the Bronx. There are photos of Julio with his wife and children. And it's his daughters' faces that do me in. I can see myself in them. My eyes are theirs and I finally know where I got my curls from. The phone slips from my hand onto the floor.

"Winter? What's wrong?" Lauren kneels on the floor in front of me.

I point to my phone on the floor and she picks it up.

My heart is beating so fast I think it's going to break through my chest. "All my life, she wouldn't tell me. And now she tells a fucking magazine. For money? What kind of person does that?"

I stand up and my friend is not far behind. "Come sit down. Please."

"I don't want to sit down." I wave her away. "I've been ignoring everything, all her interviews, her so-called begging for forgiveness, her reveals, her grandstanding outside this building. But look at where she hits me—"

My breath hitches.

"It's okay. Come on. Let's breathe and talk about this. Think about your health and the baby's. Don't let her get to you."

The baby. *Avelyn.* I need to calm down. I let her pull me to the chair again.

"What's going on? I heard screaming," Adri rushes back in the room.

"Her mom did another article."

Adri sighs. "I know what it's like to have a toxic parent. All three of us do. We can't let that jeopardize what we have."

"I know. I know. I'm sorry, I just need to—"

Pain shoots through, low in my belly, and cuts the words. It rocks my entire body and I'm helpless to do anything but to open my mouth and brace against the first thing I can find, the seat of the couch.

"Winter?"

I can't tell which of my friends is calling my name because just as the pain is ebbing, another wave of pain rips a gasp from my throat. And I know. I don't know how I know but I do.

I manage to say the words. "I think I'm in labor."

My words only make it worse. It's like they summon the monster to life as undiluted agony wracks through my body, stabbing through my underbelly like a jagged piece of glass. It throws me off balance but my friends are there, holding me so I don't fall.

Time drags like a video in slow motion. One filled with so much pain I can't hear anything but my torment. The attack is coming from all sides, a needle to my lower back, pressure that tries to tear at my hips. There's so much going on I don't know what to do or how to brace against it. I can't even help my friends as they try to help me.

They're running around, looking for my things and then we're off to the elevator. I lean against the wall and close my eyes. The move-ment makes me nauseous and I think of the Bradley classes and breathe. It's shallow because shallow is all I can manage.

The elevator bell dings and my eyes fly open. The doors open and we step out just in time. Our car is pulling over and I see heaven because I need to sit down. I can't stand anymore. Grayson flies out of the backseat. He doesn't ask, just throws his arms around me and helps me into the back of the SUV. I bury my face into his shoulder as the assault on my body continues. But he's here now, everything will be okay.

33

Winter

"You're almost there," Grayson tells me for the umpteenth time.

But almost where? I've been lying in a hospital room, shifting from side to side, for the most part of a torturous hour since Dr. Sahiner decided the C-section has to be done tonight. Even if I could move, I don't have the strength. I've been pricked and prodded. I've had so many fingers in my vagina tonight, that Sister Aveline would order me to do twenty *Our Fathers* and sixty *Hail Marys*.

I suppress the where-the-fuck-are-we-going at the tip of my tongue and grind my teeth. I'm in so much pain, I can't even fear the C-section or the needles. I just want the pain to stop.

"Winter?"

"Fine," I manage to grunt.

He nods. "Good. You're—"

"Doing good? Almost there? Being strong? Got it."

His head rears back, his hand stilling on my arm, two inches above the IV incision. He blinks a few times and then grimaces. "I'm sorry. I don't know how else to help."

229

The door opens to Dr. Sahiner. "We're going to have to go in and get this little girl. The anesthesiologist is on the way to apply the epidural. When she gets here, we will sit you up and you will bend forward so she can administer the pain medication. You'll receive two shots. The first is a local anesthetic to numb your skin. The second will be with a larger needle and that one is injected directly into your spinal fluid."

"Is that going to be painful?" Grayson asks.

"She will feel uncomfortable pressure but not real pain. She's in a lot more pain right now." She looks at me. "The whole process, from prep to you lying down again is about fifteen to twenty minutes. It's important for you to remain still and calm through it. In only a little while, you'll be holding that precious little crocus in your arms."

Grayson turns to me with a smile. He presses a kiss to my forehead. "We almost have her."

His lips are so warm and I try to hold on to that. But another wave of pain knocks the air out of me and I sag against him.

"Let's count this one out. Winter, we count, you breathe," Dr. Sahiner says. "Inhale one...two...three...four...five...six. Exhale all the tension one...two...three...four...five...six...seven...eight."

Grayson joins in the count and so does the nurse. We go through it several times, all together. I close my eyes and go with it. Somehow, breathing gets a little easier.

When I open my eyes again, there's a woman in scrubs next to the doctor. They're going over the folder I've become way too familiar with. She lifts her gaze, smiles and offers her hand to me. "Hi, I'm Doctor Vianna and I'm your anesthesiologist. We're going to get going soon. Do you have any questions for me?"

I shake her hand. "I just need you to make it stop."

She nods, her eyes full of understanding. "Of course. We're going to take care of you but there are some risks. Do you want to hear about them?"

Hell no, just fucking shoot the shit into my veins. I start to say no but Grayson nods.

"Well, there is a risk of bleeding and infection, but here that risk is minimized, as we disinfect that area of your skin and all our instruments are sterilized." She points at a nearby tray. "There's a special kind of headache called a spinal headache that some women develop within twenty-four hours of the injection. If your head starts to hurt, let us know immediately and we can treat it. There's also a risk for nerve damage. It's very rare for it to happen because we inject the medication right below where the spinal cord ends. Do you understand all of these?"

I nod.

"Do you have any questions about them?"

"No." I don't even want to think about any of it.

"One more thing. Sometimes the epidural doesn't work as well as it should. If you feel pain at any point after the first twenty to thirty minutes, you need to let us know and we can administer something stronger." Dr. Vianna nods to the nurse. "Let's get started."

Dr. Sahiner flanks me on one side and Grayson in the other. The nurse helps with my legs and the three of them guide me into a sitting position on the edge of the bed. The nurse coaches me into the right position with my shoulders hunched and my upper back on a slight curve. Grayson's hands are on my shoulders, steadying me.

The anesthesiologist parts my gown from behind. "I'm going to talk to you and tell you everything I'm doing so you know. The first thing I'm going to do is clean up your back with disinfectant. It's going to feel a little cold and I have to do it three times."

It's like ice brushing over my skin. Her fingers run down my spine and she asks me to curve my back some more and then to hold still.

"Now, this is the most painful part. It's the local anesthetic into your skin. Are you having a contraction now?"

"No." *And thank God for that.*

She counts to three and proceeds to inject what feels like pure fire into my flesh. It hurts like hell and I hiss. Then the familiar pressure begins to build. "I'm having a contraction."

The pain intensifies and then there's pressure that threatens to shatter my spine. My hands ball up in Grayson's shirt and when I think I can't take it anymore, the pain clicks off.

And everything goes black.

I wake to pats on the cheek, Grayson's ashen face, and his ragged breath on my face. I can't hear what he's saying. Have I gone deaf? My eyes ping-pong everywhere and I can't seem to focus. His hand cups my chin and forces me to look into his eyes.

"You're okay. You passed out but you're okay. You're back now." His voice is thick as his eyes are huge.

I swallow a few times and it hits me that I'm no longer in pain. There's also a flurry of movement around me and one nurse is holding onto the IV bag and they begin to roll me away.

"We're moving you to the birth room. We have everything we need there and just in case..." Doctor Sahiner says.

"In case of what?" I barely recognize my own voice.

"In case anything goes wrong, but we don't anticipate it," she explains.

The nurse places the IV bag at my side. "Don't you worry. You're at St. Raymond's. He's the patron saint of expectant mothers. He always protects the ladies who come here."

I lift a silent prayer to St. Raymond to be with us today but when I look at Gray, the world opens. "It's almost over and we get to hold her."

I concentrate on him. He's really all I need right now. Him telling me I'm strong and I can do this and just being there. I'm just going to listen to him.

I exhale, this time without agony. I don't rattle, even at the pressure of the blade sliding across my lower belly, or when they pull my flesh apart. I know when they reach inside and my breath stalls when I don't hear cries or noise. That makes my heart speed.

My gaze jumps straight to Gray's as my heart leaps to my throat. It thumps loud in my ears and for seconds that's all I hear. My mouth drifts open but the loud cries break our stare and I whip my head as Dr. Sahiner comes around the blanket with the little slimy baby in her hands.

"She's so beautiful mom and she wants to meet you."

I'm dazed as they pull my gown down and place her on my chest.

She's tiny but her cries are so strong. She's trembling and yelling so loud and I just don't know what to do.

Gray's fingers ghost over her back, so gentle and loving. I look into his eyes and there's so much wonder there. "We have her, Winter. She's here."

He kisses my lips but his eyes never leave her.

I touch her back in tiny circles until she's calmed down some. The nurse tries to pick her up. My right hand shoots out to still hers.

"It's okay, Mom. We're just going to clean her and tag her for her security and yours. Dad will have to come with me for that."

Dad? Adrenaline rushes straight to my head. He can't leave. I begin to shake my head and grab on to Gray's hand. "Don't—"

"I know. I know. I won't let anything happen to her. I'll be right back, my love." He gives me a quick kiss and I have no choice but to let him go. I want to beg him not to leave me alone but he's already walking away. And I feel it all, the way they place my organs back in place. The pressure of the needle weaving through my skin.

But I don't feel pain.

"You did a great job," Dr. Sahiner says from behind the sheet.

"Yes, you were great," her assistant echoes.

A great job? Is that what this was?

But I don't feel great.

If I was so great at it, why am I alone? It's my childhood all over again. Alone with the staff because no one's here for me. Just for her, for the baby.

And as I look over at my husband, already in love with the baby in his arms, I can't help it...

...I don't feel anything at all.

***

Grayson

My eyes don't know where to go anymore. My gaze continues to move back and forth between my sleeping wife and our daughter. Avelyn is on a bassinet a couple of feet from Winter. She's swaddled tighter than a burrito at Taco Fiesta. Her face is turned in the direction of her mom's bed, her lips puckered and her arms on either side of her head.

A tiny little angel that causes a big uproar when she's hungry or uncomfortable. She has a temper. I smile, with my ears still echoing from the last time she was awake. She raged through the night, her hands bundled into fists, her whole body shaking with every scream.

"Oh, good, Mom's still sleeping."

I turn around to look at the head nurse, whose gaze is on Winter.

"Yes," I answer. "Is that normal? She's been sleeping a lot."

She nods. "She and her body went through a lot the past couple of days. She woke up in a lot of pain after you left and the baby had a hard time latching on. After the feeding, we gave her a strong painkiller. It's easy for her body to give out like this. Plus, you know the golden rule, if the baby sleeps, you sleep."

Shit, I wasn't here when she woke up.

"Oh." I was only gone for about an hour.

The nurse checks Winter's vitals and then the baby's. "I'll be back in an hour. Call me if you need anything."

I nod and resume watching my girls. My phone vibrates. It's a text from Simone.

The old man wants to strike a deal. He'll give you back all his actions in Grayson Global and Astrid's part of the fortune, in exchange for you and Winter staying quiet about Stephen's involvement.

The he-can-go-fuck-himself is at the tip of my fingers. He hurt us. But just then my gaze drifts to my baby. She wouldn't be here if all that had not happened. I wouldn't have met her mother.

But it's wrong and he should pay. I just can't seem to hold on to thoughts of revenge while staring at her. Avelyn stirs and I rub my hand over her belly, softly, like I saw the nurse do earlier. She stills again.

I turn around to check on her mother and find her intent gaze on me. "Hey, you're awake."

THE WINTER OF MY LOVE

I move next to her bed and bend to kiss her but at the same time, she scrubs a hand over her face and my lips land on her knuckles.

"How are you feeling?" I take her hand.

"I'm fine."

She sounds everything but fine. Her voice is flat, as it's been for hours and her skin is sallow. I wish she didn't have to go through so much.

"Can I get you anything to eat or drink?"

She shakes her head. "They gave me broth earlier."

"I'm sorry I missed that."

She's staring beyond me to the window. "Don't worry about it."

"I should have been here. I just went home to shower and get some stuff. I didn't think you would wake." She doesn't say anything. I kneel by her. "Are you sure you're okay?"

"I'm just tired, Grayson. I'm going to go back to sleep. She'll be up soon to eat."

"When you wake up, we'll have to talk. Bryce has made contact. He wants to negotiate so we don't release his son's involvement."

Her eyebrows knit together. "Negotiate? What is there to negotiate?"

I shrug. "He's offering us all their stock in Grayson Global and Astrid's fortune, which would go to you and Avelyn."

She stares for a while. "He gets to go scot free after what he did to us in exchange for money?"

Her cutting tone is effective, like a double-sided blade. "We don't have to take it. I'm just keeping you in the loop of what is being said and asked."

"Sounds to me like you're considering it. You can do what you want. I don't want any of the money." She turns her face away from me and just like that, our conversation is over.

I brush off the burn and touch her shoulder. "I'm not making a decision without you. I'll wait 'til you feel better."

"You don't need to wait for me. Do what works better for you." She doesn't even bother to turn around as she shoots the words my way.

Her shoulders relax and soon so does her breathing. I don't know what to make of today, of this conversation, of the fact that she can go to sleep like I'm not even in the room.

But she's tired. I get that. If only it weren't for this nagging thought.

"She's back asleep," Dr. Sahiner says from the door. "You should do the same. Go home and get some shut eye. The nurse will call you if she needs you."

"I don't want her waking up and me not being here again. She doesn't like hospitals."

The doctor smiles. "I think she's learned to manage. She doesn't bat an eyelash anymore when one of us comes in. You'll both deal better with each other when you're more rested. You should enjoy every chance you have to sleep because we are sending you guys home tomorrow."

I get to take them home. At home, everything will be better.

I don't know if it's because she told me I was tired enough times, but the weight is at my shoulders and behind my neck. I kiss my daughter on the forehead and then do the same with my wife. Neither stirs.

From the car, I call Simone. "Set up a meeting with Bryce and Stephen."

"Hello to you too, Grayson, and got it."

I sigh. "Sorry. Thank you and let me know when it's done."

"Are you okay?" she asks. "You were over the moon less than two hours ago."

"I'm tired. I guess yesterday and today are catching up with me."

"Did Winter not pay attention to you?"

Fuck. She's way too perceptive.

"She's too tired. Both her and baby were asleep. I barely got to talk to her and the little we talked was tense." The silence is almost deafening, and I need to cut the conversation. "Listen—"

"Are you going to tell me or what?"

I rub my forehead. "It's nothing. I told her about Stephen and she told me to do what I want. Let's just say she's not keen on the idea of a deal."

"You blame her? He messed up her life."

"Thanks a lot, Simone."

"Oh, shut up." I bet her hand is waving me away like a pesky fly. "I meant what he did to you both is a nightmare. It ended up great but that's still a crime. And you know she is very 'by the book.'"

Why can't I just be happy with Avelyn and Winter? Why can't we just enjoy this time? "I don't want to be responsible for Bryce's death. Astrid loved her father and Stephen is his only living child, weasel that he is. But I don't want to risk my marriage. I don't want Winter to hate me."

"Don't be an idiot, Grayson. She loves you."

"She doesn't seem happy," I blurt out. And the air is heavy, like I barfed a boulder into it.

"She can't be happy yet. It was a difficult pregnancy, a difficult delivery, way too many emotions, and I'm sure she is in a lot of pain at times."

I shake my head like she can see me. "You didn't see her. It's like she would rather I wasn't there."

"People think that babies immediately mean rainbows and unicorns and soft music. It doesn't happen like that for every woman and even when it does, it doesn't happen with every pregnancy..." She pauses. "Trust me on that one. Go home and rest. I'll set up the meeting for next week."

I nod and hang up. At home, I don't bother with food and simply drop into the bed. My last thought is of Winter's vacant gaze. But tomorrow, she comes home and I get to start helping her get back to happy.

34

Winter

"Your husband is on his way up." The nurse smiles at me through the reflection in the mirror. "We're going to miss this little angel."

I smile at her as much as I can. "Thank you so much for everything you've done for us. You, Doctor Sahiner, and the whole staff were amazing."

She turns to Avelyn and starts wrapping her back up in her swaddle blanket. I go back to combing through my tangled curls to the sound of her hums and baby talk.

"You're just the best baby, aren't you? And you have to come back and visit us."

Pain shoots through my incision and I bite the inside of my cheek. I breathe through it, finish tying my hair into a chignon, and peer behind me through the mirror. The nurse is staring at me. I suppress the wince and the sigh. I don't want to let on about how much pain I am in. I don't want them to have any reason to keep me here.

I need out of here, away from the constant prying into how I feel. I can't keep schooling my face and I hate the lingering looks I get because I am not a smiling mom. I don't know what the hell they want from me.

I told her to keep Avelyn by my side all night. She wouldn't stop crying when they put her in the bassinet and only stopped when she was next to me. I don't know why. I don't coo or tell her how beautiful she is like everyone else. *And she is.* She's the most beautiful thing in the world. She looks so much like Grayson...and me. I can see so much of me in her face and that little mouth.

She won't even be happy with her dad for long. *Just me.*

"She wants her mommy," the nurse said last night, inadvertently twisting a knife in my chest.

Avelyn wants me and I want only to be alone. I don't want anyone talking to me or to hear her cries or the thoughts that whisper she is better off without me. I can't even do the basic things like feed her without pain.

I spent the whole night with her next to me, soft skin rubbing against my arm, and my eyes wide open. I couldn't sleep. I was afraid to crush her. I just watched her all night, the way her little chest rose and fell, and the pouty movements of her mouth.

Even as I leave the bathroom and head for the bed, her face is turned my way. And I see myself there, too, the way my eyes used to stay on my mom every time they took me away from her.

The nurse looks up at me, too. Her smile is soft and so warm. It makes my whole chest tighten. I want to look away but can't because she's staring right into my eyes, reading me.

"The swaddling helps keep her calm but now that you're going home, there will be times when she's just restless or not able to latch on right away. It's important that you breathe and stay calm. There's nothing wrong with you just walking away for a few minutes if you're feeling too overwhelmed. She will cry but that's just her only way to complain. She will be okay. She won't be calm unless you are."

I nod. It's all I can do because she can see it. She can see I'm not good at this. She knows I'm not cut out for it. I'm my mother's daughter. And I hear her now, clearly.

I went home with you and I still felt nothing. So, I started finding things that made me feel me feel happy, angry, high.

My heart starts to hammer against my chest. I hate her so much for those words. I banned her from my life and I'm just like her. How long until I start needing something other than this pain?

"You're going to be just fine. You have a husband who adores you and your baby. The two of you have a lot of help to make it through." The nurse chuckles softly. "You have wonderful Aunt Millie, who's been calling to check on you, and your friends seem very involved."

I nod again. Adri and Lauren have been by a couple of times. It was devastating to watch the way they held my baby with tenderness I can't feel or emulate.

The walls of my chest begin to push together and I close my eyes for a second, summoning the will to smile.

I can't stay here.

"Who's ready to go home?"

My eyes fly open and Dr. Sahiner is at the door with Grayson. The smile splits his face and my heart. He's holding the car seat we spent hours arguing about only a month ago. He's happy and I want to try harder. *For him. For her.*

He crosses the room in less time than it takes me to exhale and kisses me, soundly enough that I can taste his joy, along with every other flavor of feeling he can incite in me. "My girls are coming home."

I don't get to say anything because he moves over to kiss the baby on the forehead. The imprint of his lips on mine hasn't dried but it's the reverence when he bends toward her, the absolute adoration in his eyes, that knots my throat and makes it harder to breathe.

I need to get out of here.

I want to run but I can't. The doctor, the nurse, Grayson would all think I was crazy or that something's wrong and they would keep me here, locked up like the monster I am.

I pray, asking God to let me get through this.

I channel my interviews with the lady from Social Services when I was a kid. *Smile, engage, but don't talk more than you have to.* I fix a smile on my face and I nod through the doctor's instructions. I'm so intent on keeping my smile that I'm barely aware of her explaining about the services for moms and telling us about pamphlets in a bag.

"Do you have any questions?" she asks.

"No," I say.

Grayson's mouth drifts open and then closes. There's something he wants to say but he shakes his head. "Let's get out of here."

The nurse helps him place Avelyn in the car seat and we thank her. Then, we're off. In the elevator, the doctor is still talking to me.

"Call or text here at any time if you need me. I have kids and grandkids of my own. Between work and family, there is nothing you can tell me that I haven't heard." Dr. Sahiner's smile is so sweet, I can almost feel everything is okay.

"Thank you."

The weight of Grayson's stare is on the side of my face but I don't turn to meet his gaze. *Everything's going to be okay.*

The car is waiting for us. The hospital doors slide open and I step out of the building, expecting to breathe easier, but my world starts to get smaller. The car door closing feels like a prison. Next to me, Avelyn's asleep. And I'm so jealous. I wish I was unconscious. That there wasn't an elephant sitting on my chest.

Grayson turns around from the front seat. "Are you okay? You're pretty quiet."

"I'm fine."

Except I'm not and my breath is wheezing out.

"You sure?"

I don't answer him. I can't. My heart is pounding faster and my hands start to tremble. I'm trying to keep it all in but he's turned all the way around.

My mouth opens and I blurt it out. "I can't do this, Grayson."

"Can't do what?" he asks.

"This." I gesture around him, the baby and me. "I want to go home, to my place in Patterson Park. I need to be alone. I need to think. I can't think."

Grayson

At first, I don't think I heard her well, but she's rocking in place. Her hands are clutching onto her purse so tightly. My stomach starts to churn but I manage a low tone when I speak to her. "Winter, you're overwhelmed. After you get some rest, you'll feel better."

She shakes her head hard and adamant. "No. I can't think with all of you around. And there's no air. I need to breathe. I need to go. I can't be here."

She cracks the backseat window and inhales.

Jesus. What the fuck is going on?

"You can't go to the Patterson Park apartment. That place has been closed up and you've had major surgery. It's not safe for you and Avelyn there. Let's just go to our house. We can give you some alone time. But let's talk about this when we get there."

"No," she says loud enough to draw a protest from the baby. Then, her gaze flies to Avelyn and when she looks back at me, her eyes are huge and full of unshed tears. "I can't do it. I'm no good. I just need to go home."

She starts to sob and my heartbeat explodes. My stomach is so tight it's painful, my whole body is wracked. *Should I tell the driver to take us back to the hospital? Should I call the doctor?* This is so wrong. So fucked. I knew she wasn't happy, but I thought she was just in pain.

"Please. Please. Just let me go."

It breaks something inside me the way she puts her head down and keeps crying, softly but strong enough for her shoulders to shake. I turn to look at the driver, who has stopped the car and is staring at me. He's waiting for me to tell him what to do.

"We have to go home and get your key." *Good, that's good.* I have time to convince her. I can get Aunt Millie to take Avelyn and I can just spend some time talking to her.

She shakes her head but doesn't lift it up. "I have the key."

My stomach drops and I swear it drags all my insides down with it. She has the key. The key she hasn't used in months. She has it with her. Is this what she planned all along?

"Why do you have that key with you?"

"It's on my key chain." But she doesn't look at me as she says it.

I swallow and look at my driver. I try for casual. I don't want to show him how desperate I am.

"You heard the lady. Let's take her to Patterson Park." The crack in my voice unleashes shame all over me. I'm weak but I don't want to see her like this. I don't want to force this on her.

I turn around and look out at the road. I can't look at her. I can't even look at my daughter because I don't know what this is. Her mother wants to go home. She can't breathe around us.

My phone beeps with an incoming text from Lauren.

Are you almost here? Aunt Millie wants to make sure the food is warm.

She's at my house to help settle Winter and now Winter won't be there. Just Avelyn and me. It was what I planned at the beginning, but after months of a different dream, I can't see that as a possibility. It's noon time, so there's a little traffic on the streets. People are on their lunch breaks and congesting the Inner Harbor area.

We're on our way to drop her off at her apt in Patterson P. She wants to go stay there.

Lauren calls but I send the call to voicemail. I can't say this shit out loud.

You should head to the apartment. She shouldn't be alone.

Her reply is swift, as always. *On my way.*

I'm thankful that she doesn't make me explain. But heat explodes through my body and I have to grind my teeth not to scream out loud. *Why the fuck am I still thinking of her?* She's leaving us. There's a little girl in the backseat that won't have her mom because she's decided she doesn't want this. And what about us?

There's no us, you idiot. She hangs around with a key to her old place in her purse. My hands ball so hard into fists.

I don't hear any noise from the backseat and I don't turn around. I can't. I just need to get through these next few minutes. I need to let her go. We don't need her. I chant that in my head for four miles. I have my daughter and she needs me. I can't worry about someone who doesn't want us.

But my chest tightens more and more as we turn onto her street and move onto her block. My throat thickens and tightens but I swallow it. I won't give my tears to another woman who leaves me.

She's leaving me.

The car stops and I jump out. I don't know what I want to do, keep her from getting out, beg her not to go, or destroy the fucking building so she can't go inside. So she has no choice but to come home.

In the end, I do none of those things. I get out of the vehicle, slam the SUV door closed and I open her door. "Let me help you."

"No, I can manage." She still can't look in my eyes.

That sets me off. "I insist."

"Sir, I'll help her," Franklin says. The concern smeared over his face.

He unbuckles his seatbelt, but I stop him from getting out with a hand up. I want to walk her to the door. I want her to look at my face before I walk away.

"I'll help *my wife* inside." I throw the word with force, hoping it hurts her as much as it hurts me to utter it. "Give me the key."

I take her arm and she lets me. We walk to the door like nothing's wrong, like this is not the end of something. I unlock it and am proud that my wrist doesn't even shake. I see her inside.

We stand there, with the door open, only the noise of the street behind us.

"Look at me, Winter."

She does. Her eyes are red and she doesn't even look like herself. And that's good. That's what I want to remember her like in the end.

"Gray—"

I shake my head. "You don't need to say anything. You didn't want this from the beginning and like I once said, there is no shame in that. Well, there is. You got my hopes up only to leave me, like my mother did. You're turning your back on Avelyn, like your mother did to you.

But I get it. Don't worry. In the interest of not putting our daughter through what you went through and what I spent my whole childhood praying for, don't bother to come back. We can manage without you."

Her face goes pale and her gaze drops to the floor.

She doesn't care enough to fight back. My throat thickens and I can't stand here anymore.

I turn around and rush to the car. I get in the back seat, sitting in the spot she left vacant. The baby stirs when I close the door and I reach to touch her swaddled body. There are heavy layers of clothing between our skins but that seems to calm her.

Franklin drives us home. My phone is on my lap. It doesn't ring like I hope. The screen stays black and blank.

35

Grayson

I rub another circle into my daughter's back as I bounce lightly on my feet. Another two days of this and I can stop my Tuesday leg workouts. The hours since midnight have been marked by her cries. I hold her raging little body in awe and heartbreak. How does someone so tiny scream so loud and why can't her father fix this? I've rocked her, stood with her, put warm compresses on her belly, even sang to her.

She only slept after Aunt Millie went into Winter's bag and pulled out the night gown she'd worn at the hospital. I was angry, sick, and terrified by how quickly she calmed down and how fast she went to sleep after. She wants her.

The woman who left us. The woman who has yet to call. The same woman I curse every time I remember her.

Avelyn bellows as if to remind me she's still pissed off and I can't do anything about it.

"It's okay. Daddy's here."

She bellows again and I chuckle because I could swear it's the baby version of, "Who cares?"

"Someone's got a temper."

"The doctor is on her way up," Aunt Millie announces, walking into the nursery. In her hand is yet another cup of coffee, which she places next to my chair. I want nothing more than to tear into that cup but I'll wait for the doctor. I don't want to put Avelyn down when she's screaming bloody murder.

The doctor said on the phone that crying won't hurt her but God, I just can't let her. I feel so impotent. I can't even make my own baby stop crying. How am I supposed to raise her and help her? And what if she's sick?

There's a knock on the door and our maid shows Dr. Sahiner in.

"Thank you for coming. I think something's wrong with her."

"Well, it's not her lungs," she says, chuckling. "Give her to me. Let me examine her."

I don't like that she's making light of this, but I give her the baby anyway. She gives her back a few rubs and as if by magic, manages to calm her down some. Then, she places Avelyn on the changing table to examine her. She pulls out her stethoscope and the second the chest piece touches my daughter's skin, the bellowing resumes.

The doctor chuckles and I grind my teeth so I don't scream at her. This is not funny. Avelyn's a baby and if she's crying it's because something's wrong. Babies don't cry just because. No one should be laughing at her. And she doesn't have her…no, I'm not going to think about her mother. She's not thinking about us.

Winter doesn't know the hell she's left us in. But we don't need her. We will figure this out. I go stand on the other side of the changing table, focusing on what the doctor is doing.

"She's okay, Grayson. There's nothing physically wrong with her, except I think this little princess is extra hungry. How is she doing with the donor milk?"

"She drinks it but doesn't finish it."

"It's not her mommy's milk," Aunt Millie says and doesn't even bat an eyelash when I try to eviscerate her with my eyes. "It's the truth."

"I believe it," the doctor cosigns.

I roll my eyes. "You're a medical professional. You can't believe in that mumbo jumbo."

"I'm also a mother and grandmother. Babies know their mothers. I bet you she's soothed by anything that smells like Winter."

My gut twists up. I want to disagree but I can't. It makes me want to punch a wall. The one thing my daughter needs is the one thing I can't give her. I can't make her mother want to be here with us.

"There's got to be something else that we can do to help her." My voice is tight and pained and I hate myself for it. Avy is a baby but I'm not. I need to tend to her pain and forget my feelings.

"Mom will come back. It's only a matter of time. She's scared and there's some trauma from the past few months. She just needs to clear her head and heart. That's what the baby—"

I raise a hand. "I don't want to hear it. If she wanted to work things out, she could have done it here. Running away doesn't do anything for any of us."

Dr. Sahiner shakes her head. "Sometimes it's not that easy. She's scared and upset and recovering from major surgery. You couldn't begin to imagine what's going through her head. You interrupted me when I was talking about the baby blues, post-partum. It manifests in different ways. Don't close yourself up because you're angry with her. Keep your mind and the door open so she can see her."

The blood rushes to my head. "The only person keeping Winter from Avelyn is herself."

"Are you sure? If she were to knock on that door right now, would you let her in?"

I laugh now, loud enough to rattle the baby out of her cries. "She doesn't need to knock. There's a key to this house on the same key chain she kept for the one to her place."

My tone is cutting and both the doctor and Aunt Millie stare at me with sad eyes and something else. Maybe disappointment or disgust. I guess they hate it that I'm angry. They're not the ones who got left, my daughter and I are. "Excuse me. I'm going to take a shower."

The doctor clears her throat. "Grayson, I'm sorry. I can't begin to imagine what you're going through and don't mean to minimize it. I just want you to stay open, give Winter a little longer. I know she'll come back."

"I—"

She stops me with a shake of her head. "—just something to chew on. Go take a shower and try to relax. We're going to try to soothe this little one but remember, you can't calm her down if you're not calm yourself. A baby can feel how rattled you are."

I nod. "Thank you."

I leave the bathroom door open and Avelyn's screams follow me there. After a while they manage to calm her down, but they still echo in my head. What the hell am I going to do? I will give her mother some more time but I can't stand to see her like that. If Winter doesn't come back, I'm going to have to beg her and offer her whatever it takes to at least give Avelyn some love until she is weaned off. She needs her and not me, so I will do whatever to make sure my daughter gets what she needs. She doesn't care about money, what the fuck can I offer her?

Winter

My eyes bounce between the crocuses I painted this morning. I've been awake since two in the morning and the only thing that kept me from wailing all night was painting. I feel like hell, every part of me— my incision, my head, my heart, my skin—hurts. All because I heard my baby cry and it brought it all back.

I'm no longer sleeping, so I can't escape the facts. I left her and Grayson and my whole world is messed up. I can't eat or sleep. I gave in and took a painkiller at midnight but I woke up disoriented and weepy at two. I laid in bed, listening to my pain and anguish until I couldn't take it. I got out of bed slowly and found the mini canvases and paint sets I keep around for younger students and used them to paint from my couch.

And all that came to me were crocuses and inside them Avelyn. Her full little mouth. Her sleeping form. Her big eyes and long lashes.

The door lock clicks but I don't move. Lauren has been checking on me. Last night, she only left after I promised to sleep. This time she's not alone. Adri waddles in behind her, her belly so big it blurs all the rest of her.

I bite back a sigh. I didn't want her to come last night but I can't avoid her today. She's here, reminding me of the failure that I am. She is able to keep her baby in her belly until his due date. And she won't freak out and walk away. And through this pregnancy, she has been cool as a Whole Foods cucumber. But she's not here because of that. She's here because she cares. I need to just sit here and keep my mouth shut.

She heads straight to the kitchen with the bag in her hand.

"We brought you some hot tea and breakfast," Lo says.

I take the foam cup from Lauren's hand and all I can do is nod. I can't thank her without crying and I've done enough of that. The last thing I need is for my friends to think they need to call an ambulance and have me committed.

Adri comes back without her bags and sits next to me. "How are you feeling?"

Her voice, so soft, cuts through me like a knife.

I can't look in her eyes so I keep my gaze low. "I'm fine."

"You don't look fine, honey. You don't look like you've slept at all. You didn't eat much. Even my mom's chicken soup is in the fridge, untouched."

I shrug. "Thank you for all that again but I haven't been hungry. I drank some broth."

"Yeah, that's good. You need to eat, though," Lauren says, sitting next to me. "You need your strength and you had surgery."

"I can't."

Lauren clears her throat and looks to the canvases at the other end of the couch. "You've been busy. You were supposed to be resting."

I take a sip of the tea. It's warm and sweet but hard to get down my throat. "I'm sorry. I know I told you I would rest if you went home, but

I had to do something. I was too wired to sleep and there are too many thoughts in my head."

"It's okay." Adri flanks me on the other side. "You can talk to us."

Go away. I shake my head. "I can't. You're the best mom. You don't know what this is. You would never leave your kids."

Adri scoffs. "Are you kidding me? Do you know how many times I wanted to run away when Bron was a baby?"

"But you didn't. You stayed and raised a beautiful girl and you were practically a kid yourself and someone was threatening you and you still managed to get through school and stand by your baby. I left my baby and my husband because I'm no good for this. I'm just like my mother."

I fling my hand and the drink slips from my fingers and lands on the area rug. Lauren drops on the floor to wipe it up. My hands fly to my face to nestle my ragged breath.

"You're not your mother, Winter." Her voice is so calm, like I didn't just scream at her.

"She didn't feel anything for me when I was born. She told me so."

"You love Avy, though." Lauren says. "You've been texting me since yesterday, asking how she's doing. You were gentle with her and you fed her and you kept her by your side all night when she was restless."

And I can still feel her warm skin next to my left breast when I close my eyes and hear her little grunts when I nursed her. "But I still left her. I walked out of the car and didn't even look at her—"

Adri takes my hand in hers. "You got overwhelmed. It's part of being a mom. For some women, the first days are heaven because they had dream pregnancies and they feel this instant love. But your pregnancy was hard. You went through shit that a lot of people couldn't take. Even your birth was traumatic. Excuse the hell out of you, if you're not one hundred percent ready."

"I woke up this morning to her screams." And to her smell deep inside my nostrils. "I couldn't sleep since. I lay in bed until the pain became so real and it won't stop—"

I press my hand to my chest. The tears run down my face, like they had all night. Prayer didn't take this pain that stabs through me with every sob.

"It hurts. My heart and chest hurt, because I left her behind. Why did I listen to Aunt Millie's voicemail? I can still hear Avelyn cry like she's here, next to me. It hurts so bad. I'm an awful person—"

Adri's hands shoot to my chest, pressing on my boobs.

I flinch. "What are you doing?"

"Your heart doesn't hurt, not literally. Your milk is coming in."

"What?"

"Your breasts are engorged. You need to go home to feed that baby. She needs your milk. She doesn't like the donor's milk because it's not sweet like yours and she doesn't get to smell you when she nurses. She doesn't need Grayson or anyone else right now, only her mom, only you, Winter. And you need her."

I can only shake my head because she has to be lying to me.

"Go home and hold her. Put her to your breast and I promise the pain will stop and all those thoughts will calm down and everything will begin to make sense. You both have separation anxiety. You and Avy have been one for a long time and now she cries because she doesn't know where you've gone."

My heart jumps, pushing against the tight walls of my chest. *She's crying for me. All that crying was for me.* I need to go to her. I need to go be her mom. But… "I can't just go back."

Lauren stops mopping the floor. "Why the fuck not? That's your daughter. No one's going to stop you from going in there to be with her."

"Grayson told me not to come back."

Lo shakes her head. "He was mad when he said that. Give him time and you'll work it out. For now, he'll just have to get over it."

I shake my head. I did the same thing his mom did to him. He won't forgive me but I need to go back for my baby. Avelyn needs me. "I'll go."

Adri pats my leg. "Good."

I push off the couch with Lauren's help. I manage to shower and get dressed in an old pair of yoga pants, tank top and hoodie sweatshirt.

My hair's wet but I don't bother to dry it. It would take too much time and I just want to go home.

All the way there, in the back of Adri's nifty new minivan, my nails dig into the back of my hand. My heart is trying to beat its way out of my chest and my stomach is a giant pretzel. I'm trying to concentrate on seeing my daughter, on being with her, and being well. But I can't help but being sickened at the thought of facing Grayson.

He has to hate me and I deserve it.

I try not to think about him.

I can't help it. Even the scenery reminds me of him, the top of his building, where we lived, where he and my daughter are right now, stands like a beacon. A reminder that all I left behind has been so close. I'm scared to death that his hatred is so deep he won't let me in but I'm prepared for anything.

To beg for forgiveness or scream in the lobby until he faces me.

36

Grayson

"Grayson?"

I startle awake, my hands pressing against my chest, but Avelyn's not there. My heart gallops and I look straight down to the floor. She's not there, either. I look around the room, scared as hell. Did someone take her? My gaze lands on the bassinet only a couple of feet away from me. I cough out air. I didn't drop her. No one took her. She's still asleep and I dozed off on the phone.

"Grayson," Simone calls out again.

I pick up my headphones and insert one in my ear. "I dozed off. Then woke up thinking I had the baby in my arms. Which is stupid because I always have her strapped to my chest in that damned contraption."

Simone laughs. "Baby Bjorn. You really are a parent now. You haven't really slept for days, fall asleep during conversations, and wake up afraid something's happened to her."

I rub a hand over my face, over my thick stubble. I need to trim it but that's down on my list after sleeping for more than an hour or two at a time. "When do they start sleeping through the night?"

"It depends. Mine didn't until they had full bellies, which meant putting a little cereal in their milk. You've got a couple of months to go before you can do that. Is the garment still working?"

My lip curls up. That damned nightgown is there whenever she does sleep. I swear it's mocking me right now. "Yes."

"Whatever you have to do to get her to sleep, Grayson."

"Easy for you to say."

"Her mom will come back soon—"

"Spare me the speech, Simone. I'm tired of you, Doctor Sahiner, Aunt Millie, Lauren, everyone advocating for her. I'm not in the mood for it today."

She sighs. "Fine. We'll talk about it another time but you need to be ready because she's going to come back any time now. Now, let me tell you what's going on at the office before your new boss wakes up."

"Very funny." But true. I've never worked for someone as demanding as Avelyn before. "Go on."

"Bryce's lawyer called. I told him your terms and every stipulation. He agrees. The meeting is set as you requested and they have no clue that Alice is going to be there."

"Good. I want this dealt with and him gone from my company as soon as possible. Did you work out the details for Avelyn's trust?"

"Yep," she says. "The reports for the Gray Matter stock will be released today. It was a great idea. It's going to be profitable with all the new products you'll be introducing. By the way, the graphic tablets are kicking ass."

The ones Winter helped me evaluate. *Fucking great.*

"Good. Put the profits from the tablets in Avelyn's trust too."

She sucks in a breath. "Wow. She's the richest baby I've ever met."

That makes me smile. "That's the goal—"

My desk phone beeps and I put Simone on hold.

"Yes?"

"Sir, your wife is on the way up," the security guard says.

Ice prickles over my skin. *My wife.* Winter's coming up. My first instinct is to tell him to turn her down, but one look at my sleeping daughter and I sigh. "It's fine."

I hang up and pick back up with Simone. "I have to let you go. Winter's on the way here. I need to deal with this."

"Wait, Grayson. Don't do anything you'll regret. You're mad at her and you have the right to be, but remember she's Avelyn's mom. And the baby needs her. Let her see her daughter."

Rage blows up inside me. "What kind of monster do you all think I am? I'm not going to deny my daughter. I know she needs her mother. I need her mother to know that this is not a revolving door."

Avelyn starts to wail. *Shit, I must have screamed that.*

"Simone, I have to go. The baby woke up."

"Yeah...I know. Call you later." She hangs up the phone.

I slam the receiver down and make my way to the bassinet. "I'm sorry, I didn't mean to yell."

She doesn't forgive me. Instead, she rages and no matter what I do —bounce, hum, beg—I can't get her to calm down. Great, now it's going to look like I can't take care of her. "Come on. Don't do that. You need to calm down."

"She's probably hungry."

Her voice is like a blade through my chest. I close my eyes for a couple of breaths, trying to brace myself to face her. It's different and more difficult with the baby in my arms. I can't say what I want to.

I turn around and she's standing closer than I expected, only a couple of steps away. I don't know what I was expecting but it's definitely not what I find. She's so pale and not well at all. Her eyes are swollen and her hair wet. The are-you-okay is at the tip of my tongue but I shake it off.

"You should sit down," I say instead.

She shakes her head. "I'm fine standing."

Her voice is loud enough to carry over the baby's cries. She extends her hands. I take an instinctive step back.

"May I have her, please? I need to feed her."

"Is that why you're here, Winter? To feed her? Because she's been eating without you for two days."

She flinches but doesn't retreat. "I'm sorry I panicked and left. It was too overwhelming and I didn't know how to deal with it. But I'm back for my daughter. She's hungry and I would like to feed her."

She steps closer, with her arms still extended and I'm out of options because Avelyn does need her and I won't let my daughter be in distress.

I force myself to place the baby in her arms. Her scent is the first thing that reaches me and sneaks inside my nose. How many times did I breathe her in when I held her? It still clings to our closet. I step back quickly. I am not Avelyn, who's easily won over by Winter's fragrance and is already nuzzling her chest.

"We'll talk."

Winter's gaze snaps to mine. "We will. I have a lot to atone for. But now, I want to spend time with my baby. I have to ask her for forgiveness."

She turns around and walks out of my office. Only then do I notice Aunt Millie standing a few feet away and smiling.

"She came back like a mama lion. She went to the nursery first and then came here to face you. I offered to come get the baby. She wanted to do it herself."

I say nothing.

"It's a good thing, Grayson. Your family is back together."

I still say nothing. What the hell else can I say? Everyone's so hopeful but I don't know. "What happens when she gets scared again?"

Her smile deepens. "You'll work it out. She won't leave again."

"What makes you think that?"

"She needs Avy and you."

I snort. "She didn't act like it. She got the baby and left."

"She's thinking like a mom first. I'm going to heat her some soup. Lauren says she hasn't eaten anything in two days."

She leaves and I go to my desk. I turn on the baby monitor. She and I designed this surveillance together. So we could see the baby and whoever was caring for her from wherever we are.

She walks into the nursery and hands the baby over to Adri, then, with Lauren's help, removes her zip-up sweatshirt and takes the baby back, snuggling her against her chest. She sits down and it's clear how uncomfortable it is for her to move around. But she smiles as she grazes her cheek against our daughter's.

I have to turn the camera off. It's everything I've wanted but I can't stand to watch.

Winter

Avelyn's face moves around my breast. Her open mouth keeps missing the nipple. It's so cute but she's getting frustrated. So, I lean forward and she lands on the right spot. I can only yelp when she latches and the pain shoots through my breast.

I distract myself by rubbing her little hand and placing it on my chest. Her skin is softer than I remembered. They've been using the baby lotion Gray and I had made specially for her. Lavender and chamomile mixed with her own scent. The scent that woke me up and made me weep in the middle of the night.

"You're so hungry," I say, moving my free hand to support her lower body.

Her mouth is quick and eager, like she can't get enough milk into it. I chuckle when her little fingers knead into my flesh.

Aunt Millie brings the breastfeeding pillow and I lift Avy so she can place it under her, then lean back on the chair to get more comfortable.

I smile at her. "Thank you."

She smiles back and rubs a finger over the baby's head. "She missed her mommy's milk. The other just couldn't compare."

My face tingles so badly I need to look away. My baby didn't want the other milk and I wasn't here to feed her. She kept crying because she was hungry.

"I'm sorry," I tell my daughter. I don't think I'll be able to say it enough.

Aunt Millie places a hand on my shoulder. "No, hon. I didn't mean it like that. I was just pointing out she loves your milk. You're fine. You came right back."

"I—"

Avelyn's eyes drift open and she's staring right at me, setting off a humming in my chest that gets bigger and bigger. I can't help but stare back into those little eyes that are so much like her father's.

"I think this is our cue to leave."

I look up and blink for a bit. "I'm sorry?"

Adri laughs. "It's okay. Enjoy her. We have to go anyway."

I turn back to my baby and she's still looking at me.

"I guess you do forgive me. I need to explain, though. I got scared and overwhelmed, but I promise you that no matter how scared I get in the future, we're going to work through it together. I won't leave you again."

I rub my fingers over her cheek and breathe. The air fills my lungs all the way and I'm able to lean back. Her eyes stay open and I keep talking to her. I switch her to my other breast, commending her for latching on faster the second time.

"You're a fast learner, which is good because I want to teach you about colors and painting. Your daddy will probably want you to know the ins and outs of his company. But I hope you're an artist, just without the temperament."

When she gets that glazed, satisfied look, I hold her against my shoulder, smiling as I burp her. Then, I lay her back so I can stare at her face. Her eyes finally drift close. I don't know how long we've been here and I don't care. I'm so at peace right now, with her. How could I leave?

I should have looked into her eyes. I should have held her from the beginning. I was so caught up on my own stuff that I didn't think. I did to her what Gray's mom did to him. *Oh my God. I did to her what Gray's mom did to him.*

My throat knots again. I know all about his pain and trauma with that, but I didn't think. He tried to tell me, to get me to come home. I didn't listen. How will he ever forgive me?

I don't put Avelyn down in the crib. I can't. I've been away from her for too long and just need to hold her for a while. My gaze strays out into the view of the city but returns right back to her. Her lips do the sucking motion and it's the cutest thing in the world.

Adri was right. All the noise in my head shuts off and I don't hear anything but her soft breath. I'm finally relaxed and I probably could sleep but I'm afraid she may slip from my arms. I also don't want to change this. This feels right. No, right is too light. It doesn't fit. This, right now, is almost perfect.

"You should put her down." Gray's voice is thick but soft and I don't know if he's trying not to wake up the baby or trying not to spook me.

He's standing by the door like he belongs in a baby's room as much as in an office. And he does. It was so natural, the way he held her in his office when I came in. His big hands gentle around her back and his measured bounce trying to quiet her, it crumpled everything inside me. He loves her. He's always known. He's not scared of her or the situation. He's so sure of everything. He won't understand me...or forgive.

"You look exhausted," he says.

"So do you," I counter. Because he does. There are circles around his eyes. Except his circles are from taking care of her. "I'm sorry I wasn't here to help with her."

A muscle in his cheek jumps but he wipes a hand over his face. "Let me take her."

"No. I want to hold her."

"Jesus, you're so fucking stubborn. You're about to keel over. That's not good for you or her."

My throat swells. I get his meaning. *What if I drop her?*

He sighs. "Let me help you up. You can both lie in bed."

He stands in front of me, reaching with both hands to help me stand. For a second, it feels perfect. Avelyn in my arms and he's about to pull me into his arms. But he pulls away and steers me in the direction of our room, on the other side of the nursery.

The room is now cold, except for the baby pressed next to me. I don't want to go to our bedroom. I don't deserve that.

"No, I'll go lie with her in the guestroom. I'm not taking your bed."

"I'll take the guest room. You need to rest."

Our room feels the same. It's big and cool. I used that as an excuse to snuggle up to him so many times. The bed has been made but the co-sleeper nest I got as a gift from Adri is between his pillow and mine.

My throat expands. "She slept here with you."

"Define sleep." The hint of smile on his lips raises my hopes. "Apparently, she only sleeps with you."

And down my hopes go.

"Gray, we need to talk..."

He shakes his head.

I need him to hear me out. "Look, I got scared and I handled it all wrong. I'm sorry—"

"Not now. You need to sleep and I need to think."

"Can we talk when I wake up?"

He nods. "Oh, Doctor Sahiner called that she's coming by tonight."

"Yes, I called her when I was on my way back. She's going to check my stitches and she's bringing a friend of hers, a counselor. I think I need to talk to someone."

His mouth opens but he pauses and then says, "Okay. I'll see you at dinner time."

He leaves me standing there. I don't want to sleep here without his arms around me but at least I'm not alone. I've got Avy to keep me company in this big bed. I place her in the nest and lie down next to her. I'll rest for a bit but tonight, he's going to hear me out.

37

Winter

She's finally asleep again.

I lift my gaze to the sky and send a million prayers. My eyes are so dry I can barely blink and my body is so tired I could sleep for a week. For the third straight day, I've been awake before the sun. I greet it with resentment, as my scar is on fire from the pain. But today, I'm in my daughter's nursery with Avy's little cheek pressed against my neck. I spent parts of the night taking care of her and not sobbing. I rub a couple of circles on her back.

Fast footsteps tap along the hardwood and I stiffen. It's not Aunt Millie's soft gait. I turn as Grayson appears at the door with bed hair, an A-shirt and pajama bottoms. *Holy Davidoff commercial, I'm about to swallow my tongue.*

"No wonder the building wasn't shaking," he says.

"Huh?"

"She's usually screaming bloody murder through the night. Why didn't you call me? You didn't have to do this alone."

I shake my head. "I was okay. You looked really tired and I'm the one with the boobs, anyway."

I'm half-joking but his gaze drops to my chest and my pulse sets off.

"Aunt Millie sent you some tea."

"Oh." I didn't see the mug before. "Thank you."

He places it on the table next to me and then stretches his arms toward me. "Here, I'll take her so you can drink it."

I lean forward and he picks her up, his warm fingers grazing my skin. But it's the way he secures her against his chest, his hand gentle but protectively pressing against her back. It floods warmth all over my heart.

"What?" he asks.

I shake myself off. "Nothing. I just love the way you hold her."

He looks away and I busy myself with the tea mug.

"How are you feeling?" he asks.

I swallow and clear my throat. "Better. Just tired."

"The two of you were sleeping hard when I came to check on you."

He checked on us. Well, probably on Avy. But he said "you."

"Thank you for checking on us. I'm sorry we didn't get to talk last night. After the doctor and counselor left, I fed her and I passed out."

He nods. "I get that. I was exhausted, myself. I fell asleep watching TV."

And that's why I didn't wake him. He's been doing this for days. "We can talk now, if you have time."

He sighs. "I can't. Today, I am meeting with the Millers."

My hand freezes on the way to my mouth. "What? Why?"

"They've asked to meet so we can discuss the settlement."

My palms grow sweaty and I have to put the mug down. "Without me?"

Ice flickers in his eyes. His glare is so intense I want to back away. "You told me you didn't care what I decided. Remember?"

Heat flashes up my throat and rises to burn my cheeks as my words come back to roast me. I press my hand to the armrest of the rocking recliner. Jesus, I have so much to apologize for. "I'm sorry, Gray. I wasn't thinking straight back then. I think we need to…I need be a part of this. They messed with my life, too."

His neck is stiff, the tendons popping out. He's so angry with me. I don't blame him and I need to take the heat for what I've done.

"I'm going with you," I say.

His gaze snaps back to mine. "No."

Fuck this. "What do you mean no? It wasn't a question. I said I'm going."

He sighs. "Winter, these are not good people. You are not well. And I have a surprise for them, so things may get ugly in there."

I lean forward and push from my knees, bracing one hand on the armrest to stand. He's there in the next second, hooking a hand under my armpit and helping me up while still keeping Avy secured.

He doesn't move back this time. "Look, you shouldn't be there. Not in your condition. Stephen's a rat. God knows what he'll do when he comes face to face with Alice."

"The surrogate? She's here already?"

He nods.

"Then I definitely should be there. These people tried to screw our lives. Someone's dead." He shakes his head but I grab his hand. "Besides, we have security and you won't let anything happen to me. So, what time do we have to be there?"

He steps back, walks to the bassinet, and places Avy in it.

"I'll tell Aunt Millie. The meeting is in an hour." He walks out of the room without sparing me another glance.

My heart plunges way past my belly. He's never going to forgive me. I know it's too soon to expect anything, but damn. I have a right to be at this meeting.

You told him to do what he wants.

I can't dwell on that forever. I head to our bedroom but he's nowhere to be found. I make my way to the closet but a knock on the door stops me. Aunt Millie comes in with her unflappable smile.

"Good morning. I heard the princess had you up early."

I can't help but return the smile. She's been so sweet and has not judged me. "She's a hungry girl. Thanks for the tea."

"You're welcome, hon." Then she shakes her head. "I hear you're going out."

"Yeah. He's not happy but—"

She places a hand on my arm. "You have to do what you have to do. I think it's good you're going. It will keep him from doing something crazy. Just take it easy."

I nod.

She helps me get ready. It's not easy putting on the recovery wrap. I keep things easy with a long-sleeve cashmere dress, matching sweater, and knee-high boots. My makeup is minimal, enough so I don't look half dead. It's a meeting at Grayson's company, after all. My hair is up in a bun.

One look into the nursery and I'm questioning everything, mostly why am I leaving her. She's still sleeping and so beautiful. I don't want to go. She wouldn't be here without all that happened. Shouldn't that be enough to make me forgive those people? I gained so much because of what they did, what I never had, a family. I still haven't gained Grayson, but I wouldn't have had even an inkling of what happiness is like, if this had not pulled us together.

I caress the top of Avelyn's head, rub my knuckles over her soft cheeks. *I can't leave.*

"Winter, you have to go," Aunt Millie says, her gaze somewhere over my shoulder.

I take a breath and turn to face Grayson. He's at the door, waiting in his suit, handsome, angry, and worried.

I have to go. I have to show him we are still a team.

"I'm ready," I say like an idiot. He can clearly see that.

He gives me a lingering once over and nods. "I'll call the car."

He turns around to talk.

Aunt Millie wraps me in a hug. "I think he likes what he sees."

"You think?" I'm unsure. I still don't feel very well.

She nods.

"Car's all ready," he announces.

I take a last look at Avy and follow him out.

We ride the elevator in silence and when we get to the car, he helps me inside. I look at him every so often. When our gazes meet, he looks away first. How am I going to make him listen?

"Simone is going to be there and so is Elias. I'll warn you again, Stephen is a sleaze. If you feel uncomfortable at any moment, let me know," he says.

"I will," I say. I grab onto his hand. "Will you let me know if you're not okay?"

He blinks a few times, as if caught unaware. "I don't know."

And I don't know where we stand but I'm going to fight anyway.

Grayson

Everyone's happy. Simone, Sandra, and my whole executive staff have been coming in and out of my office. It's like they forgot it's a workday and that I'm here and that we have a meeting in less than fifteen minutes.

"I can't say enough how wonderful you look," Simone says to Winter.

And she does. She's smiling like I haven't seen since way before she went into labor. If things were still the same, I probably would send everyone out of the room so I could put my lips all over her blushing skin. I would kiss her until she was panting. But we're not like we were.

"Thank you," she says to Simone but her gaze is on me.

I go back to examining the email on my screen. Why couldn't she just stay home? I don't want to expose her to Stephen, for her to hear any venom he may spew. Or worse, believe it.

"Right, Grayson?" Simone asks.

I look up and all of them are staring at me. "What?"

"Sandra was asking who Avelyn looks like and I'm saying she is gorgeous like her mother." Her eyes sparkle and I know exactly what

THE WINTER OF MY LOVE

she is doing. Winter apparently does, too, because she's staring into her hands.

No matter how mad I am, I can't lie. Avy looks so much like Winter that sometimes it hurts to look at her. I also won't make my wife look bad in front of others.

"She is beautiful like her mother," I say and she meets my gaze. I so badly wish we could put it all behind us.

My phone beeps. "Mr. Grayson, the Millers are here."

I break our gaze and answer. "Show them to the conference room, Janine. We'll be right there."

Simone stands. "It's showtime. I'll go get your legal wonder."

I go around my desk to help Winter. I hook a hand under her arm and she stands but she doesn't let go. Instead, her hand slips into mine. I frown at her but she smiles.

"United front, Gray. We're in this together."

The warm light in her eyes snatches my breath and I just stare. I can only nod and walk because the knot in my throat thickens. What is she doing to me? We'll have to talk soon.

Tonight, after we put this shit out of our lives.

The air in the conference room is thick and my gaze lands on Stephen first. A rancid tang builds under my tongue and spreads all over my mouth. I want to smack the priggishness off his face. The family lawyer is to his left and his father to his right. Bryce's expression is unreadable. Next to him, and closer to the head of the table, is an older, paunchy man who I recognize right away. It's Astrid's primary Doctor Cooper's son. He's the director of the clinic where the embryos were frozen. *What the hell is he doing here?*

My gaze meets Simone's and she gives me a slight shrug. She doesn't know either.

Unease breaks a hole in the pit of my stomach. I force myself to keep walking but the still, small voice tells me something's changed. Something that's bound to fuck this up.

Winter's hand tightens around mine on our way to my chair and I give her a reassuring smile. I help her into the chair to my right and then sit.

"Let's get on with it," I say.

Their lawyer stands up. "Mrs. Grayson, I am Joseph Barnes, the Miller Family's lawyer. In the interest of not wasting anyone's time and because my clients want to be considerate of your newborn baby at home, we want to make this as quick as possible— "

My spine stiffens. They need to not refer to Avelyn. Simone jumps right in.

"Your clients chose an interesting time to be considerate, given Stephen created this whole situation. Also, in the interest of keeping things strictly professional, you will refrain from using my clients' child in your vitriol."

Barnes cocks a head to the side. "I thought we were going to be civil, counselor."

Simone reaches into her bag and slaps a folder on the desk. "Yes, and that was a civil request. Now, let's get on to reading and signing the terms of this agreement so we can be considerate to each other and never have to be in each other's presence again."

He clears his throat. "Well, things have changed."

"Changed how, exactly?" I blurt out. Because I sense bullshit.

Barnes clears his throat. "We've acquired new information that puts a spin on this whole situation. That's why Doctor Cooper is here. Doctor, can you explain to them why you're here?"

The man wrings his hands. His eyes are on the table and not meeting mine. "My father retired two years ago and passed away last year from colon cancer. He personally oversaw the freezing of the embryos with Astrid. I never had any part of it. When your specimen was requested, the staff sent it to Better Maryland. I had no reason to be involved."

"Quit stalling. We know all that already. You didn't have to bring the doctor here for this." Simone's tone is sharp.

Winter's biting her lip and the unease inside me spreads.

"Let him finish, counselor. Continue, please," Barnes says. He's calm and confident but there's an expectant light. He's Mariano Rivera in the bottom of the ninth inning. I'm the poor bastard at home plate praying for a meatball.

Because there's a hammer about to drop, but where? *And what hammer?*

"I was asked to review our records by Better Maryland and Mrs. De Castro, here, to figure out the discrepancy in the paperwork. I went through our records and my father's notes..."

He looks at me this time and there's something there, like an apology or shame or something I can't put my finger on. A heavy feeling stomps over my chest and my gaze meets Winter's. I can see it there, reflected in her frown and in her finger pinching the skin of her neck.

"Mr. Grayson, there never were implanted embryos at the clinic. Astrid's eggs were unusable when she came to us."

Heaviness spreads through my body and my breath hitches. I shake my head. This man is lying. "It's a fucking lie. I went to the clinic plenty of times with her. I donated my sample. I picked her up after the implantation procedures."

He sighs. "My father, in his own words, 'helped her.' She told him about the cancer and asked him to help her keep the secret. She didn't want you to know she was sick or that the eggs were not good. You see, he was already diagnosed himself. He had known the Millers all his life. He didn't feel he could deny her. So, he went along with it and we kept your frozen sperm there. In his notes, it says he tried to tell you at the funeral but couldn't bring himself to. He planned on telling you, but my guess is death got to him first."

No, this can't be.

"This is not possible. Astrid wouldn't lie. She wanted a baby, wanted to try. She did many treatments." I'm grasping, my brain refusing to accept this. Could this be a trap? Something to get the Millers off. It just can't...

"My father's notes do confirm that. She did want a child. We took several eggs, but none were useful and her ovulation issues didn't allow her to produce enough."

She lied. My God, she was lying the whole time. We went through so much. It was all a lie. My fist is balled so tight, my knuckles are screaming. I need to breathe. I need to finish this meeting. I need to get the fuck out of this place.

A hand presses over my fist. I turn and Winter's closer than I expected. "You're okay."

It's not a question but a statement. I hold her gaze, needing what I see there, wishing the rest away.

"So, this changes everything. There were no embryos to destroy, no evidence of wrongdoing, nothing you can blackmail my clients with to doing your bidding."

Before emotion can rise, Winter's hand closes tighter over mine.

"That's not what was happening here and you know it, Barnes." Simone's voice rises.

"But it was." Bryce speaks for the first time. "Grayson was trying to get our shares of Grayson Global and Astrid's money."

I come off the table then. "I wasn't trying to get Astrid's money. You offered that so the police wouldn't find out what your precious boy tried to do."

Bryce shrugs. "Well, since there were no embryos, there was no crime, really. Just a doctor with a gambling debt, pressured by a surrogate who changed her mind at the last minute. A woman who can't be found anyway."

Stephen smirks and I take two steps, but Winter's voice stops me.

"Jesus, you don't care. You're not even sorry there were no embryos. You don't care that your son is a low life or that something was obviously so broken with your daughter she made up this lie. What if he had really destroyed your possibility for grandchildren?" Her face goes red.

Bryce points a forbidding finger at her. "You don't know me, child. Don't speak like you do. My daughter spent her whole life doing dumb, impulsive things. Her last act of defiance was this one." He waves a hand in my direction.

She stands up way too fast and winces. "Don't talk about him like that. He actually cared about her. He wanted to make her last wish come true. He's the victim here." She shakes her head. "Money is the only thing you care about, so we're going to hit you where it hurts."

My heart is hammering my ribs. I manage breaths because seeing her this upset brings out something murderous and I so want to hurt Stephen and Bryce and Dr. Cooper, if he were alive. But she's right. Money is the only language they speak.

I signal to Simone and she goes to the door.

The smugness in their eyes, the way they look at one another, their celebratory faces are too much to take. I look at Winter and she shakes her head. Like she can't understand or refuses to believe.

And then the door opens and the two security guards bring Alicia in. An icy wave descends over the room. Slimy smiles slip off, there's a gasp, and the tide turns.

"Alice here has told us everything and is willing to testify against you. We have no doubt she will be able to get immunity, in exchange for her testimony," Simone says.

Stephen's sputter is the sweetest sound I've heard in my life.

3 8

Grayson

She hasn't run again. Not even after the bullshit yesterday or when I came home and locked myself in the office. I needed to think and to be alone. What Astrid did was so…fucked. I can't even fathom her lies. I couldn't understand it so I spent the afternoon researching places to donate her fortune. Winter didn't want any of it and she also didn't want it to touch Avy. I agreed. I want my daughter far away from that shit, too.

I fell asleep at my desk, woken up by Avy, as always, screaming bloody murder.

I ran to the room but Winter was already feeding her. Her hair was all over her face and she was half confused. It was a dead-on portrait of my life since coming out of the hospital.

"Get in the bed, Grayson," Winter snapped. "You look like hell."

I laid in our bed for the first time since she came back and slept most of the day. In the afternoon, Dr. Sahiner and the counselor showed up again. They talked a lot with Winter. I was in the room for part of the conversation. During another part, I was asked to leave.

THE WINTER OF MY LOVE

"Are you going to keep seeing the counselor?"

Jesus, Grayson. Is that how you want to start this?

But she looks up from her dinner and smiles. "Yes, I'm going to keep seeing her. I want to make sure I'm always balanced, so I can manage things easier."

"Good. Doctor Sahiner said you're recovering well. I could've done without her excessive mentions of how sweet your milk is."

She laughs. "I actually loved hearing that part. My baby knows my milk. Anyway, the doctor wants me to try to keep taking it easy for a bit longer. I strained my stitches when I was at the apartment alone."

The apartment. Patterson Park. Leave it alone, Grayson.

"I didn't know about that. How did you do it?"

"We haven't had a chance to talk, but I painted when I couldn't sleep or concentrate on anything else." She puts another forkful of food in her mouth.

"What else did you do when you were there?" I wracked my brain and in my worst moments, I pictured her happy and sleeping.

She places her fork down and pushes the plate away.

"Cry, worry, panic." Her fingers gracing over Avy's feet. "Smell her... Miss you."

She looks into my eyes when she says it. No hesitation or smile, like she means it.

"Did you really?"

'There's no need for me to lie." Her voice is soft but firm.

"Then, why did you leave? Why not let me help you? Why not come with me?" I can't help how harsh and accusatory my tone sounds, even to my own ears.

"Because you had everything you ever wanted, Gray. You were happy. I'm the one who wasn't. I was the one that kept hearing my mom's words. The last time I saw her here, she told me all about my birth. She was hopeful when she was pregnant and then everything got tough and it was a difficult birth and she couldn't feel anything for me. Sound familiar?"

What the hell? She didn't tell me all of this. "Winter—"

She shakes her head. "No. Let me tell you. Since then, I've been

273

scared shitless. I was worried it was going to be the same and then things kept happening. The bleeding, the placenta previa, Stephen *fucking* Miller, and then her interview. She revealed my father's name like that, when she wouldn't tell me. I couldn't handle it and then I was in so much pain and we had to do the C-section and you went with the baby and left me alone..."

"It was just to tag her. I was right there."

"I know that, now, when I'm thinking clearly. At that moment, I just wanted you not to leave me alone."

"I'm sorry."

"No. It's not your fault. Everything just conspired. I was tired and overwhelmed. You were so happy and holding her so gently. You looked at her with all this love and adoration. I wanted that so bad. I wanted to look at her and feel what I do now—" Her voice cracks.

She looks over to our baby and her features smooth out as if Avelyn's a buffer. "I was okay with her. I didn't mind feeding her, even if I was tired. When she fussed, I had them put her in the bed. She seemed calmer around me. I didn't get that. I do now."

I cover her hand with mine. "Why didn't you come to me with your fears? Why did you hold that in since that day with your mom?"

"Shame. She looked me in my face and said that she had to turn to alcohol and drugs to feel something. Remember how surprised the doctor was that I didn't need more painkillers to manage the pain?"

I nod.

"I was in pain the whole time. But I needed that pain. I was feeling something. The day we left the hospital, I kept wondering how long until I'd need something more. I didn't want Avelyn to go through what I did. A mother who's never really there. Someone only there to mess up her life."

I can't take it anymore. I push out of my chair and go kneel in front of her. I put my arms around her.

"I'm sorry, Gray. I didn't mean to be like your mom and run. I just couldn't cope."

It's like a fist to the gut and I flinch. I pull back and look into her eyes. "You're not like her. You came back to us."

THE WINTER OF MY LOVE

"I hurt you. I could see it in your face. You meant it when you told me not to come back."

I'm nauseous. Not only was I blind to what she was going through, I made it worse. "I did mean it but I was wrong. Thank you for not listening."

"I'm good at not listening."

I laugh. "Yes, you are."

We move to the family room and she sits next to me. Our daughter is in her bouncer. She stirs and Winter picks her up.

"Aunt Millie is going to yell at you for that. She's going to say you're going to get her used to being picked up all the time."

She shakes her head. "It's going to take me a bit to be able to let her be. I need to hold her as much as I can."

I run a hand over Avy's feet. "I get that."

She stares at me for a while and I hold my breath.

"Thank you."

I frown. "For what?"

"For understanding, for letting me back in again. I love you. I want you to know that."

I swallow and catch my breath. "I love you, too. There was never a moment when I stopped. No matter how mad I was, I never would have kept you away."

I lean over and kiss her. Her lips are soft and pliant and I savor their sweetness, the flavor that's so hers.

"I want you to tell me whenever you're feeling overwhelmed. In turn, I promise to be more observant."

She nods. "I can do that. I may also need you to come with me to see the doctor. I think, after yesterday, you probably need to talk to her, too."

I move closer, so I can nestle her next to me. "I will."

"Gray, as soon as I'm feeling stronger, I'm going to face my mom."

Hell no. I don't want her anywhere near that heartless bitch. But I just need to see where she is going with it. "Are you sure? If you're trying to change her—"

She tilts her head to look at me. "I'm not but she and I need to talk.

275

There are things I need to say to her and get off my chest. I also need her to stay away for good."

I can only nod. I don't even know what to say.

She leans back and kisses the corner of my mouth. "Let's forget about her for now. Let's just work on us."

I run my tongue over her bottom lip and catch it in my mouth. "I like that."

Then I run my hand over her thigh.

She chuckles. "You gotta wait six weeks for that kind of work."

I groan. "I forgot about that."

She gives me another peck on the lips. "We can use the next six weeks to get ready for that. We can kiss and do romantic things, tease each other. Everything couples do before they get pregnant."

"Sounds intriguing. How do we do that with our third wheel?" I point to Avy, whose eyes are wide open.

"We'll figure it out."

I kiss her soundly one more time. "I'm looking forward to trying."

EPILOGUE

Winter

"Grayson, one more question." The *Maryland Times* reporter asks, ignoring that Gray's body is half turned away from them.

His eyes flash with impatience and he manages to keep a straight face, but the soft groan he lets out under his breath rumbles in my ear. "Yes?"

Don't laugh, Winter.

I bite the inside of my cheek and manage not to double over.

"I wanted to get your comment on the recent donations made by Grayson Global to the Brain & Behavior Institute for Postpartum and Psychosis research and to the campaign against drunk drivers."

The laughter evaporates and instead, the familiar burning explodes inside my chest. I recite the usual litany in my head. *We knew these questions would come. We're prepared.*

"These are two causes my wife and I feel extremely close to. My father was the unfortunate victim of a drunk driver. Anything we can do to bring more awareness and help to the families." There's emotion and passion in his voice and traces of his pain, too. They were there when we made the decision to donate the Millers' money.

"What about the other donation?" The reporter follows up.

My spine stiffens and the burning intensifies. It's my turn to talk. Grayson's hand closes tighter around mine and I breathe. Our eyes meet and I nod to let him know I'm okay.

"It's also a very personal cause to our family. Approximately one in seven women experiences postpartum depression. I'm one of those one in seven women. Fortunately, I have the support of a loving family and friends, as well as the financial means to battle this condition. We believe our donation will not only help with research but it will assist mothers and families who truly need it."

I meet Gray's eyes and I'm grateful for the warmth there. We answer a few more questions and then make our way through the room, but Grayson doesn't stop walking until we're outside. Our car is waiting for us.

"We're leaving? It's a Grayson Global party. We shouldn't leave so early."

He helps me into the back of the car and he gets in behind me. "Because it's our party, we leave whenever the hell we want to."

"Gray—"

I find myself in his lap, with his lips on mine. One hand sneaks behind my neck and the other up the hem of my dress. I hum as his tongue plunges into my mouth and am halfway thrusting against his fingers.

"You were amazing tonight," he says between kisses.

"Is that why you almost dragged me out of there caveman style?"

He chuckles. It's dark and deep, like the look in his eyes. "I couldn't share you anymore. One, I would've had to fire all the men who kept staring at you. Two, I needed to stop trying to figure out the trick to getting this dress off you. I had to put my plan into action."

His fingers trace over the exposed skin that divides my off-the-shoulder dress. He's been eyeing me with curiosity all evening and now I know why.

I peek at our driver to make sure his eyes are not on us. Then I bring my mouth to my husband's ear. "It's two pieces, Gray. One is the skirt and the other is a bodysuit. I think you're really going to like this."

I guide his hand farther up my skirt and spread my legs a little, letting him feel his way up until he stiffens.

"Franklin, we're going to need to get home in a hurry." His voice is strained and he doesn't remove his hand. Instead, his knuckles brush back and forth and I have to bury my face in his neck so I don't moan like I want to.

By the time we get home, I'm so wet I'm ready to let him fuck me in the elevator, but all we do is dry hump and make out like teenagers who can't help themselves.

"We're almost there," I gasp when he pins me to the wall outside the apartment. His cock presses against my front and I rub myself against him as he fumbles around for the key. We rush down the hall, careful not to make any noise. If Avy hears us, it's over.

And it can't be over. I need him now. We make it to our room and I drop my purse on one of the chairs. He flings his jacket on the way. I back him toward the bed, push him on it, and lift my skirt. There's surprise and need in his eyes. He stares into my eyes as he pulls out his beautiful, hard cock.

"Yes," I say. "I need that now."

I have a knee on the mattress and his hands on my ass when a wail rattles the whole room. We fly apart, staring at each other in shock. The door to the nursery is open and I tiptoe my way there.

"Oh no. Someone woke up hungry." Aunt Millie shuffles inside the room, her voice is soft against my daughter's angry cries. "I thought we both fell asleep. Let's get you some milk."

"Later?" I whisper to my husband, who's stuffing himself back in his pants.

He nods. "Definitely."

"It's okay, Aunt Millie. We're here. I'll feed her."

Thirty minutes later, Avy's still nursing, pausing sometimes to smile and grab chunks of my hair. Gray's on the floor by the glass windows, watching us and taking pictures with his phone.

"I'm blowing this one up." He scoots closer and shows me.

Avy pauses and tries to swipe his phone. He grabs her little hand and blows a bubble in her palm. She giggles and we laugh and then he kisses me.

"Thank you for giving me everything, Winter, my love."

THE END

Please turn the page for some important information.

PLEASE READ

Winter Grayson is a fictional character but the statistics she quoted in the epilogue are very real as is the struggle with postpartum depression (PPD) for many women. Sometimes the symptoms are hard to recognize and can get lost in the joy of a new baby's birth. It's important that you talk about it and seek help when you're feeling overwhelmed or anxious.

If you are struggling with PPD, please know you are not alone. There is help available for you.

Here are some organizations that can help:

Postpartum Support International – 1-800-994-4773

Substance Abuse and Mental Health Services Administration – 1-800-662-4357

In an emergency:

You can reach the National Crisis Text Line from any where in the United States by texting: **HOME** to **741741**

Or call National Suicide Prevention Lifeline at **1-800-273-8255.**

If you know anyone who is struggling with PPD or any mental health issue, please refer them to any of these places. Let's take care of ourselves and each other.

ACKNOWLEDGMENTS

Thanks to Deranged Doctor Designs for this beautiful cover. Thank you to my awesome editor Nina S. Gooden and to the sweet Katie Testa for proofreading.

My critique partners Shadow Leitner, and Laralyn Doran and a very special *thank you* to Audrey Couloumbis and Cate Tayler for feeding my muse and cheering me every step. My Alpha readers Angil, Crystal, and Vera. Your comments and feedback give me life!

A special mention to my sweet *Citlali*. She may not have a store yet, but those macarons are real and delicious!

Thank you to my group of supportive friends John, Vivian, Maria, Felia, Marisol, Kakazi, Nancy, Robin, The Lake House Writers, The Domingo crowd, and my LPHIDs.

Thank you to, my amazing family. Papi, Mami, my stepmom, my brothers and sister, uncles, aunts, nieces and nephews, and my beautiful Nin, I mean, Trin. I wouldn't be here without any of them.

Thanks to you and everyone who supports me, reads my books, and indulges my muse. Your support means the world to me.

ABOUT THE AUTHOR

J. L. Lora is a Dominican-American author. Her stories explore the dark side of good characters, people living in the gray areas of life while playing the cards life has dealt them. She loves strong heroines and their equally powerful Men. She currently lives in Maryland, pursuing her dream of writing compelling, sexy, can't-put-down stories about empowered, badass alpha heroines and take-your-breath-away alpha heroes. You can find her and or chat her up on Social Media.

Sign up for my newsletter and learn more about new releases, events, news, freebies and much more at **www.JLLora.com**.

facebook.com/AuthorJLLora

 twitter.com/jtothelove

 instagram.com/jllora

BOOKS BY J. L. LORA

The Trinity

BOSS

MADE

DAMNED — *a short companion book*

STEEL

A Love for All Seasons Series

THE SUMMER I LOVED YOU

ALL I WANT *a free holiday short story*

THE WINTER OF MY LOVE

THE AUTUMN YOU BECAME MINE (Fall 2019)

THE SPRING OF MY HEART (Spring 2020)

Standalone Books

SOME NIGHTS

EMPIRE (Summer 2019)

Made in the USA
Middletown, DE
23 March 2019